"Audrey, wait!"

His hand wrapped around her upper arm, brought her to a halt. "I didn't notice the flour in your hair until just now when we were talking. It was barely visible. Truly. I was only teasing."

Blake was so close she could feel his warmth on her back. She glanced at his hand on her arm, so strong yet gentle, and held her breath against the quivering in her stomach, the ache in her throat. "I know. I was only having a…a 'redhead' moment."

"Then I'm forgiven?"

The bell on the door jingled. "Of course. Now, I have bread waiting to be baked, and you have a customer…" She stood quietly, waited for him to release her arm.

"You back here, Latherop?" Garret Stevenson strode through the doorway, came to an abrupt halt. "Oh, sorry, Mrs. Latherop, I didn't mean to intrude."

Blake's hand fell away from her arm. She felt him take a step back—no doubt embarrassed to be seen in what could be interpreted as an intimate moment with her. She turned to rescue him. "Not at all, Mr. Stevenson." *The only thing you intruded upon is my foolishness.*

Award-winning author **Dorothy Clark** lives in rural New York. Dorothy enjoys traveling with her husband throughout the United States doing research and gaining inspiration for future books. Dorothy believes in God, love, family and happy endings, which explains why she feels so at home writing stories for Love Inspired. Dorothy enjoys hearing from her readers and may be contacted at dorothyjclark@hotmail.com.

Books by Dorothy Clark

Love Inspired Historical

Stand-In Brides
His Substitute Wife

Pinewood Weddings
Wooing the Schoolmarm
Courting Miss Callie
Falling for the Teacher
A Season of the Heart

An Unlikely Love
His Precious Inheritance

Visit the Author Profile page
at Harlequin.com for more titles.

DOROTHY CLARK

His Substitute Wife

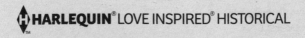

Recycling programs
for this product may
not exist in your area.

LOVE INSPIRED BOOKS

ISBN-13: 978-0-373-42507-5

His Substitute Wife

www.Harlequin.com

Printed in U.S.A.

Who can find a virtuous woman?
for her price *is* far above rubies.
The heart of her husband doth safely trust in her...
—*Proverbs* 31:10–11a

To my first great-grandchild—
may you read this when you are older
and know the joy you have brought to me.

And Sam. Once again. Thank you.

"Commit thy works unto the Lord,
and thy thoughts shall be established."

Your Word is truth. Thank You, Jesus.

To God be the glory.

Chapter One

Medicine Bow Mountains, Wyoming Territory
August 1868

"Next stop, Whisper Creek!"

Audrey Prescott caught her breath. They were almost there! A sharp spasm in her stomach pulled her gaze from the mountains she'd been watching outside the soot-filmed window. More than a few of the soldiers sharing the passenger car on this last leg of her long journey from New York were staring at her with open admiration. Heat crawled into her cheeks. She locked her gaze on the lanky conductor standing just inside the door, his legs splayed against the rocking of the train.

"We'll be stopping at Whisper Creek long enough to take on water and coal. You're all welcome to get out and stretch your legs if you're of a mind to, but we won't be more than twenty minutes at most, so don't wander off. The town's raw and there's no food available—and no drink. Town's dry." The conductor's piercing gaze slid her direction; a smile warmed his face. "I'll be unloading your trunks for you, Miss Prescott." He stepped back outside onto a small platform and closed the door.

Her trunks. Another spasm struck her stomach. What would Blake Latherop think when he saw her standing beside them at the station? The rhythmic clack of the train's wheels against the rails, the rocking of the car as they rolled down the tracks were suddenly a comfort she did not want to stop. The train swayed around a mountain wall, blasted its whistle, then chugged through a growth of tall pines and entered a long, broad valley. She stared out the window at the vast field of grasses bisected by steel rails, her stomach roiling.

What had she been thinking, coming to Whisper Creek in Linda's place? Her plan was foolishness—pure foolishness. She winced, opened her purse and withdrew Blake Latherop's last letter to her sister. The paper shook. She frowned at the display of nerves and scanned the words she'd read so often she knew them by heart.

My Beloved,
At last! My dearest Linda, it is with great joy I write to tell you the construction of my store is finished. The first of the goods and supplies I have ordered came on Tuesday's train, and I stocked the shelves this very evening. Tomorrow morning, I will hang the Open sign on the door.

My beloved, there is nothing to stand between us now. Our living quarters upstairs over the store are also completed. It is my hope that the furniture I've purchased comes in time for me to have it in place for your arrival.

My dearest Linda, hurry to me. As I told you when I asked for your hand before I came West, the contract I had to sign in order to receive the free land and building lumber in this new town states that I must marry within thirty days of opening my business or I lose the store and all I have invested in it to Mr. Ferndale, the town's founder. That investment, dearest, is the total of the inheritance I received from my mother that I told you of. But do not fret. Once the town grows, I am confident the store will provide us a comfortable, even prosperous living.

I am enclosing the railroad ticket for your journey to Whisper Creek, as well as money enough to cover any expenses you may incur. Don't waste a moment, my dearest. Our future depends on you. And I am emboldened, as your betrothed, to tell you I am eager to again look upon your beautiful face and form and to hold you in my arms and pledge to you my undying love.

Until you arrive, I remain your impatiently waiting, always faithful,
Blake

The train's whistle blew again. Audrey closed her eyes, fighting a rush of panic. What was she doing here? How could she ever have thought of such an insane scheme? The clacking of the wheels slowed. It was a matter of minutes now. The knots in her stomach twisted tighter. She opened her eyes and stared down at the letter fluttering in her hand, guilt swarming. She should never have answered Blake's letters when Linda asked her. But she'd wanted to believe her sister had changed, that Linda really did intend to marry Blake. And when Linda had gone off on her month-long visit with friends, what else could she do with Blake so far away and anxiously awaiting a response from his betrothed?

She refolded the letter and ran her fingertip along the crease. Blake wrote beautiful letters full of plans and hope for the future. They deserved a respectful reply, not a careless dismissal! Still, she should have warned Blake that Linda liked to string a beau along until someone new took her fancy. But she'd hated the thought of hurting him—and of being disloyal to Linda. Oh, if only she'd known about the contract Blake had signed on the strength of Linda's pledge of marriage!

Our future depends on you. Her face tightened. The guilt that had driven her to board the train for Whisper Creek surged. She drew a deep breath and pressed her hand against her stomach, hoping she wouldn't be sick—though it was no more than she deserved. *Dear Lord, I know it's foolishness, but please let my plan work. Please help me to make amends for writing those letters. I didn't know the true situation, and—*

The train jerked, jerked again and came to a stop. Her oft-repeated prayer blurred into an unarticulated plea from her heart. She peered out the window at a long, plain building shadowed by two huge tubs sitting high on splayed legs and attempted to gather her courage. The engineer and fireman hopped from the train, trotted to the second tub and swung its black-stained chute into place above the coal car. The fireman pulled a cord and coal tumbled down the chute, black dust puffing against the rose-streaked dusk sky. She shifted her gaze to the wood sign hanging from the deep eaves of the depot's roof—Whisper Creek Station, Union Pacific Railroad.

If you're so worried about Blake, Audrey, you *go marry him!*

Bile crept into her throat. Challenging Linda to do the right thing and keep her promise to marry Blake had only made her sister more determined to have her way. Nothing interfered with Linda's "fun." Certainly not a little thing like a promise! Audrey swallowed hard and slipped the letter back into her purse. She never should have picked it up when Linda threw it at her and flounced from the room. But it was too late to think of that now. It was too late for anything but clinging to the foolish mission that had brought her here.

Movement caught her attention. The soldiers were standing, waiting for her to detrain first. She dipped her head to acknowledge their politeness, lifted her satchel off the seat beside her and walked to the door. *Blake!* She froze, stared at her sister's fiancé hurrying toward the steps the conductor had shoved into place. The strength left her legs. She grabbed for the edge of the door and turned back, but her way into the passenger car was blocked by the line of soldiers behind her.

"Linda, dar—*Audrey!*" Blake stared up at her, blinked then made a visible effort to collect himself. "I didn't know that you were—I mean— How nice to see you again, Audrey." Blake stumbled over the polite words, reached up to take her satchel.

"And you, Blake." She took a steadying breath, placed her hand in his proffered one and stepped down. He peered behind her, and the eager joy in his expression died. His gaze lifted to the soldier who followed her from the train, raised to the next, then came back and fastened on her. She forced herself to look into his eyes and answer the question that hovered there. "Linda's not on the train, Blake. She's not coming."

"Not com—" His face paled. "Is she *ill*? Or—"

She shook her head, pushed at the unruly curls on her forehead and wished she hadn't come either. How could her plan ever have seemed *sensible*? "No, Linda's not ill. It's—" She glanced at the soldiers milling about, took another breath to squelch her nerves and looked back at Blake. Worry shadowed the handsome face she remembered so well. "It's…complicated. Is there some-place we can go to talk?"

"My store." He took hold of her elbow and led her toward the steps.

"Wait! My trunks…" She stopped, glanced over her shoulder at the two trunks sitting on the platform close to the tracks.

"Trunks?" His gaze bored into hers.

"It's a long journey." She winced inwardly at the lame response, but she couldn't just blurt out the truth. She needed time to prepare him for that. She did her best not to squirm beneath his long, measuring look.

"They'll be safe here at the station. Fortunately, an eastbound train arrives in about an hour." He frowned and urged her forward. "Forgive me, Audrey. I don't mean to sound rude or unwelcoming. But there is no place in town for you to overnight."

"But, I'm—" She bit off the words and nodded. "All right. If you're certain they will be safe."

He gave a curt nod, ushered her down the steps, then released her elbow. A sound of hammering vied with the whisper of coal sliding down the chute and dropping into the tender car. She lifted the hems of her green gown above the trodden dirt and walked forward eyeing the new buildings framed on either side by the skeletons of more buildings under construction at the end of the road. Behind the raw, unpainted structures, a waterfall gushed from a mountain to splash and dance down a massive rock face to where dark pines sprawled in dwarfed splendor. A creek shimmered its way between the trees and flowed away down the length of the broad valley. The cluster of buildings looked puny against the towering mountains. She stopped and tilted her head back to look up at the snowcapped peaks. "I've never seen anything like these mountains. They're breathtakingly beautiful but…frightening. I—I feel so…small."

"They take you like that at first."

Blake's tone didn't invite any more casual comments. She walked on beside him, looking at the beginning of Whisper Creek village. Would the new town become her home for a while? She glanced at Blake through her lowered lashes. He looked distressed, concerned. Would he even listen to her plan after he learned—

"Here we are." He shifted her satchel to his left

hand, helped her up the steps, then crossed the deep porch and opened the door.

She moved forward into his store and inhaled the scent of newness, then waited for Blake to lead her to where he intended for them to talk.

He closed the door, set her satchel on the floor and faced her. "Again, I don't mean to be rude, Audrey. But where is Linda? We're supposed to be married today. If she's not ill, why is she not here? What has happened to her?"

The strain in Blake's voice brought the guilt washing over her. She clenched her fingers around the cord on her purse and wished it was her sister's pretty neck. "I don't know where Linda is, Blake. She...married two weeks ago and left town. I've not heard from her since. Of course, I've been traveling the last—"

"Linda is *wed* to another?"

She couldn't tell if his harsh, choked tone was caused by pain or anger—probably both. "Yes." She rushed to push out words to ease the shock of the news. "I'm sorry—"

"*Sorry!* My *betrothed* has given herself to another, and you're *sorry?*"

The words exploded from him. She flinched, then pressed her lips together against the useless words of sympathy. There was nothing she could say. It was too late. She should have warned him of Linda's flirtatious nature when he first started courting her—though he wouldn't have listened. None of Linda's conquests did. They were all too blinded by her blond beauty, too smitten by her womanly charms and coquettish manner. Still, she should have tried. The guilt held her mute.

Blake strode away from her toward the interior of the store and stopped. He sucked in a sharp, ragged breath. "I *believed* her. I built this store—our home upstairs—on the strength of my faith in our love. How could I have been so *wrong*? Her letters were so full of love and caring…"

My letters. The guilt bit deeper. There was no mistaking the agony in Blake's voice. She glanced at the door wanting to leave, to not have to witness the pain Linda's selfish behavior had caused, but Blake's situation was dire and time was short—and she was his solution. *Dear Lord, give me strength.* She braced herself for his reaction to her absurd plan. "That's why I've come, Blake. Because of the store."

He turned, stared and raked his fingers through his hair. "Forgive me, Audrey, I forgot that you were here. I— What?"

"I said that I'm aware of your situation, and I've come because I believe there is a way you can keep your store." *Please, Lord, let it be so.*

"Keep my store?" Awareness flickered through the shock in his eyes. His face went taut. "No. That's impossible now. There are only four days remaining before—" He clamped his lips shut, turned away.

"Before you must marry." How cruel that sounded.

Blake stiffened, spun back around and walked to her, anger in every line of his body. "I appreciate you coming all this way to deliver the news of Linda's betrayal in person, Audrey. But, as you've experienced betrayal yourself, I'm sure you'll understand that I'm in no mood for polite commiseration—no matter how sincere." A muscle along his jaw twitched. His hands clenched. "As I said earlier, a train headed east comes through in about an hour. It's the last one today. As there is as yet no restaurant in town where you can wait in comfort, I'm afraid the bench at the station will have to do. I have to go tell Pastor Karl there will be no wedding. He will have heard the train arrive and will be expecting—" Pain flashed in his eyes. His lips clamped tight again. He bent and picked up her satchel. "I'll walk you back to the depot."

She shook her head, his reference to her ex-beau John Barker bringing the pain of being a second-best castoff surging forth and strengthening her resolve to spare Blake as much pain as possible. "I'm not going home, Blake. At least, not unless you tell me to." He jerked away from the door and stared at her. She looked at his tight mouth, at the pulsing vein at his left temple and blurted out her plan before he dragged her out the door. "I came to marry you."

Audrey's words slammed against the shock of Linda's betrayal with stunning force. His mind reeled. Blake drew breath to speak, but no sound came. He gave his head a quick shake, struggling to grasp the incomprehensible thought. "I'm sorry, Audrey, but—" He gave his head another shake and stared down into her hazel eyes. Surely, he'd heard her wrong. "Did you say, you came to *marry* me?"

"Not for *real*!"

The skin over her cheekbones turned redder than her hair. He rubbed at his throbbing temple, tried to make sense of what she was saying. "I don't understand. How—"

"The *marriage* would be real. But you and I wouldn't—" Her gaze jerked from his, focused on the floor. "That is to say, the marriage would be…"

Her embarrassment brought the word springing forth—*"Impersonal?"*

"Yes."

The color on her cheeks flared. He gaped at her, his mind numbed by the shock upon shock. She burst into speech.

"When Linda left, I opened your last letter to answer it and tell you what had happened, but the railroad ticket and money were there, and that's when I learned that you had signed a contract that states if you do not marry within thirty days of opening your business all that you have invested will revert to the founder of Whisper Creek. And that you had signed that contract because of Linda's promise to marry you as soon as you had your store and living quarters built."

"And so you came here to marry me." It was so preposterous he could hardly credit it, let alone relate the idea to the young woman standing before him. Audrey had always been quiet…reserved…*sensible.*

"It wasn't like *that.*" Her chin lifted. "The letter had lain unopened for over two weeks. Had I responded in kind to explain what had happened, by the time you received my missive there would have been no time left for you to do anything to save your store and all you have invested." Her shoulders squared. "So I've come to honor my sister's promise."

"To marry me."

"Yes. And, as you just stated, there are only four days left for us to do so."

Four days. "Audrey, I—"

"—think I'm insane." She stepped closer. "I know it sounds mad, Blake. But I've thought it over quite carefully, and it's the only way I can think of to save your store. The contract states that you must *marry*—not how you must *conduct* that marriage. Correct?"

The pain of Linda's betrayal hit afresh. Bitter gall rose in his throat. "And how long would this pretense of a marriage go on?"

"Until you find another solution to your problem."

"Until— That could take some time."

Her gaze lowered to her satchel gripped in his hand. "I'm prepared to wait."

His mind jolted backward, pulled up an image of her trunks sitting on the station platform. She was serious. She'd come prepared to stay. What sort of man did she think he was? She should have known he wouldn't consider letting her do such a thing! He set his jaw, shook his head. "That's generous of you, Audrey. But… Linda's… behavior is not your responsibility." His throat tightened at the taste of his beloved's name on his tongue. "Nor is saving my store. That is my problem. I'm the one who signed the contract."

"But you did so because of Linda's promise."

Of course I will marry you, Blake darling. I love you. Go to Wyoming. I will join you when you build our home. Our home. How wonderful that sounds! Pain constricted his chest at the memory of Linda's words. He squeezed the satchel's handle, fought down the urge to throw the case across the room.

"I can do nothing to ease your hurt over my sister's

betrayal, Blake. But I *can* do something to stop it from costing you your inheritance. I hope you will let me."

The desperation in Audrey's voice caught at him. He yanked his thoughts from the painful memory and fastened his gaze on her. "I'm sorry, Audrey. I can't—"

"Please don't refuse me! My plan will *work*, Blake." She stepped close and peered up at him, her eyes imploring. "Surely you can see it is the only way to save your store! And it will only be for a short time."

"You can't know that."

"I know that you are an intelligent, resourceful man. You will find a solution."

He put down her satchel and scrubbed his hand across his eyes trying to think through the cloud of shock. "Your faith is misplaced, Audrey. I have no idea what that solution might be. I can't think..." He drew in a ragged breath, swept his gaze around the store. "Perhaps, given some time, I might think of something, but... I don't know..." He turned and stared out the window, jamming his hands into his suit jacket pockets. Pain jolted him at the touch of the ring. It was over. His love had chosen another. What did anything else matter? He might as well let Audrey have her way—whatever her reason. He pulled air into his aching chest and motioned for her to join him. "Do you see that small church, down a ways across the road?"

"Yes."

He fingered the ring, forced out words. "That's where Pastor Karl lives. He's waiting to perform the ceremony that would have made your sister and me man and wife." Bitterness swelled, drove him on. He pulled his hand from his pocket and looked down at her. "There is no place you can stay in Whisper Creek but upstairs in the living quarters with me, so be absolutely certain you want to do this, Audrey. We will have to marry immediately. There will be no opportunity for *you* to change your mind." *Like your sister.* He waited for her answer, his jaw set, the vein at his temple drumming.

"I've had days to think about this plan, Blake. I've thought of nothing else since I read your letter and boarded the train in New York. I'll not change my mind."

Her voice was soft and steady. There was determination in the lift of her chin. He dipped his head in curt acceptance. "There's one thing more. We will have to play the part of loving newlyweds in front of others. If Mr. Ferndale were to discover that the marriage is a pretense it might void the contract and your...kindness will have been in vain." Her eyes widened, her posture stiffened. Clearly, she had not realized what her offer entailed. But he understood. He reached for her satchel to walk her back to the station.

"I understand. I shall do my best."

He straightened, looked at her. It should have been Linda standing there—rushing into his arms... "Look, Audrey—"

"I'm not going home, Blake." Her hazel eyes bored straight into his. "Not until you have solved the problem Linda has caused you with the store."

The resolve in her eyes, her stiff posture—everything said she meant it. Well, he'd given her every chance to stop this foolish plan and go home. And she was right—marrying her was the only way to save his investment and not walk away from the store penniless. At least he would salvage something from the ruins of his hopes and plans for the future. And what did the marriage matter? The farce would be over soon enough. He'd think of something. "Very well, then." He ignored the sickening ache in his chest, pushed her satchel aside and opened the door. "Let's go. I don't want to keep Pastor Karl waiting. And, remember… we're supposed to be in love."

May the Lord bless your union with many years of health and happiness.

The pastor's parting words echoed in her mind with every step she took back to the store. Audrey stole a quick glance at Blake through her lowered lashes and wished she could say or do something that would ease his tension. But that was unlikely as she was the cause of that tension. She took a breath and glanced down at his hand holding her elbow, grateful for its support as she forced her shaky legs to climb the steps to the porch.

Blake released her elbow, led her inside and picked up her satchel. "This way."

His voice sounded as if his throat had gravel in it. Her heart squeezed. How horrible for him to have had to endure that marriage ceremony with her when he'd just learned the woman he loved had wed another. She remembered the raw hurt when John had cast her aside to make an advantageous marriage. She bit back words of apology and commiseration and followed Blake into the dark interior. Sympathy would do no good. Words could not ease the pain of an aching heart.

She stole another glance at Blake, but the store was

too dark and shadowed to see clearly. He led her through a door at the back into another, smaller room, his footsteps and the rustle of her skirt loud in the silence. How much effort it must have cost him to pretend to be a happy bridegroom when he was suffering from her sister's betrayal. What inner strength he had! Even she hadn't detected his hidden emotions until the pastor pronounced them man and wife, and he'd kissed her.

She raised her hand and touched her fingertips to her tender lips. Thankfully, the pastor had interpreted Blake's vehemence as love, not anger. Tears stung the backs of her eyes. How he must have hated being forced to kiss her, to pretend—

"Wait a moment until I light the lamp, Audrey. It's not safe for you to climb the stairs in this dim light."

She blinked the tears away and squared her shoulders. A match flared. Blake lifted the globe of a hanging lamp and touched the match to its wick. Light spread over the area and highlighted the taut features of his face. She looked up the open stairs into a soft circle of light at the top. The home he'd meant to share with Linda was up there. Her breath shortened. *Oh, Lord, what have I done? This is madness! I can't—*

"Do you want me to go first?"

Blake's strained voice snapped her thoughts back to him. Her discomfort was nothing compared to the turmoil of emotions he had to be experiencing. She shook her head, gripped the railing and started to climb.

The stairs led to a U-shaped interior hall lit by a pewter oil lamp sitting on a shelf centered between two doorways in the wall they faced. Blake gestured toward the door on the left. "That's the sitting room. You'll find it sparsely furnished. I thought—" He stopped, stood beside the door for her to precede him.

He's thinking about what was to have been. Talk about things! Distract him. She stepped into the dark room and swept her gaze over the furnishings: lamp stands, a chest, two armchairs with cushions facing a settee. Light from the hall lamp shone on the padded arm. Blue damask. Linda's favorite color. She looked at Blake and forced out words. "It's lovely. And more than sufficient."

He nodded, and she followed him back out into the hall, glanced toward a door he indicated on their right. "That's my office." He swept his hand toward a door at the end of the short hallway. "And a bedroom."

She drew a breath, found a bit of courage and spoke before it fled. "Is that where I—"

"No. The room is empty but for a cot. I'll sleep there."

She started to protest, noticed his taut face and kept quiet.

Lamplight gleamed on Blake's dark hair and broad shoulders as he walked past the stairwell and gestured toward that second open doorway now on their left. "That's the kitchen."

She glanced into the dark room. The light from the hall gleamed on the polished wood of a dining table surrounded by Hitchcock chairs. It was all she could see in the quick glimpse. She stifled a wish to look around the kitchen and hurried after Blake, almost bumping into his back when he stopped at the door centered in the short hall at the right of the stairs that formed the second arm of the U.

"This is the dressing room. You'll find everything you need in it—piped-in water, a bathing tub…" That muscle along his jaw jumped. "Towels and other necessities—soaps and creams and such—are in a cupboard."

All bought for Linda. Her stomach flopped. She couldn't—

"I'll light the lamp." He did so quickly then stepped back out into the hall and opened the door across from the kitchen at the end of the short hall. "This is where you will sleep. You can hang your gowns in here." He yanked open a door on a cavernous wardrobe, set her satchel down, strode to a nightstand beside a four-poster and lit the lamp. Golden light glittered on a small heart-shaped silver box, spilled onto a beautiful blue-and-white woven coverlet on the bed.

Her gaze froze on the heart-shaped silver box and the thumb of her left hand turned inward, touched the ring on her finger—Linda's ring. She lifted her gaze to Blake's rigid back, remembered the tremor that had shook his hand when he'd pulled the ring from his suit coat pocket and put it on her finger. She slipped the ring off and cupped it in her hand.

Blake scrubbed his hand over his eyes and turned, his face as fixed as stone. "I'll go to the station and get your trunks. You'll be wanting to settle in." He strode out into the hall and walked down the stairs.

She lifted her hand, stared down at the circle of gold on her palm and thought of all it stood for—of what it meant to Blake. Tears blurred her vision. She blinked them away, walked to the nightstand and put the ring in the box. It was difficult enough to live with the knowledge that your betrothed rejected the love you carried in your heart for them without seeing a reminder all day. She might stand in Linda's place, but she'd not wear the symbol of Blake's love for her.

Blake threw a blanket over the cot he'd slept on while his store was being built, then turned away before he broke the folding bed into pieces. The quiet sounds from the other bedroom stabbed into him like knives. He wished Audrey would put off unpacking the trunks he'd brought from the depot until tomorrow when he was downstairs at the store. But he had no good reason to ask her to do so. He couldn't tell her the truth—that every rustle of movement reminded him of Linda's betrayal, of what should have been. That she was sleeping on the bed that had arrived only yesterday. His and Linda's wedding bed.

He clenched his fists wanting to smash something the way his dream had been shattered. But there was only the cot. Or the walls. He stared at the wood partition separating him from his *bride* and jerked his mouth into a bitter smile. If he started punching the wall, he'd likely frighten Audrey into a faint. And how would he explain his bruised and bloodied hands to any customers tomorrow—to Mr. and Mrs. Ferndale, who were certain to come around to wish them well?

His stomach curdled at the thought of the town founder and his wife. They would want to meet his bride. How would Audrey handle that? How would he? He'd best do better than he had at the wedding! His face tightened at the memory of his agony during the ceremony. He'd been so angry over Linda's betrayal, he was shaking. Still, he shouldn't have kissed Audrey like that. Remorse washed over him. Audrey had come all the way out to Wyoming to help him keep his store, but there had been nothing of gratitude in that kiss—only anger and frustration. She didn't deserve that.

What a mess his life was! All of his hopes and careful plans were brought to ruin by Linda's fickleness. A strangled moan burst from his throat. He shoved his hands through his hair and looked around the empty room that was meant for the children he'd hoped to have someday. His gut twisted into a painful knot. If only he could get out of here and go for a walk, but the moon was too bright. He couldn't take the chance that one of the few people in town would see him striding down the road. Men didn't go for solitary walks on their wedding night. At least he could get some air to breathe! He strode to the door leading to the porch that roofed the store's loading dock and grasped the knob.

A floorboard in the next room creaked. The sound shot through him like an arrow from a warrior's bow. He froze. There was a door onto the porch from the other bedroom as well. If he went out there and Audrey heard him and came outside… He released his grip on the doorknob. It wasn't worth the risk. He couldn't bear to see her again tonight.

Linda… Oh, my heart's desire…

Memories exploded. Images of his beloved laughing up at him, her blue eyes glowing, her soft, full lips enticing him to kiss her. The silky feel of her blond curls beneath his hands, the warmth of her arms sliding around his neck, the ardor of her return kiss. Pain ripped through him. *How could you betray me like this, Linda? How could you turn your back on our love?*

He leaned against the door, shaken, ill, furious, fighting for control.

Dear God, what have I done? How will I get through this sham of a marriage?

He paced around the empty room, his steps keeping time with his tumbling thoughts. There were only three things he knew for certain: he owed Audrey an apology for that angry kiss, he would never trust a woman again and there would be no sleep for him tonight. And one more—he had to find a solution to the problem with the store so he could free Audrey from her commitment and get out of this farce!

Chapter Two

Gray light poked through the slatted wood shutters on the windows and formed dim streaks on the carpet. Dawn was breaking. Was Blake an early riser? Audrey blinked her dry, burning eyes and rose from the chair in her room.

She tucked the hem of her white bodice farther beneath the waistband of her long, dark blue skirt then shook out her hems. Her chosen outfit was functional, with the barest nod toward style in the high ruffled collar and the large, flat bow that rested on the fullness of gathered fabric at the back of the skirt—not exactly the sort of dress one would expect a bride to wear on her first day of marriage. But then, she was only a pretend bride standing in her sister's place. Her hands stilled. Tears stung her eyes. *Oh, Linda, where are you? Have you reached San Francisco? Is your husband treating you well?*

Her uneasiness, carried since Linda had stormed out of their house, swelled into a band of tightness around her chest. She'd seen Linda's prospective husband only a few minutes when Linda had come home to get her jewelry and withdraw her share of their inheritance, but something in his eyes had made her uncomfortable. She'd taken an immediate dislike to him. That wasn't like her. Of course, that could be because he was the reason Linda had broken her promise to marry Blake—if she had ever intended to do so.

She closed her eyes and rubbed at the ache in her temples. Maybe things would have turned out differently if their father were still alive. Or if she hadn't challenged Linda to do the right thing and marry Blake that day. Perhaps if she'd been less ardent in defense of Blake's expectation, she could have talked Linda into at least coming West to see Blake again before she married another.

Oh, what did it matter? It was done. Thinking about it would change nothing. She would simply have to live with her guilt. And Linda— She gasped, lowered her hands to press against her chest. Linda did not know she'd come to Whisper Creek! And she was the one Linda relied on since their parents had passed. How would Linda find her if she needed help? Oh, everything was such a mess! And she couldn't even confess to Blake about the letters. It would only deepen his hurt, and make their situation untenable.

"Dear Lord, please watch over Linda and keep her well and safe. And please help me to be all that Blake needs me to be until he finds a solution to save his store. Help me to play the part of a newlywed well in front of others—to atone for writing those letters. And help Blake's heart heal. Oh, Lord, please don't let Blake suffer because of Linda's selfish ways and my imprudence. Let him heal and find love with another, I pray."

Tension thrummed along her nerves. Some planner she was. She hadn't thought beyond the point of marrying Blake to save his inheritance. Now she was caught unprepared. *Play the part...* What did that mean? How did a loving bride act? Thanks to John's betrayal, she'd not had a chance to learn about being a bride. An image of Linda's friend Carolyn Rogers clinging to her new husband's arm and cooing love words at him flashed into her head. Surely Blake would not expect such behavior from her. He could barely stand the sight of her. And she didn't blame him.

Tears surged, but she swallowed them back, refusing to cry any more. What was done was done. She couldn't change it. All she could do now was to help Blake save his store.

She thrust aside her troubling thoughts and hurried to her satchel inside the large wardrobe Blake had made to hold Linda's many gowns. She couldn't bring herself to place her grooming aids on the lovely dressing table he had bought for Linda, or to use the products he had provided for her sister. Thoughts of the White Rose paste for teeth, the Pears' soap and the lovely milk glass Crème Simon jar alongside the tin of Gillette safety razor blades and the jar of Swiss Violet shaving cream on the shelf above the washbowl in the dressing room sent a tremble through her. The sight of those items had brought Blake's longing to wed Linda home to her as nothing else had. They were so...*intimate*, sitting there side by side.

Her stomach churned, threatened to empty. Blake

resented her for coming to Whisper Creek to marry him, even if it was for his benefit. And he regretted yielding to her arguments and going through with the marriage. That had been clear in that angry ceremonial kiss. And in the obligatory polite way he had treated her last night. There had been no evidence of the casual friendship that had existed between them when he was courting Linda. She sighed and opened the satchel. As uncomfortable as her position was for her, it had to be unbearable for Blake. He loved Linda. And her mere presence, here in the home he had built for the two of them, had to remind him of her sister. All she could do was try to be as unobtrusive as possible when they were alone.

She coiled her long wavy hair into a thick figure eight at the nape of her neck and secured it with hairpins and the pearl hair comb that was a bequest from her grandmother. A quick glance in the long mirror affixed to the inside of the wardrobe door revealed wispy curls lying against her forehead. She smoothed them back and closed the door. Linda's blond curls looked lovely resting on her forehead. Her own red curls just looked messy. But the room was neat.

She released another sigh and looked around. There was no sign of her being there. She could not sleep in that bed with its pristine blue-and-white coverlet, so she'd sat in the rocker and dozed when she wasn't pacing and worrying last night away. And she'd made certain there was no sign of disturbance to the dressing room when she'd washed and prepared for the day.

The room was getting lighter. She glanced at the brightness filtering through the shutters. Dawn came quickly in the mountains. Should she go to the kitchen now? She tiptoed to the bedroom door and pressed her ear against the wood. There was no sound, only silence. A frown tugged at her eyebrows. Had Blake finally fallen asleep? He'd been stirring in the next bedroom all through her long sleepless night. Perhaps he'd risen when she dozed off after coming back from the dressing room.

She stepped back, nibbled at her lower lip. What should she do? When did he breakfast? Were there provisions in the kitchen? Surely there were provisions! He'd said there was no restaurant in Whisper Creek, so he had to cook—didn't he? The questions streaked through her mind, adding to her indecision. The only thing she was sure of was that she did not want to presume for her own use the things that Blake had provided for Linda, or in any way add to his hurt from Linda's betrayal.

She listened at the door again, heard nothing and turned back into the room. It would be ill-mannered of her to rise first; she would wait until she heard Blake leave his bedroom. She moved to the window, opened the shutters and watched the sun climbing above the mountains. How foolish Linda was to throw away the love of a man as thoughtful and caring and faithful and…and *passionate* in his feelings as Blake.

Blake stood with his hand on the doorknob, torn between his desire to leave the confinement of the bedroom and his reluctance to face the agony of the day ahead. He'd been looking forward to Linda's excitement over all of the things he'd bought for her comfort.

How could he face Audrey in his beloved's place? How could he watch her in the kitchen, using the utensils and pots and pans and stove he had bought for Linda, while she prepared and then shared what should have been his first breakfast with his wife?

Wife. The word stabbed deep. He sucked in a breath and glanced at the light slipping through the window shutters. Morning was breaking. He had no choice but to live through this day. And neither did Audrey. He released the doorknob and massaged the tense muscles in his neck and shoulders, then drew his knuckles along his freshly shaved jaw. Audrey had tried her best to act undaunted last night. But she hadn't been prepared for the reality of a marriage—even a pretend one. It was obvious when they came back to the store last night that she hadn't thought beyond the ceremony. There was an unworldliness...an innocence about Audrey. He'd sensed it during their short conversations when he'd courted Linda, and it was strongly in evidence last night. And now he was responsible for her.

His face tightened. He never should have married her—wouldn't have if he'd had time to think beyond his shock at Linda's betrayal and the urgency of the moment. But then he would have lost the store. He owed Audrey his gratitude and respect for saving it for him, but—*Linda*. The ache swelled, burst over him like a wave. He bit back a moan, set his jaw and reached for the doorknob. The sooner he faced this day, the sooner it would be over. He gripped the cold metal, fighting the anguish that had become a part of him. "God in Heaven, help Audrey, I pray. And please help me to hide my feelings. She doesn't deserve any of this."

A quick twist of his wrist opened the bedroom door, and he walked down the hallway into the kitchen. Light from the windows gleamed on the new furnishings. The sight of them fueled his determination. He strode beyond the worktable to the stove, opened the firebox, struck a match and lit the kindling he'd readied the day before. He'd choke down breakfast somehow.

"Good morning."

Audrey. His hand tightened on the damper. He finished adjusting the draft on the stovepipe, turned and pulled his lips into a facsimile of a smile. "Good morning. It looks like it's going to be a nice day." A bald-faced lie. It was a *wretched* day. He should be taking his wife in his arms—

"Yes. It was beautiful watching the sun come up over the mountain. Though it was quite misty."

Her return smile was shaky. So was the hand she lifted to push back the curl dangling on her forehead. An image of Linda smiling up at him while she twirled a curl around her finger flashed into his head. His chest constricted. Thankfully, Audrey didn't have blond hair and blue eyes or Linda's coquettish ways—he couldn't have borne that. He nodded, turned to the coal box on the floor and scooped up some black chunks.

"The mist rises from the snowcaps." He slid the coal off the shovel onto the kindling, closed the door and adjusted the draft. Audrey's skirt whispered against the polished wood floor. He tensed, glanced over his shoulder. She was walking toward him, her hazel eyes shining.

"What a beautiful stove." The words were a mere whisper. She wasn't talking to *him*. He watched her brush her hand across the gleaming cast-iron cooking surface, then raise it to touch the blue porcelain doors on the warming ovens above it before lowering it and resting her fingertips on the chrome handle of the oven door. "Just beautiful…"

It was the exact response he had hoped for—but from the wrong woman. He clenched his hands, reminded himself of what he owed Audrey and cleared his throat. "I'm glad you approve of it. I wasn't sure—"

"Oh, it's wonderful! Just look at that spacious oven! Why, I could bake—" She caught her lower lip with her teeth, stepped back and slid her palms down the front of her skirt. "I mean—any woman would love to have this stove to cook and bake on."

"I'm glad to hear it, because any man likes to eat." The attempt to ease the awkwardness of this first morning with humor bore fruit. She lifted her head and gave him a tentative smile.

"Would you like me to fix you some breakfast?" She glanced around the kitchen. "Are there provisions…?"

Trapped. Now he had to eat. His stomach clenched at the thought. "There are supplies in the refrigerator, and in the cupboard beside it. If you don't find what you need, just ask. I will likely have it in the store." He turned back to the coal box, scooped up more chunks and moved to the corner.

"What is that?"

Fabric rustled. Her dark blue skirt hem floated into sight at the corner of his eye. He glanced up. She was standing in front of the tin-lined sink cupboard gazing toward the column in front of him.

"It's a water heater." He opened the door of the fire-box and dumped the coal onto the glowing embers.

"A *water* heater?" She leaned closer, her eyes sparkling with curiosity. "There's no spigot. How does it work?"

"The water comes from outside into the bottom of this reservoir…here." He touched a pipe that came up through the floor. "The coal heats the water and it rises to the top. Then the hot water from the top of the reservoir flows out through this pipe—" he raised his hand to a pipe midway up the tank "—into the washbowl and bathing tub in the dressing room."

"Oh, I see." She glanced his way and smiled. "I *wondered* where that wonderful hot water came from." Her gaze slid back to the water heater. "What are those other pipes for? Does that one— Oh, my!" She leaned forward, peered over the end of the cupboard. "That one comes to this sink!"

He grinned, caught up in her enthusiasm. "That's right. It brings the hot water here—" he stepped closer, stretched out his hand "—to this spigot. And this one—" he touched another pipe that ran along the wall to the sink cupboard "—brings in the cold water from outside."

She straightened and looked up at him, her hazel eyes shining bright with gold flecks he'd never noticed before. "And the wastewater?"

"You dump it into the sink and it flows down this screened hole through a draining pipe to the outside."

"Truly?" Her gaze dropped to the sink cupboard. She gave a soft sigh and slid her fingers along the wood cabinet. "I never would have thought a kitchen in Wyoming Territory would be more luxurious than ours in New York."

Ours. The thought of Linda took him like a fist to the stomach. He sucked in a breath, looked away. "I wanted the best..."

"Yes, of course."

She sounded stricken. He glanced back, saw the knowledge of his hurt in Audrey's eyes. She'd understood what he'd left unsaid. He'd have to do better at hiding his emotions, but how? It was as if Linda stood there between them. He took refuge in honesty. "I'm not really that hungry, Audrey. Coffee will do for me. There's a bag of Lion's—freshly ground—in the pantry." He dipped his head toward the large floor-to-ceiling cupboard at the other end of the stove.

She met his gaze for a moment, then nodded and moved back to the stove. He set his jaw, watched her lift the new coffeepot from the cooking surface, set the insides on the worktable, then turn to the sink cupboard and reach for the tap.

"Wait!" Too late.

Water gushed, hit the rim of the pot and splashed onto Audrey's hand and blouse. She gasped and jumped back. He reached to turn off the deluge and their hands collided. She jerked hers away, grabbed her blouse and tugged at the wet spot, flapping it to make it dry. "That water is freezing cold!"

Her uneasiness at his touch was plain on her face. Guilt pricked him. She had come all this way to help him. The least he could do was show some appreciation and try to make her as comfortable as possible under the circumstances. He tugged his lips into a slanted grin. "Sorry. I tried to warn you. The water is melt-off from the ice cap piped in from the waterfall. There's a lot of pressure."

"I noticed."

He chuckled at her dry tone.

She looked up, an uncertain smile playing at the corner of her lips. Their gazes met and she looked down, opened the tap slowly and ran water into the pot. "How do you like your coffee?"

"Strong and black."

She nodded, set the pot on the worktable and moved to the pantry. "Father liked his coffee that way. Two spoonsful for every cup."

"You made it for him?" The stovepipe crackled. He turned the draft down for a slow burn.

"Every morning." There was sadness in the smile that curved her lips. "I'm an early riser—like Father was. There's something special about shar—" Her lips clamped closed. She carried the bag of coffee to the worktable. "Where are your spoons?"

"Here in this drawer." He stepped beside her and pulled a drawer open while she placed the insides in the coffeepot. "There are towels and things in the drawer in front of you."

She accepted the spoon he handed her, opened the bag and peered inside, then tipped it from side to side, probing the coffee with the spoon handle.

The rich aroma rose to tempt his nostrils. "Looking for the picture card?"

She stopped searching in the ground beans and glanced up at him with a self-conscious little laugh. "Force of habit."

She saved them? Linda wouldn't bother with a picture card. She was too sophisticated and worldly for such things. Obviously more worldly than he'd known. His lungs constricted, cut off his breath. The muscle along his jaw twitched. "I tossed the card away when I ground the coffee." He moved to the water heater, pretending to adjust the damper on the firebox door.

"It's of no matter." The spoon clinked against the coffeepot. "As I said, it's only habit. I save them for Lily Chaseon—the daughter of our neighbors back home."

Where she would be had she not come West to help him. His hand stilled. Why would she do that? She was not responsible for Linda's behavior. He watched Audrey place the coffeepot on the stove, fold down the top of the bag and carry it back to the cupboard, her movements neat and precise. Everything about Audrey was neat—her hair, her appearance in that plain gown…even the way she arranged her thoughts into a sensible argument that had left him no room for disagreement—except on an emotional level. He frowned, shoved his fingers through his hair and determined to stop acting like a graceless boor. At the very least, he owed her good manners. "Audrey…"

"Yes?" She moved to the step-back dresser displaying blue-and-white-patterned dishes and lifted a cup and saucer off the shelf.

"I want to apologize for my behavior last night." Her posture stiffened. She glanced at him then started for the table.

"There's no need for an apology, Blake."

"I think there is. I had no right to kiss you like that—

to take my anger out on you. Or to treat you in such an unwelcoming manner after you came all this way to—"

"Please stop, Blake. I realize how…difficult…all this is for you." The cup rattled against the saucer. She set it on the table and clasped her hands. "I'm so sorry for…everything."

"You've nothing to be sorry for, Audrey. It is—" his tongue refused to speak the name of his beloved "—your sister who broke her promise to me. You've come to help me. And I recognize that that was very hard for you—as is this farce of a marriage in which we find ourselves. And I appreciate what you are doing for me—though my behavior toward you last night did not, in any way, reflect my gratitude. I'm sorry for that. I hope you will forgive me." He cleared his throat and moved to stand beside her. "It's early. Dawn has not yet fully given way to the day. Shall we start again?"

Her gaze lifted, the uneasiness that had shadowed her eyes replaced with a hint of the friendliness he remembered. "As you wish."

"Then we'll need another cup and saucer." He grabbed the dishes from the dresser and carried them back to the table. "We'll have a cup of coffee to toast our…er…*partnership* in saving my store. Thanks to you, I will have the time to come up with a plan to do so. And we need to discuss how we will make this charade work meantime." The thought soured his stomach.

"That sounds like the sensible thing to do." She gave a delicate sniff, glanced toward the stove. "Excuse me, I don't want the coffee to boil." She took a dish towel out of the drawer in the worktable, gripped the coffeepot and set it down toward the back of the stove. "That's better—it's not as hot there." She placed the towel on the worktable and gave him another of those tentative near smiles. "It will be a few minutes until the coffee is ready. Shall we begin?"

He dipped his head. "Ladies first."

"Very well." She brushed her palms down the front of her long skirt, then raised one hand and gave a small all-encompassing wave. "I am not concerned about cooking or household matters. Since Mother passed away, I have cared for our house and for Father and Li—" She caught her lower lip with her teeth, looked down.

Linda. Pain flashed. He clenched his hands, took a breath and nodded. "That's good to know. We should know about each other's lives, should someone ask us." He ignored the ache gripping him and pressed on. "One question I'm certain will be asked us is how we met."

Her head jerked up. "What would you have me say?"

"The truth. That we met while I was courting your older sister." The vein in his temple throbbed. He moved to look out of one of the windows that bracketed the dish dresser to avoid the compassion in her eyes. "The problem is, Mr. Ferndale knows Linda is…*was*…my fiancée. I often spoke of her by name." He scrubbed his hand over the nape of his neck, ignoring the knot in his gut. "We'll have to think of something to explain why we married. And it would be best to stay as close to the truth as possible so we don't get our stories confused."

A train whistle sounded, echoing down the valley. "That's it!"

"What is *it*?"

"The train." He pivoted, met her confused gaze.

"We'll tell people we corresponded, and when…Linda… wed another, you came out of friendship to tell me in person." The constriction in his chest tightened. He fought for breath to continue. "I think it would be best if we not mention the store, so I will tell Mr. Ferndale when you stepped off the train and I saw you again, I realized my feelings for you had deepened beyond friendship. That I had fallen in love with you through your letters. That we talked, I confessed my feelings for you and you… professed a fondness for me, and agreed to marry me." He stepped closer, studied her face. "Are you all right with this, Audrey? You look pale."

"I'm fine…only a trifle uneasy. I've never been good at…at dissembling. The coffee's ready." She snatched up the towel and turned to the stove.

He watched her lifting the hot brew. Guilt reared. What depths had he sunk to, putting his need to save his fortune ahead of his honor? He squared his shoulders. "Forgive me, Audrey. It's wrong of me to put you in such a position. There is a train going east early this afternoon. I will put you on it, then go and tell Mr. Ferndale the truth."

Steam spiraled from the hot pot, misted the air between them. "Thank you for your consideration, but I'm not going home, Blake." She walked to the table, poured the hot coffee into their cups and returned the pot to the stove. "And you did not put me in this position—I did. And I would do it again. It's only right after what my sister did to you."

The hem of her skirt swished across the floor, a quiet accompaniment to her firm words. He studied the resolute look on her face. A different Audrey than he'd ever seen. She'd always been so acquiescent to Linda's wishes.

"And what you said about me is true. I *did* come in friendship to tell you what had happened. And we *did* talk. And I *did* agree to marry you when you asked me—well, that's backward, but it's close enough. The... conditions...of our marriage will remain our private knowledge." She moved to the refrigerator and opened the door, glanced inside. She closed the door again.

"Sorry, I got meat and butter, but forgot about milk."

"That's all right—I can drink the coffee black."

A real smile tugged at his lips. "That shudder you just tried to hide says different. I have some Eagle Brand in the store. I'll get it."

Audrey listened to Blake walking down the stairs, every step driving his words deeper into her conscience. *That I had fallen in love with you through your letters.* It wasn't true, of course. Blake didn't love her and he didn't know she'd written the letters. But still, it was a plausible explanation. The warmth of Blake's letters had drawn her. And she had responded to that warmth— though as Linda, of course. Still, the attraction was sincere. But then, she'd always enjoyed her conversations with Blake...

She eyed the steaming cups of coffee, picked up hers and took a cautious sip hoping to settle her churning stomach. All she achieved was a scalded tongue and a shudder at the bitter taste. Tears filmed her eyes. "Father God, You know I'm sorry for helping Linda deceive Blake. I was wrong not to have warned him she was fickle when he began courting her, but— No. No excuses… Please help me to make amends. Please help Blake—"

Footsteps on the stairs halted her choked words. She blinked her eyes, wiped her cheeks and ran on tiptoe to look out of the window over the coal box beside the stove. A muted hammering came from the raw structure next door. The hotel. He'd written to Linda about—

"Here's the milk. I'll open it for you. These cans are hard to puncture, even with a can opener."

Blake's thoughtfulness brought another surge of tears. She was too tired and too unnerved by their situation. She nodded and blinked, struggled to get her emotions under control.

"There's some ground sugar in the bowl—if you use it."

He'd ground sugar for Linda. "No, only milk." It was another way she differed from her sister. Linda used spoonsful of sugar in her coffee or tea. She swallowed hard and jerked her thoughts from Blake's love for her sister before her guilt overwhelmed her and she blurted out the entire story. It would only hurt him more. "I can hear them working on the hotel."

"You know of the hotel?"

Her stomach flopped. She shouldn't know about the things he'd written Linda! She groped for a way to cover her error. "Linda shared the things you wrote about Wyoming Territory and Whisper Creek with me." It wasn't a lie. Not really. It was only…misleading.

"I see." His voice was flat, terse.

Another mistake. She shouldn't have mentioned Linda. She hurried to the dish dresser for the creamer and poured some of the milk into it. "Thank you for opening the can." Blake nodded and put the can in the refrigerator, but she'd seen the taut line of his mouth, the shadow of pain in his eyes. Her hands tightened on the creamer and spoons she carried to the table. "To continue our discussion—I will need to know your routine in order to plan my household tasks, when to prepare meals and such."

He held her chair for her, then took the chair across the table and bowed his head. "Thank You for Your provision, Lord. Lead me—*us*...through this day, I pray. Amen."

Us. The word hung in the air, awkward and uncomfortable. She stared down at her cup, swirled milk into the hot dark brew and watched the color lighten, knowing Blake wished it were Linda sitting in her place. So did she.

"This is good coffee."

Was he being polite? "I can adjust the amount if—"

"Nope. It's perfect as it is." His smile looked forced. "About my schedule... I really haven't established one yet as I've only just opened for business. Until now it's all been orders from those building new homes or businesses. That number has been very few, but it's growing. Still, having only a few residents in the town limits business." He took a swallow of coffee, glanced over at her. "I'm up at dawn, so I open the store at seven. The first train comes through at seven ten and I'm hoping the passengers will come in and buy things they need—though none have as yet."

"That's not surprising."

"I beg your pardon?"

She stopped stirring and looked up. "The conductor on my train told the passengers there is no food or drink available in town and advised them not to wander away from the station as Whisper Creek is a short stop for refueling and taking on water only."

"I didn't know the conductors did that." He frowned and set his cup back on the saucer. "I'm sure some of those soldiers on their way to their postings farther west would come in for tobacco and other sundries if they knew of my store. Not to mention the civilians. At the moment, my store is the last chance for them to purchase necessities and small luxuries before they continue on their journey."

She sipped her coffee, weighed the idea that had popped into her head. Would he think her forward if she mentioned it? A foolish worry. How could he think her any more forward than he already did for suggesting they marry? "Perhaps a sign would help."

He gave her an odd, sort of surprised, quizzical look, then shook his head. "The Union Pacific does not allow signs on their property. I'll speak to the stationmaster, ask him to tell the conductors that my store is open for business so they can pass the word along to their passengers."

Her pulse quickened. His descriptions in his letters had made her curious about Whisper Creek, but she'd been too nervous last night to pay much attention to the buildings and surroundings. She took another sip of coffee to keep from asking to accompany him, certain he would prefer to be alone.

The hammering from the building next door grew louder. Blake glanced toward the window. "It will be expected that I take you on a 'tour' of Whisper Creek—such as it is. Would that be acceptable to you?"

She grasped at the chance to be away from this home he'd hoped to share with Linda. It would be good for both of them to forget how Linda had altered their lives—at least for a little while. "Yes, of course. I would enjoy seeing the town—'such as it is.'" She set her cup on its saucer and took a breath, spoke what had been on her mind all morning. "But, before we do, I'm concerned about, that is, I'm not certain I know how to play the part of a newlywed, Blake. What do you want me to do?" The muscle along his jaw jumped. Pain sharpened the planes of his face. She looked away, stared down at her coffee. "If you'd rather wait—"

"No. We'll take the 'tour' now. As for how to act—just follow my example. And bear in mind that I, too, will be acting my part. Don't flinch away if I should… touch you."

The vein at his temple was pulsing again. She nodded, hid her clenched hands in her lap. "I'll be ready as soon as I clear the table."

"I'll await you downstairs in the store." He rose and slid his chair under the table. "You may need a wrap of some sort. Early mornings are cool in the mountains."

She stared after Blake as he strode from the kitchen, then sighed and carried their cups and saucers to the sink cupboard. *Don't flinch away if I should…touch you.* Why would he say that? She'd never had men swarming about her the way Linda did, but it wasn't as if she'd never had a beau. And he knew she'd been promised until John Barker decided Alicia Blackwell's sudden inheritance was the wiser move for his future and broke off their betrothal to court the spinster. She frowned and dumped the rest of her coffee into the sink. It was only that this odd situation made her nervous. She wrested what comfort she could from that thought, then set herself to act the part of a new bride.

Chapter Three

"I'm ready."

Blake pivoted toward the door to the storage room and was struck again by Audrey's neat, trim appearance, and how well it matched her personality. Linda would be swathed in ruffles and lace that drew a man's eye to her curves and— He jerked his mind from the conjured image of his beloved and stepped forward. Audrey moved slowly toward him, her gaze sweeping around the store before coming to rest on him.

"Your store is larger than it seemed las—in the dark." She stopped by a display of Bull Durham tobacco sitting beside piled boxes of ceramic doorknobs on the counter and looked up at him. "There are so many choices. How do you decide what to stock?"

The question halted him. How like Audrey to try to distract him from their ridiculous circumstance. He'd forgotten how kind she was. Her intelligence demanded a well-considered answer. He gathered his thoughts. "I try to think of what will be required to build the town and then keep those items in stock for the men doing the work. Right now, that's mostly foodstuffs, tools and hardware and other construction needs, along with tobacco products and a smattering of household items."

"Oh, I see…"

Her gaze slid toward the back corner. A frown formed a small line between her delicately arched eyebrows. He glanced at the tables that sat there, a large one covered with piles of denim pants and cotton shirts, a smaller one covered with a few bolts of cloth and some small baskets of buttons and other notions. "Is there a problem with my dry goods section? I know it's small. But until your…arrival, there were only two women in town—Mrs. Ferndale and Yan Cheng, the laundress."

She looked up, met his gaze full on. "Do you want my honest opinion?"

Probably not enough ribbons and lace to suit her. Still, if she was nice enough to pretend interest in the store, he should humor her. "Yes, of course."

"Very well." She took a soft breath. "I understand your reasoning—and it makes perfect sense to cater to the majority of your customers. But, if you are hoping to sell to the women passengers on the trains passing through, then—in my opinion—you should bring your dry goods forward out of that dark corner." She crossed to the table and touched the basket holding ribbons. "It is hard to see what you have displayed here. And the dim light afforded by the overhead lamps does not show the fabric or trimmings in a true light. It is most frustrating to buy a piece of fabric or trim and find when you get it home that it is not the right color at all." She turned back to face him. "Also, women will not like walking through an entire store of men's tools to find the few items of interest to them."

He stared at her, taken aback by her sensible detailed answer. "I see."

Pink spread across her cheekbones. "Forgive me, Blake. I got carried away—"

"Not at all. I appreciate you explaining a woman's thoughts on such things to me." He shifted his gaze away from her face. Linda had never blushed like that. It was surprisingly touching. "I will move the dry goods. Where would you suggest?"

"Me?"

He nodded at the gasped word. "You must have had a place in mind." The shock on her face turned to dismay.

"No, I didn't. Truly! I only noticed the darkness of the corner. I wasn't trying to—"

"But you would place the dry goods at the front of the store?"

"Well…yes. But—"

"Where?"

She stared at him a moment, then walked to a tool-covered table situated at the left front corner of the room. "I would put them here—in the natural light from the window. And—" Her teeth caught at her lower lip. She glanced at him, then looked away and gave a small, dismissive wave of her hand.

"And what?"

"Nothing. I'm sorry, Blake. Please forgive me for being so bold as to offer you advice on your store. I have no experience as a shopkeeper." She smoothed her skirt, looked toward the door. "Shall we go now?"

"Not yet. I'd like to hear what you were thinking." The dismayed look returned to her face.

"It was nothing of importance. I only thought…" Her shoulders squared. She waved her hand toward the window. "If you feel you could spare the space, you might want to put a bolt of fabric and a basket of notions, ribbons and such in the window." She glanced toward the shelves behind the long counter. "And perhaps one of those large ironstone pitchers… And a pewter candlestick… And perhaps a crock of that marmalade…" She met his gaze again. "My thought was—with only tools and hardware items in the window—how are the women passengers to know the store sells things they may want or need?"

"How indeed?" He pushed aside his shock at her astute suggestions, focused his attention on the window. "You make excellent sense, Audrey. A few household items in the display would draw a woman's eye. I believe I will make those changes before I—*we* go to the depot to talk to Asa." He strode to the back table, lifted the bolts of fabric and carried them to the counter. "Which would you suggest for the window?"

Her expression brightened. She hurried to his side, touched a rose silk, an apple-green organdy with a delicate white embroidered flower trim at the edge, then sighed and shifted her hand. "This blue taffeta. Most women are partial to blue."

He stared down at the taffeta the color of Linda's eyes, fought back memories of her gazing up at him through her long lashes and shook his head. "I'll use the green." The words came out more brusque than he'd intended.

Audrey withdrew her hand, stepped back. "Forgive me, Blake. I—I didn't think about—"

"No reason why you should." He cleared the gruffness from his throat, looked over at her and read the understanding in her eyes. "What happened, happened, Audrey. You had no part in it, and you've no reason to keep apologizing because of my...feelings. I'll get over them." He headed back to the dry goods table.

Will I? Will I ever forget the feel of Linda in my arms? Will the longing to hold her and kiss her, to have her for my own, ever go away? He stared down at the baskets and clenched his hands to keep from throwing them at the wall, busting the table in pieces and walking out the door to never return. It would cost him all he had to leave, but he could find employment, make his way somehow. At least he would be away from all these things that brought back the memory of his plans for a life with Linda. But he had Audrey to think of now. She had come all this way to save his store for him; he couldn't walk out on the debt he owed her for that. He had to figure out a plan that would release them both from this sham of a marriage!

His temple throbbed. He unclenched his hands, piled the baskets one atop the other and carried them to the counter. Audrey had that stricken look in her eyes again. He groped for something to take her mind off Linda and their situation. "Show me where you would place the things in the window and I'll clear the spot. If you're of a mind to, you can put the things you suggested there while I finish switching the goods on the tables."

She nodded, picked up the bolt of green organdy and followed him down the length of the counter toward the window. "I think it would be good to put them in the center front, where those saws are—if that's all right?"

"Makes sense." It was the best response he could manage. He lifted the saws out of the window and carried them to the storage room, fighting the swelling pain of betrayal.

"I'll tell them if I ain't too busy—or they ain't."

What an officious little man! Audrey held her smile and stared back at the stationmaster peering out at them, his balding gray head and slumped shoulders framed by the ticket window in the depot wall.

"But I can't promise you. Things get busier than a hornet's nest 'round here when a train stops. Them conductors only got but twenty minutes to get any messages from dispatch, see to their passengers and the loadin' and unloadin' of freight before they're out of here. And we got to see to the consignments and waybills. And I got the telegraph and all."

Blake nodded, let go of her arm and shoved his fingers through his hair. "I understand you have a job to do, Asa. And I know it's against the Union Pacific rules for any signs to be placed on their stations. But I was wondering if a small one sitting here at the window would be acceptable? That would—"

"I'm afraid not. Rule says clear, no signs nowhere on the property. There's the telegraph! Got to answer it." The balding gray head dipped her direction. "Pleasure to meet you, Mrs. Latherop."

"And you, Mr. Marsh." She was talking to air. The stationmaster had slipped off his stool and disappeared. Clicking sounds drifted out of the open ticket window.

"Well, that puts paid to that idea." Blake frowned, grasped her elbow and turned toward the steps. "I'll have to wait for the train passengers' patronage until I get the store sign made. A large sign, big enough to be read from here. I'll hang it on the board across the top of the porch."

"And that will teach Mr. Marsh there is more than one way to skin a cat!"

Blake jerked to a stop. His eyebrows rose. "'*Skin* a cat'? Why, Audrey Prescott…er Latherop. You've read Major Jack Downing's adventures!"

She lifted her chin. "Hasn't everyone?"

His smile turned into a grin—the crooked kind he used to wear when he teased her about something. "Men, yes. But I don't know any other *women* who read Seba Smith. They read Godey's Lady's Book." The grin faded with his words. He released her arm, looked off into the distance.

Godey's Lady's Book. Linda's favorite—for fashion. Linda didn't read the articles. She took a breath and prepared to throw herself on the sacrificial pyre of Blake's teasing. Anything to draw his thoughts back away from her sister. "Father and I read Major Downing's adventures together. We discussed them over his morning coffee." Blake didn't respond. She moved closer to the edge of the platform, looked down the dirt road to the beginning of the town and returned to their purpose in coming to the depot.

"A large sign will be easily read from here, Blake. And I'm certain one will draw the passengers to your store." She glanced over her shoulder at him, then lifted her hems and walked down the steps. "Twenty minutes is a long time to simply stand around this station trying not to get in the way of the other passengers or the train crew. And the short walk will be inviting to those who have been sitting in a swaying passenger car for hours."

"I'd forgotten how optimistic you are, Audrey." Blake trotted down the steps and stood beside her. "You're right about the sign. But it has to wait until the store is painted and the trim finished, so there's the meantime— and it's obvious Asa Marsh will be of little help. But it's my own fault. I should have waited to open the store. I was too eager to—" He bit off the words, grasped her left hand and tucked it through the crook of his right arm. "In case anyone sees us walking while I show you around Whisper Creek."

"Such as it is…" She took a skip to catch up with his long strides.

"Sorry." His steps slowed, stopped. He stared down at her hand resting on his arm. "Where's your ring?"

"The ring is safe in its box." She lifted her chin, looked full into his eyes. "It's too large and I don't want to lose it—should anyone ask." The muscle along his jaw twitched. He nodded and moved forward. She cast about for something to distract him from his tormenting thoughts. "The hotel looks finished outside, except for needing paint and trim like your store. But, I can hear them working inside. When does Mr. Stevenson expect to open for business?"

"Mr. Stevenson?" Blake stopped walking, gave her a puzzled look.

Featherbrain! You distracted him all right. How would you know the hotel owner's name? She widened her eyes in a look of confusion. "Am I wrong? These things were only mentioned in passing." *Oh, wonderful! That will keep him from thinking of Linda.*

She pressed her lips together and slid her gaze back to the large raw building before more of her knowledge of Whisper Creek and its residents slipped out. Blake was too much of a gentleman to question her explanation, but she could almost hear him wondering how much of his letters Linda had shared with her. *Blessed Lord, please don't let him guess that it was the other way around. That I—*

"The name is correct. Your memory serves you well." His arm relaxed beneath her hand. She held back a sigh when they started walking again. "To answer your question—Garret Stevenson hopes to open by the end of September on a limited basis. It will be winter before all of the rooms are finished. And then, of course, they will have to be painted and furnished before they can be occupied."

"And he will buy the paint and the furnishings from you? That's wonderful, Blake!" She smiled up at him. His strained look brought her back to reality. "I mean— if you still have the store then."

"Which I will—if I can't come up with a plan." Bitterness laced his voice. "I've tried, but I've thought of nothing that will work. If it weren't for that contract I signed…"

Her heart ached for him. "It's not even been a full day, Blake. And this is an…unusual circumstance. You will think of something."

"More optimism?"

His teasing tone fell flat. "No, not optimism. I have faith in your abilities." She waved her hand forward. "What is the building on the other side of your store going to be?"

"An apothecary. The owner is not in town yet." His gaze shifted to their right. "I assume he and his wife will come when the store and their house are finished."

She looked away from the twitching muscle along his jaw and followed the direction of his gaze. A narrow path to the side of the stores led into the tall grasses. She lifted her gaze into the distance and gasped at the sight of a large white house with a porch and a round turret situated by the creek that flowed down the long valley. "What a beautiful house. It could sit on the finest street in New York."

"It belongs to Mr. Ferndale, the town founder. The smaller, octagon-shaped house under construction is the apothecary's."

"Octagon-shaped? I've never seen such a house!" Framework for the eight-sided structure sat beside the creek a fair distance beyond the Ferndale home. Movement caught her eye and she shaded her face with her hand, made out the figures of two men crawling along the roof. The muted sound of hammering floated off down the broad valley. She looked into the distance beyond the homes until her gaze collided with the encompassing snowcapped mountains. "I thought the West was full of cows and cowboys and such." She drew her gaze back to look up at him. "Where are the ranches?"

"There aren't many in Wyoming, though ranchers are beginning to move in because of the land opening up and the railroad coming through. I've heard some cowboys bought the land in the adjoining valley and are building a cabin and pens and such. Rumor is, they plan to go back to Texas and bring a herd of cattle up next spring. But it's only rumor. What I know for certain is that there

will be no ranches in this valley. Mr. Ferndale owns all
of the land and he refuses to have Whisper Creek turn
into what he calls a 'rowdy cow town' with drinking and
gambling and other…disreputable pursuits. He envisions
Whisper Creek as a town modeled after his home village
back East. That's why he advertised for—why he won't
allow bachelor businessmen to invest in the town. He
wants men who will build stores and homes and raise
families here." He turned his back, cleared his throat.

She stared at his rigid shoulders, snagged her lip
with her teeth and clenched her hands. *Linda Marie
Prescott—or whatever your name is now—it's fortunate for you you're not here, because I could cheerfully
shake you until your teeth rattled!* She looked around
for a safe subject, found it in the water gushing and
splashing down the mountain behind his store. "Is it
possible to get closer to the waterfall, Blake? I've never
seen one."

"Yes, of course." He turned and offered her his arm.
"It's a bit of a walk—if you don't mind."

"Not at all. It's a lovely day."

"All right then. We'll go around the hotel to reach
the path. I'm afraid it is not a good one, merely beaten-
down grasses."

He led her between a small copse of pines and the
side of the hotel, then turned right and walked along
a rutted dirt path that ran behind the buildings. She
glanced up to get her bearings, stopped and stared at
a wide, odd-looking wood barrow sitting beneath the
floor of a deep, roofed porch. "What is that?"

"My cart. It's how I get my supplies from the depot
to the store. That's my loading dock."

She lifted her gaze. "Is that another porch above it?"

"Yes."

"And that building that adjoins the porch?"

"My stable."

Her pulse jumped. She'd always wanted to ride a horse. Perhaps— "You ride?"

"No. I need a horse to pull the cart. Mitchel Todd—he runs the logging operation here in Whisper Creek—has been allowing me the use of one of his horses until I can buy one." He released her arm. "The path is this way. Take care where you step—the grasses are treacherous and the ground is rough where we buried the pipe for the water supply. The trail is too narrow to walk together. I'll go first in case—"

The blast of a train whistle drowned out his words. His head turned toward the tracks.

The look in his eyes pricked her heart. *He's hoping Linda is on that train. He wants her to come back to him.* Her hope for a pleasant, distracting walk to the waterfall died. She lifted her skirt hems and started up the few steps to the loading dock.

He pivoted toward her. "What are you doing?"

"I've changed my mind. I think it would be best if we stayed here."

"But the waterfall…"

She shook her head and continued up the steps. "You can show me the waterfall another time. I forgot that Mr. Marsh might tell the porter about your store. You need to be here if any passengers come to make a purchase." She hurried across the deep porch, wrenched open the door and rushed through the storage room and up the stairs, aware of him following behind her. She reached the top, swung around the newel post into the short hall on the right and peered over the railing. Blake paused at the bottom of the stairs, then walked on. Tears stung her eyes at the anguish in his unguarded expression. She listened to his footsteps fade away as he entered the store.

Every part of her being longed to help him, to right the wrong done him, but it was impossible. She knew from experience that only God could heal his wounded heart. She shoved away from the railing, grasped hold of her skirts and walked into the bedroom she was using—*their* bedroom. Everything here was either built or purchased with her sister in mind. There was no place in the living quarters she could go that did not remind her of Linda. And if it was that way for her, how much worse it was for Blake. What had ever made her think coming here to save Blake's store would ease his agony over Linda's betrayal? How could he forget what had happened when everything around him was a constant reminder of his lost love? Including her. She never should have come.

Her back stiffened. It was another mistake she would have to live with. She was here now. And she would make the best of it for Blake and herself until he came up with a different plan to save his inheritance. There was no doubt that he would—or that his plan would be much more sensible than hers. Meantime, she would stop trying to ease his pain over Linda's desertion and concentrate on making his life, and hers, as comfortable and pleasant as possible under the circumstances— starting with this room.

She marched to the bed, stripped off and folded

the beautiful blue-and-white coverlet, then opened the blanket chest at the foot of the bed. She snatched out a wool blanket the mustard color of an autumn leaf and put the coverlet inside. The silver ring box gleamed at her. She spread the blanket on the bed, snatched up the ring box and shoved it out of sight at the bottom of the chest. The throw on the back of the rocker worked nicely to hide the ornate dressing table. She arranged her grooming items on top of the woven wool, straightened and looked around. Much better. At least she would be able to sleep in this room now.

Now, for Blake's room. She set herself, walked the U-shaped hallway around the stairwell, grasped the knob on his bedroom door and froze, unable to open it. It was too…intimate. She whirled about and started back down the hallway.

The room is empty but for a cot.

She stopped, turned and stared at the door once more. A deep breath steadied her. She squared her shoulders, marched back and opened the door. A cot stood in the middle of the room, a sheet, blanket and pillow tangled together on top of it—mute testimony of a sleepless night. She blinked away a rush of tears and opened the doors of a sizable wardrobe on the inside wall. There was a canvas bag on the floor with a rumpled white shirt sticking out of it. She closed the doors and hurried back to her bedroom to get clean linens.

It was a challenge. Audrey eyed the cot she'd moved so it sat between the two shuttered windows in the side wall and nibbled at her lower lip. How could she make the bed linens stay in place? There was nowhere to tuck them, unless— She smiled, snapped the sheet through the air, let the excess fall to the floor and then tucked the corners beneath the feet of the crisscrossed legs. That should work. Blake's weight would hold the corners of the sheet firmly in place. She added a top sheet and then the blanket, tucking only the bottom corners under the legs at the foot of the cot, then shoved the pillow into a clean pillow slip, fluffed it and laid it on top. There!

She gathered up the dirty linens, shoved them in the bag in the wardrobe, then stepped back and eyed her handiwork. At least the cot looked more like a bed now. And, if her idea worked as she hoped, Blake would be able to sleep without the linens strangling him in a tangled mess. But he needed a bedside table, and an oil lamp—the days were getting shorter. There had to be one she could use somewhere.

She rushed out into the hallway, glanced toward the door to Blake's office on her left, then walked ahead to the sitting room. She did not want to overstep her wifely role in this strange marriage. She wouldn't enter his office unless he gave her permission to clean it. She swept her gaze around the sitting room and spotted a lamp table in the far corner. Would Blake be upset if she took it for his use? Perhaps not, once the deed was done. She carried the table and oil lamp back to Blake's bedroom and placed them beneath the shuttered window on the right side of his cot. Perfect!

Now, for his clothes. They would be in a dresser in her room—the bedroom he'd planned to share with

Linda. Guilt tightened her chest. She pushed it aside and concentrated on the task she'd set herself. She had to bring Blake's clothes in here where they would be handy for his use. If he didn't have to constantly enter that bedroom it would be one less reminder of Linda's betrayal.

She returned to her room and opened one of the large bottom drawers of the highboy. Shirts. She'd guessed right—it was Blake's dresser. Propriety blended with modesty and brought warmth crawling into her cheeks. She closed the drawer and stared at the dresser. This was *too* intimate. How could she possibly move his clothes?

Pillow slips.

The idea brought a smile to her lips. She ran to the blanket chest and pulled out a pillow slip, returned to the highboy, covered Blake's shirts and pulled the drawer free. The bulky weight plopped her to the floor on her backside. "Oh!" She shoved the drawer off her legs, scrambled to her feet, lifted it tight against her stomach and headed for the door. It was a close fit. She turned sideways and edged out into the hallway.

"Audrey, I heard a scraping sound. What are you doing?"

Blake! She whipped around toward the stairs, caught her toe in the hem of her skirt, stumbled and pitched forward, still clutching the drawer that rammed straight into Blake's abdomen.

"Oof!"

His warm breath gusted by her cheek, his hands clamped onto her shoulders, held her steady. She came to a heart-pounding halt bent forward over the drawer with the top of her head pressing against his chest.

"Are you all right, Audrey?"

The question was a little breathless. Small wonder with the drawer jammed into his stomach. She was breathless, too. "Yes." The word was smothered by the cloth pushing against her face. She tried to straighten and failed. He tightened his grip on her shoulders, gently pushed her back until she was upright.

"Why don't I take this?" His hands brushed against hers as he grasped hold of the drawer. "Just out of curiosity... What are you doing with my shirts?"

The shirts and pillowcase were all askew. So was her hair. She could feel the curls tumbling every which way onto her forehead and temples. Wonderful! They would match the red of her burning cheeks. She tugged her bodice back into place, shook her skirt hems straight and looked up. "I thought it would be...handier for you if your clothes were in...your bedroom." His gaze lifted over her head toward the open door behind her. She snagged her lower lip with her teeth, wishing she could say one thing that did not bring that strained look to his face. "I was taking them there—one drawer at a time so I could manage them."

He nodded and cleared his throat, lowered his gaze back to meet hers. "And how were you going to move the dresser?"

An excellent question. She shoved her hair comb back into place and lifted her chin. "I hadn't thought that out as yet."

"I see." He frowned and blew out a breath. "I appreciate your...concern, Audrey. But I don't need to be protected. Nothing can change what has happened. Linda chose another. And while that knowledge is raw and painful, I will come to grips with it given time. Now, come and show me what you intend to do in… my bedroom. And the next time you get an idea like this, call me. I don't want you hurting yourself." He stepped aside.

She swallowed back a protest that she was not protecting him, only making things more convenient, and walked ahead of him to his bedroom. She glanced up at his face when he entered. He looked in the direction of the cot and the table, stopped and stared.

"What's all this?" He put the drawer down on the floor, bent down and looked at the corners of the blanket and sheets trapped beneath the legs of the cot. He shook his head, straightened and scrubbed his hand across the back of his neck. "That's clever, Audrey. I wish I had thought of it. My feet would have been a lot warmer these past couple of months." A smile touched his lips, then faded.

She released her breath, thankful he wasn't angry with her presumption in making over his room—or was pretending not to be. "I hope it works."

"It looks as if it will." He headed back for the door. "I'll get the rest of the drawers, then bring the dresser."

She looked at his set face and stepped into his path. She'd meant to spare him pain, not cause it. "There's no need for you to interrupt your work in the store, Blake. I can manage—"

"No. I'll do this."

Her stomach sank. Did he think she was overreaching her position in their arrangement? "But the store…"

"I have no customers demanding my time. Won't have, until I'm able to put up that sign." He glanced around the room. "Where do you want me to put the dresser once I get it in here?"

"I thought on the back wall next to that door, but you—"

"That's as good a place as any. I'll be back."

And she'd be gone! She wasn't going to stand here and watch him do the work she'd started. "Before you go…"

"Yes?"

"I was wondering about dinner." Would he eat anything, or was this another mistake? She squared her shoulders and pressed on. How could things get worse? "I saw packages of meat in the refrigerator. Would roasted beef suit?"

He nodded and looked away. "Roasted beef is fine."

His taut features said he was only being polite. Probably he had as little appetite as she. Still, they had to eat—and she needed something to do. "Then, I'll go start dinner." At least she wouldn't make any mistakes while—

"Can you manage the fire?"

The question rasped along her already frayed nerves. She jerked to a stop and spun about to face him. "I have been doing the cooking, tending the house and caring for my family ever since my mother died four years ago, when I was sixteen. Of *course* I can manage a fire. And I can do anything else I set my mind to as well—including moving that dresser!"

She snatched at a strand of hair tickling her neck, jammed it back into the loosened figure eight twist at her nape and jutted her chin into the air. "I may have stumbled with that drawer, Blake Latherop, but that's because you *startled* me! I am *not* incompetent. Or clumsy!" Tears stung her eyes. She whirled and headed for the hallway, her skirts swishing.

"Whoa, wait a minute!" Blake's hand clasped onto her wrist, drawing her to a halt.

She stiffened and blinked to clear her vision, swallowed hard when he grasped her shoulders and turned her around to face him.

"I meant nothing disparaging by my question, Audrey. It was not a comment on your capabilities, only a statement of my ignorance of them. I can't know if you can manage a fire, any more than you can know if I like roasted beef. We have a lot to learn about each other."

She drew a breath and nodded, shamed by her outburst. "You're right, of course." She pulled her lips into a rueful smile. "I guess you've just learned that I can be a little...overly sensitive at times. Though I try not to be." His lips twitched, slanting into that grin he used to give her when they were friends. Her stomach fluttered. She lowered her gaze from his face, sought for something to say to dispel the odd feeling. "Father said it comes from my having red hair."

He let go of her shoulders and peered down at her. "I thought it was red hair and a temper that went hand in hand."

She crinkled her nose and headed for the kitchen, her shoulders warm from his hands. "I'm afraid I also have one of those—on occasion."

"I'll keep that in mind." His teasing tone took any possible insult from the words. He walked with her as far as the door, paused there with his hand braced on the jamb. "If there is anything you need and can't find, come and tell me. I'll get it from the store."

"All right." She watched him walk away, then took a package of meat from the refrigerator and hurried toward the stove, her steps quick and light, her spirits buoyed by their brief moment of shared banter. Perhaps they could make this unusual arrangement work after all. Perhaps they would even become friends again. She lifted a cast-iron Dutch oven from a shelf on the wall and began preparing their meal, hope warming her heart.

Chapter Four

Blake hurried down to the store, spotted the dark-haired man standing by the hardware and smiled. "I thought I heard the bell. Good afternoon, Garret. How can I help you?"

"Afternoon, Blake." Garret Stevenson nodded, walked to the counter and set down a box of door hinges. "I guess congratulations are in order. I heard your fiancée came in on the six ten yesterday, and you were married last night."

"You heard right." Blake tugged his lips into a smile, shook Garret's offered hand and steered away from the topic of his marriage. "Are those hinges all you need today?"

"No." Garret jiggled the wood bucket dangling from his left hand. "Mitch and his crew are running short on nails."

"Not surprising—I hear a lot of pounding going on over at your place." He led the way to the kegs of nails sitting against the back wall. "How many of what size?"

"Five pounds of the fours, and one small keg each of the tens and fourteens."

Blake piled the small kegs on the cart beside the display, weighed out and dumped the four-penny nails into Garret's bucket, then walked back to the counter and pulled out his account book to enter the charges. "How's the hotel coming along? I can't see what's going on now that it's all closed in. Do you still think you'll be open for a few guests by the end of next month?"

"Actually, it's coming along faster than I expected. Mitch has got his crew working sunup to sundown finishing the rough work on the second and third floors." Garret slid a box of cabinet hinges over beside the box of door hinges and added one of cupboard door pulls. "Might as well get these. Mitch is starting on the kitchen. He's framing out the food cupboards and pantry today. You'd better order the stove and refrigerator we talked about. I'll be needing them soon."

"I'll place the order right away. They should be here before the end of the month."

"Good enough. Oh, and order two of those new flush down water closets and two bathing tubs like the one you've got upstairs. My hotel is going to be so comfortable the guests won't want to leave." Garret carried the boxes over to the cart, placed them in the bucket sitting on top of the piled kegs and grasped the handles. "I'll bring your cart back as soon as I unload these things."

"You can just leave it on the loading dock. I'll get it when I need it." He watched Garret disappear into the storage room headed for his back door, then wrote out, addressed and sealed the orders for the requested items. Pride spurted through him. His judgment in taking a chance on coming West to Whisper Creek had been sound. The store was making a nice profit due to all the building going on in the new town. And the families who would come as the stores and homes were completed meant a good steady business for the future. Along with the train customers he hoped would swell his coffers. He swept a glance toward the back room. He'd planned on moving the hardware items back there as the construction slowed, then using the present space for a larger stock of groceries, dry goods and household things that would be in demand as the town grew. Not that it mattered now—he wouldn't be here.

His sense of accomplishment fled and his mood soured. He entered the cost of postage for the orders in the debit column, shoved the account book and writing materials back on the shelf beneath the cash box and picked up the orders. Another of his plans ruined. There was no need to seek to have the Whisper Creek Post Office located in his store. He'd be gone by the time he could be given formal acceptance as the postmaster.

He slid the orders into his pocket, took a coin from the cash register and glanced at the clock. Twenty-seven minutes until the next train headed east came through—more than enough time to walk to the station and give Asa the orders to put in the mailbag.

He walked to the back room, grabbed boxes of hardware, carried them into the store and placed them on the displays to replace the ones Garret had bought. The activity helped to hold thoughts of Linda at bay. Soft footfalls sounded overhead. He tensed, glanced at the clock—twenty-four minutes until train time—still too long. It was only a five-minute walk to the station, less if he hurried. But it would get him away from… everything.

A shadow moved through the pool of sunlight on the floor. He looked toward the window, winced at the sight of Mr. Ferndale approaching the door. He wasn't ready to face the man. He hadn't perfected the answers he would give to the questions that were certain to come up when he introduced Audrey as his wife. How could he explain marrying the wrong woman in a believable way?

The jingle of the bell on the door stiffened his spine. He forced a smile and stepped forward. "Mr. Ferndale, how may I help you, sir?"

"I'm running low on candy." The stocky man pulled a round tin from his pocket and handed it to him.

"Yes, sir. One tin of candy, light on the lemon drops and heavy on the peppermint." He stepped behind the counter, lifted the covers off the glass candy jars, filled the tin and returned it. "Will there be anything else, today?"

"Mrs. Ferndale wants a jar of marmalade—she says you know which one she prefers."

He nodded, crossed to the shelves holding the groceries, took down a small stoneware jar of lemon marmalade and set it on the counter. "Anything else?"

"Only an invitation for you and your bride to come to our home for dinner after church service on Sunday. Mrs. Ferndale and I wish to welcome your bride to Whisper Creek."

Two days! His stomach knotted. He forced a smile. "We would be honored to accept your kind invitation."

"Excellent! Mrs. Ferndale will be pleased." A smile touched the portly man's mouth. "She's beside herself with excitement at the prospect of talking with another woman. It's been lonely for her since she came to join me." His thick fingers wrapped around the marmalade jar. "We'll see you on Sunday."

He watched John Ferndale leave the store, stood waiting until the bell over the door stopped jingling, then spun on his heel and headed for the storage room. He couldn't take any more talk about his *marriage*. He would walk to the station by the back path he used to trundle his orders from the trains to the store.

The liquid whisper of the waterfall accompanied his steps across the loading dock. He glanced at the glimmer of water peeking through the branches of the towering pines that muted the cataract's roar and clenched his jaw. He should have taken Audrey to see the waterfall. He'd known there would be no customers. It had been obvious Asa Marsh was not going to take the time to send passengers to his store.

He stopped, ran his fingers through his hair and sucked in a lungful of the brisk morning air. If only the pain of Linda's betrayal would dull. If only the memories of her would fade. He didn't expect them to go away, but if he could just bury them deep enough to get through these next weeks…

He stared at the shimmer and flash of the water between the trees, guilt piling on top of all the other emotions roiling around in him. All Audrey wanted was to see the waterfall. That was all she'd asked of him since she came, and he'd let her down. He needed to concentrate on Audrey—on his obligation to her.

He straightened, drew his shoulders back and headed for the train station, resolve strengthening with his every step.

The long blast of a whistle echoed through the kitchen, muted but clear. Another train had arrived. Audrey pulled her biscuits from the oven, snuggled them into the towel lining the bowl she had waiting and placed them in the warming oven. Dinner would keep while Blake tended to his customers. Surely, they would come this time. She smiled at the prospect, pushed the curly wisps of hair back off her warm face and hurried to the window beside the dish dresser to watch the passengers come.

The road from the depot was empty. She lifted her gaze to the passengers milling about on the station platform and frowned. Obviously, they had not yet been told about Blake's store. She rested her fingertips on the window ledge and watched them, reining in a spurt of irritation. Mr. Marsh had his job to do, certainly. But this was the third train today. Surely, he could spare a moment to—

"I forgot to tell you—"

She gasped and whipped around, stared at Blake standing in the doorway.

"I'm sorry, Audrey. I always seem to startle you."

"It was my fault. I was woolgathering and didn't hear you come upstairs." She lowered her hand from the thudding pulse at the base of her throat. "What is it you wanted to tell me?"

"That I bought a dinner bell." He strode into the kitchen, gestured over his shoulder. "It's there on the shelf by the door. It's small and I thought you might not notice it. It will be easier for you to ring the bell than to walk down the stairs to tell me when meals are ready."

"That's very thoughtful, Blake." *Of course the bell was meant for Linda's comfort and ease. But Linda isn't here...* Worry settled over her. "Thank you for telling me."

He stepped to her side, peered out the window. "What was drawing your attention?"

"The train's arrival." His face went taut. He nodded and turned away. She took a breath and fought back words. Nothing she could say could comfort him. Or her. She turned and looked at the train. Her chest tightened. *Where are you, Linda? Will I ever see you again?* Tears stung her eyes.

"I know this...situation...is difficult and painful for you, Audrey."

Blake's voice, deep and quiet, brought more tears surging. She wiped them away with her fingertips and opened her eyes. He was looking down at her, his eyes warm with sympathy.

"I wish there were some way to make all this easier for you."

His understanding flowed over her like a wave. Her throat constricted at his kindness. "And I, you."

He nodded, gave her a searching look. "Do you mother everyone, Audrey?"

Was that how she appeared to him? She flattened her palm and smoothed a wrinkle from the apron she'd found in a drawer. "I suppose I do—though I don't mean to." She raised her head and looked full in his eyes. "Someone had to step into Mother's place when she passed away and take care of Father and—" He stiffened. She clenched her hands, swallowed back her sister's name. "It's become a habit."

The quick double blast of a whistle floated through the window behind her, announcing the train's imminent departure. The twenty minutes had passed without— *"Dinner!"* She brushed by Blake and ran to the stove, snatched up a towel and pulled the roasted beef and vegetables she'd transferred to a crockery dish from the oven, then stood holding it, uncertain of his appetite. The steam rising from the dish wafted by her nostrils. Her stomach, knotted by concern for Linda, recoiled.

Blake's footfalls sounded against the floor. "I'll carry that to the table for you."

He was going to eat! She shook off her surprise, slipped out of the apron and took the biscuits from the warming oven. She followed him to the table she'd set earlier, bowed her head and glanced through her lowered lashes at Blake as he asked God's blessing on their meal. There was determination in the set of his shoulders. She drew her own shoulders back and prepared to follow his example at their first meal together as— She jerked her mind from the unsettling thought and closed her eyes. *Almighty God, please help us to find our way to a place of ease in this marriage that isn't a marriage.*

"If you hand me your plate, I'll serve you."

As a husband would. She swallowed hard and forced a smile. "Only one spoonful, please. I'm not hu—" He glanced at her, and she hastened to cover her slip-of-tongue. "I haven't a very large appetite. Father always fretted that I didn't eat more."

"Perhaps this mountain air will change that."

"Perhaps." She stared at her plate, wondering how

she would manage to eat when it felt as if Linda were sitting at the table with them.

"I used to watch the trains come and go when I first arrived. Now, I barely notice them—though it's hard to miss the whistle."

She watched Blake take a bite of his food, and her throat tightened. He was trying so hard to act normal. "I suppose you get used to them after a while. I'd never—" *Don't talk about home!* "That is, I've always traveled by carriage before." She took a breath and hurried off that slippery slope. "I never realized how *vast* this country is. The plains stretched on and on. And the mountains—" *Stop babbling!* "—are incredible." She reached for the bowl and threw back the towel. The aroma of hot biscuits rose like a cloud. Blake's head lifted. She moved the bowl toward him. "I made biscuits—if you'd care for one. I didn't know if you liked them, so you needn't be polite…"

"They look delicious." Blake lifted one of the lightly browned biscuits from the bowl, split it and reached for the crock of butter. "Perhaps I should open the window. The train passengers would come running if they smelled these."

She returned his smile, matched his effort at polite conversation. "The train has left. There aren't any passengers."

"Well, that's their loss, then." He took a bite of biscuit, raised his eyebrows. "Truly. Those soldiers would love these biscuits."

His surprised look of appreciation eased the coil in her stomach. At least he liked her baking. "Why are there so many soldiers on the trains, Blake? Where are they going?" She lifted a bite of potato to her mouth, determined to eat when he was doing his best to put her at ease.

"Most of them are going to Fort Bridger, I imagine. The Indian attacks—"

"Indian attacks!" She dropped her fork and glanced toward the window.

"You're in no danger, Audrey. I would never have sent for—" His words choked off. She slid her gaze back to him, noted the throbbing pulse at his temple. "In spite of…everything, I would never have let you stay if I thought you might come to harm."

"I know that, Blake. I'm not concerned for my safety. I'm shocked. I hadn't thought about Indians."

"That's not surprising. There aren't many in New York City."

His attempt at humor made her heart ache. She lifted the coffeepot off of the trivet and filled their cups, added milk to hers. "Have you seen any Indians since you came to Whisper Creek?"

"A few."

She froze with a bite of biscuit halfway to her mouth and stared at him.

"But only at a distance. They appear every now and then at the edge of the valley and then disappear again. I think they're just checking to be sure none of us are intruding on their land—Mr. Ferndale issued strict rules about that."

"So I need to learn where the boundaries are."

"You're fine as long as you stay in the town." He smiled reassurance. "The miners at South Pass are asking for trouble, and they've got it. We're safe enough as long as we don't break the Fort Laramie treaty."

An image of the black chunks tumbling down the chute into the tender car on the train flashed into her head. "The coal miners are the ones being attacked? How will the trains run?"

"The men at South Pass aren't mining coal—they're after gold. And they're staying in the area despite the Indian attacks." He shook his head, took a bite of food and reached for another biscuit. "Greed makes a man take risks that make no sense otherwise."

"So does love." She heard the words and rushed into speech, aghast that the thought had slipped out aloud. "Or so the poets say—Keats and Burns and Donne. Do you enjoy poetry, Blake?"

"I did."

The clink of his fork against his plate blended with the bitter words. She broke off a bit of biscuit and put it in her mouth. It tasted like dust—but at least she had an excuse not to respond. She stared down at the food on her plate and held back a sigh. She wasn't accustomed to parsing every word before she spoke, but it seemed a habit she would have to form. There were simply no safe subjects. Everything led back to Linda.

"Mr. Ferndale came to the store a short while ago."

She looked up, found Blake's gaze fastened on her. "Was it terribly…difficult?"

"No." His lips slanted in a crooked grin. "That will come on Sunday."

The grin was almost real—almost like when they were friends. Her stomach fluttered. "Why on Sunday?"

"We are invited to dine at the Ferndale home after the church service."

"Oh."

His grin widened. "Don't look so worried, Audrey. Perhaps there will be an Indian attack, and we will miss the dinner."

"An attack!" She stared at him and her lips twitched upward. "That's a terrible thing to say."

"Not if it calmed your fear and made you smile."

The flutter increased. A soft tinkling floated up the stairs.

"That's the store bell." Blake placed his fork on his plate and pushed back from the table. "Excuse me, Audrey, while I go take care of my customer. And thank you for the meal. You're a good cook."

Oh, Linda, how foolish of you to let Blake go. He's a wonderful, kind and thoughtful man. She stared down at the cold food on her plate, sighed and rose to clear away the dishes. *Sunday.* Her hands trembled as she scraped the scraps from their plates into the bucket beneath the sink cupboard, ran hot water and swished the soap holder through it to make suds. *Please, Almighty God, don't let me fail Blake on Sunday. Help me to remember the story we have decided upon.*

Her skirt hems whispered across the floor, a soft accompaniment to the litany of facts flowing through her mind as she put the leftover food away while the dishes soaked. *We met when Blake was courting my older sister. We exchanged letters after Blake came to Whisper Creek...*

They had made it through the first day. And that major hurdle had been cleared without any disagreement. Blake had been most understanding about her moving his things out of what was, after all, *his* bed-

room. He was a very nice man. Audrey gathered her
brushed hair at the nape of her neck, reached for a ribbon then paused, listened to an unfamiliar sound in
the silence—a sort of…whisper. Where was it coming from? She let the long wavy mass of her hair tum-
ble free, walked to the bedroom door and opened it a
crack. The sound was fainter. Blake must be having
another restless night. She pressed her ear against the
wall separating the two bedrooms. All was silent. The
sound must be coming from outside.

She glanced toward the door set in the wall a short
distance from the bed. It had to open onto the porch
she'd seen this afternoon. The white silk of her dressing
gown floated around her nightgown, the hem brushing the tops of her matching slippers as she crossed the
room. The whisper grew louder. *The waterfall!*

Of course! She should have realized… Was it visible from the porch? The moon was almost full. She
stood a moment gnawing at her lower lip. Blake had
been reluctant to talk about the porch that afternoon,
but surely it would be all right to go out there. He hadn't
told her not to. And he was abed… She grasped the
knob and twisted. Cold night air rushed in the opened
door, fluttered her dressing gown. The whisper grew
to a muted murmur. She stepped out onto the porch,
closed the door and moved through the shadowed darkness beneath the roof to the railing. Moonlight silvered
the face of the mountain, glinted on patches of water
showing between the feathery tops of the towering
pines at its base.

A pungent smell of pine peppered the fresh night air.
She lifted her gaze to the top of the mountain, caught

her breath at the sight of the sparkling water cascading from beneath the jagged slash of snow glittering against the dark sky, at once menacing and beautiful.

A shiver chased down her spine; bumps rose on her flesh. She wrapped her arms about herself for warmth and stood drinking in the stillness. Water rippled in the dark, calming, soothing. The tension of the day drained away. Her mind drifted free of her will, imposed an image of Blake looking down at her against the darkness.

I wish there were some way to make all this easier for you.

How kind he was, considering her while he was suffering the pain of betrayal. Linda didn't deserve him! She stiffened, jolted from her reverie. How could she be so disloyal to her sister!

She lifted her chin, turned her back on the beautiful scene and went inside. A quick puff extinguished the oil lamp. Her dressing gown slipped off with quiet sibilance against the silk of its matching nightgown, shone in the slits of moonlight poking through the slats of the shutters. She shivered in the night chill, stepped out of her slippers and slid beneath the covers, tucked her feet beneath her long gown and waited for the bed to warm. Blake's image returned, hovering against the darkness.

I don't need to be protected.

Was that what Blake thought she was doing? Was she? Was that what caused that disloyal thought about Linda? No. That was pure foolishness. A man like Blake didn't need protection; he only needed her help at the moment. And it wasn't for his sake alone she had moved his clothes. Having him come to this bedroom for them would have been…awkward. She stirred, stared into the deepening darkness of the room, discomfited by the half-truth. Well, what if she *did* think of doing so to spare him pain? It was only another way of trying to make up for writing those letters for Linda—but he couldn't, *mustn't* know that. He would be so wounded to know Linda hadn't cared enough to write, and he was already wounded enough by her betrayal.

Do you mother everyone, Audrey?

Her hands tightened on the blanket she clutched beneath her chin. What an unflattering image Blake had of her. And how unlike a bride! It was certain he didn't think of Linda in motherly terms. A worm of jealousy wriggled through her. She had always faded into Linda's shadow. Well, not now. Let Blake think what he would. She was his bride as far as anyone in Whisper Creek knew, and she would act like it!

She flopped onto her side, tugged the cover close and closed her eyes, mentally sorting through the dresses she had brought with her, wishing, for the first time, that she owned a fancy dress adorned with lace and ruffles like Linda wore. She may only be Blake's stand-in bride, but she wanted to do him proud when they went to the Ferndales' for dinner on Sunday.

The green silk. Yes… She yawned, snuggled deeper into the warmth of the blankets. It would have…to be… the green silk…

Blake froze at the sound of a door closing. He'd thought everyone was asleep. If Garret came out and saw him standing on the path to the pond—

Movement caught his eye. *Audrey*. He jerked his gaze up to the porch, hoping she was only being curious about where the door led. The hope died as she walked out of the shadows to the railing. *The waterfall*. Guilt struck him anew. He should have taken her to see it.

He glanced at the tree beside him, decided it would draw her attention to move and stayed motionless in its shadow. He didn't want to have to explain why he was out in the night instead of in bed—not that she wouldn't already know. The cold slithered over his neck and down his spine, uncomfortable now that he wasn't walking, but he wouldn't have to stand there long. She would get cold and go inside.

He pushed his chilled neck back against his collar and looked up. She had wrapped her arms about herself and was standing looking out into the distance. The moonlight made dark smudges of her long eyelashes, silvered the crests of her delicate cheekbones and played over the crests and valleys of the long curly hair falling about her face to rest on the shoulders of a white silk dressing gown. His gut tightened. He stared up at her, mesmerized by the purity of her beauty.

On the mountain a wolf howled for its mate. He jolted to his senses, jerked his gaze from Audrey and scowled at the ground. What was wrong with him, reacting like that?

A door opened and closed. Audrey had gone inside. He glanced up to be sure, then crossed the open moonlit path to the loading dock, sat down at the top of the steps and removed his boots. The moon slipped behind a cloud, hid its silvery light. He tucked his boots beneath his arm, crossed to the door and slipped into the storage room. The dimmed oil lamp lit his way upstairs to the hallway. He set his jaw, averted his gaze from the bedroom on the right—*his bridal chamber*—and made his way to the bedroom where he would spend another sleepless night alone.

Chapter Five

"Thank you." Blake looked up and snagged Audrey's gaze with his. "It feels odd, having you pour my coffee. I'm still not used to this...*marriage*."

"Nor I." Her eyes clouded. A shadow flitted across her face. "I'm praying I won't make any mistakes tomorrow."

A very real possibility if his mere mention of their situation brought that look of concern to her face. Hopefully the Ferndales would mistake her unease for a bride's anxiety. "You'll do fine, Audrey. And I'll be right there with you in case you start to feel uncomfortable. Not that I've done much to help you thus far. I'm afraid I've been too self-absorbed to consider—" He stopped at the quick shake of her head.

"That's not true, Blake. You have been most thoughtful in these circumstances. It's been two years, but I remember how devastated I was when John broke our— when he broke his promise to me." Her long skirt flared out around her as she turned toward the stove. "Truth be told, I'm surprised you can abide the sight of me."

He shot to his feet, grabbed her shoulder and stepped in front of her. "Don't ever think that, Audrey. I'm very appreciative of the sacrifice you made—continue to make—by coming here to save my store and all I have invested in it. And beyond that, I value your friendship. Linda's...*behavior* has not changed that. I'm sorry I've been so consumed by my feelings I haven't made that clear to you." He pasted on a smile, looked down into her eyes. "We are in this together, Audrey. From now on I will do better at holding up my part of our agreement— and our friendship. And to show you I am a man of my word, I am going to take you to see the waterfall later today—when it warms up outside."

"That's not necessary, Blake. I—"

"—will agree to the excursion without argument, please. Walking to the waterfall will help us to relax. It will take our minds off of this strange situation we are in and help us become comfortable in each other's company again." His words echoed in his head. He frowned, suddenly aware of the error in them. He *was* comfortable in Audrey's company—always had been. It was the reminder of Linda's betrayal that was tearing him up and keeping him in turmoil.

"But you have to tend the store. I don't want to—"

He drew his brows down into a mock scowl. "You aren't going to go all 'redhead' on me, are you, Audrey? I said 'please.'"

"Redhead!" She gazed up at him a moment, then let out a huff. "It seems I made a mistake in telling you about Father's opinion concerning the color of my hair."

"It seems so." He looked into her eyes, grinned.

She gave another huff and walked to the stove. He picked up his cup and followed her.

The coffeepot clanked against the top of the stove. She slanted a look at him over her shoulder. "I imagine it would be too much to expect an apology?"

"I imagine." He leaned back against the worktable, blew on the steaming coffee and took a swallow, reluctant to end the repartee. It felt good. "Remember yesterday when we agreed we had a lot to learn about each other?"

"Yes…" She gave him a suspicious look. "Are you changing the subject?"

"Not at all. I've just learned something about you."

"Oh?" She gave him another look—an uneasy one. "And what might that be?"

"You're not very good at feminine wiles."

"I beg your pardon!"

He chuckled at her gasp. "Take feigning displeasure— like you were trying to do over my 'redhead' comment. You *said* the right thing. But those gold flecks in your eyes brightened up and sparkled. It gave you away. You looked amused, not displeased. Didn't John ever tell you that?"

"Certainly not. John was too much the gentleman to tease a lady."

"Then he probably never mentioned that the way you blush also gives you away." The pink on her cheeks deepened. So did his grin. "Yep. Just like that."

She jerked her hands up to cover her cheeks. "You're— you're…"

"Honest?"

"I was thinking more along the lines of incorrigible."

"That, too." He laughed and took another swallow of coffee.

Her lips twitched. She turned and snatched the dirty pans off the stove, brushed by him and stepped to the sink. "I'll wash these breakfast dishes and then be ready to go whenever you choose." Water spurted out of the spigot into the dishpan.

"Good." He emptied his cup and handed it to her. "Friends?"

"As long as you don't call me 'redhead' again."

Her eyes held the glow of the friendship he remembered. "Well, I can't promise, but I'll try not to."

"You'd best do better than 'try.'"

He chuckled at the implied threat, tossed her a mock salute and strode from the kitchen. The tightness he'd carried in his chest since she'd told him about Linda's betrayal had eased with their casual bantering and the warmth of Audrey's smile.

Audrey frowned at her limited dress selection and reached for the dove-gray light wool walking dress with the bolero jacket. It was the warmest outfit she had brought with her, and, even when the sun was at its peak, it would be cool in the shade of those towering pines or walking beside that frigid water. A frisson of pleasure spread through her at the thought. "Blessed Heavenly Father, please let Blake's words be true. Please let this walk renew our friendship so that the strain of this pretend marriage is over and we become comfortable in each other's company again."

A whistle, muted but sustained, trembled on the air, froze her hand on the soft wool fabric of her dress.

Another train. Perhaps it would be different this time. Perhaps Mr. Marsh would tell the conductor and passengers about Blake's store.

She turned from the wardrobe and hurried to the kitchen window, placed her fingertips on the crosspiece and waited. The blue of soldiers' uniforms flashed among the somber colors of men's suits and the bright hues of women's dresses as the passengers milled about on the station platform. The road between the station and the town remained bare. Blake was right. Mr. Marsh did not intend to make an effort to tell the conductors about the store. If only there were something she could do to— She caught her breath, glanced down at her fingertips pressing against the window ledge.

Perhaps I should open the window. The train passengers would come running if they smelled these biscuits.

Was Blake right? She gazed at the passengers and worried the corner of her lower lip with her teeth, considering the idea that had popped into her head. Would it work? She turned from the window and walked to the shelf by the door, studied the Union Pacific Railroad schedule leaning against the wall by the small dinner bell. There were six trains a day; three going west and three going east. That gave her plenty of time.

Excitement rippled through her. Perhaps there *was* something more she could do to help Blake regain his investment. She closed her eyes, visualized her actions and laid out her plan. Two short, sharp whistles announced the train's departure. Her pulse jumped. It was time to get started. *Please let this work, Father God! Please let this work.*

She opened her eyes, took a breath and hurried to the pantry. She carried the flour, baking powder and salt to the worktable, added a jar of vinegar, then set out the baking tray she'd used yesterday. Two would be much better, but she could make do with the cast-iron griddle for now. She added it to the assembled items. What else? There was butter and milk enough in the refrigerator for this first batch. And that was all… No! She needed a container large enough to hold the biscuits.

A search of the cupboards turned up nothing appropriate. She stood by the worktable with her hands on her hips and surveyed every inch of the kitchen. The enameled dishpan! With a clean towel to line it the dishpan would be perfect! She crossed to the wash cupboard, filled the dishpan with hot water, swished the soap holder around to make suds, gave the pan a good washing, dried it and carried it to the table. Now, all she needed were some towels and a small basket. And a good hot fire!

Everything was ready. And the next train should arrive any minute. Audrey pinned on her small, flower-trimmed black hat, tugged the bolero jacket that matched her dove-gray dress into place and turned from the mirror. The long whistle that announced the train had entered the valley and was approaching the station echoed through the bedroom and reverberated along her nerves. It was time!

Please let Blake be right, Lord! Please let this work! The smell of freshly baked biscuits drifted out from the kitchen into the hall. She hurried to the stove, pulled the covered bowls from the warming oven, placed the biscuits they held into the towel-lined dishpan and covered the heaping mound. Now for the basket. She divided the last of the biscuits between two towels, placed them into the lidded basket she'd found in the pantry, grabbed the dishpan and hurried down the stairs, the basket swinging from her arm.

Blake was in the store at the counter writing in some sort of ledger. She stopped and stared at him through the doorway. Another ripple flowed along her nerves—this one regret for her impulsive action. She should have told him about her plan—asked him if it was all right. Too late now. She blew out a breath, lifted her chin and walked into the store, pausing as he sniffed, then straightened. His head turned toward her.

"I made biscuits. A lot of them."

His gaze lowered to the towel-covered mound in the dishpan. His eyebrows rose. "What—"

"They're for you to sell." She hurried forward, set the dishpan on the counter, then stepped back, gripping the lidded basket. "I'm sorry I simply barged ahead with the baking without asking you. I'm used to making all the household decisions at home. And, well, you said if the passengers smelled the biscuits they would come to the store to buy them. These are for them to smell!" She waved the basket through the air, whirled and headed for the front door at the two quick whistles that announced the train's arrival at the station. "I'll explain everything when I return. I have to hurry to catch the passengers so they can come to the store before the train leaves…" She wrenched the door open.

"Audrey, wait!"

She paused, glanced over her shoulder.

Blake shoved the ledger beneath the counter. "You can't barge off to the station by yourself. I'll come—"

"No, you can't do that! You have to be here when the customers come." She tore her gaze from his astonished one, stepped out the door, then, struck by a thought, stuck her head back inside. "You might want to put some crocks of marmalade on the counter beside the biscuits where the passengers will see them."

She shut the door and headed for the station, her long skirt swishing about her shoes, her breath coming quick and shallow. She'd done it now. It had been bad enough banishing Blake from his bedroom yesterday—but ordering him about in his own *store*! Where was this boldness coming from? Not to mention the ideas that prompted it. An image of Blake staring at her with that astounded look on his face formed against the path. Her stomach clenched. No matter the source, this idea had better work!

She snagged her lower lip with her teeth and raised her gaze to the passengers moving from the train to the station, the blue uniforms of soldiers predominant among them.

Those soldiers would love these biscuits.

Hopefully, Blake was right. She swept her gaze over the milling people, searching for the uniformed conductor. He was nowhere in sight. She took a deep breath, climbed the steps to the platform and made her way to the ticket window.

The aroma from the biscuits wafted through the store. Blake clasped his hands behind his back and rocked up on his toes, scowled out the window. He should have gone with Audrey. He was responsible for her now, and that train would be carrying troops west. All of those soldiers! And Audrey, with that air of innocence about her, looking so...so *attractive* in that gray dress.

His scowl deepened. He pivoted from the window and strode to the counter, stared at the dishpan heaped with biscuits. The memory of Audrey walking out the door carrying that lidded basket knotted his stomach. Whatever she was doing, it was because of him.

You said if the passengers smelled the biscuits they would come to the store to buy them. These are for them to smell! He stiffened, stared at the biscuits. Surely she didn't think he had meant for her to— *You have to be here when the customers come.* She did. The realization shot through him like a lightning bolt. He had to go after her! He strode to the door, reached for the Closed sign and froze, staring at the soldiers trotting down the station road toward his store. Whatever Audrey had done had worked.

Boots thumped on the porch steps. He shook off his troubling thoughts and hurried back to pull a few small crocks of marmalade off the shelf and set them on the counter. The bell on the door jingled. Soldiers trooped into the store, sniffing so deeply he could hear them.

"This the store that sells the biscuits?"

"It is." He uncovered the fluffy, lightly browned biscuits, his mouth watering at the rich aroma that rose from them. Soldiers crowded against the counter.

"What's the cost?"

"Who cares?" The soldier in front slapped a fistful

of coins on the polished wood beside the dishpan. "I'll take as many biscuits as that will buy."

"And I'll take a dozen of them. And that orange marmalade." A gloved hand slapped a folded bill on the counter.

"Save some for the rest of us, Sarge!" A man wearing a buckskin shirt pushed forward to the sergeant's side. "I'll have six biscuits and a pouch of that Bull Durham chew."

Soldiers muttered a chorus of protest and pressed closer to the counter.

"One at a time, gentlemen." Blake tore off a strip of brown paper, did some rapid calculating in his head, wrapped up seven biscuits and tied the package. The soldier peeled away from the counter and headed for the door. He jotted down the sale and swept the coins aside to put in the till later.

"And one dozen for you, Sergeant." He tore off more paper and tied the package, snipped off the string, made change and smiled at the man in buckskins. "That's six for you, sir." He packaged them, placed the pouch of tobacco on top and slid them across the counter, listening to the steady jingle of the bell as the soldiers entered and exited.

"And you, sir?"

"I'll have a half-dozen biscuits, some of that cherry toothpaste—" the soldier leaned forward over the counter "—and four packages of that water closet paper."

The muttered words brought forth a chorus of hoots. The private behind the soldier thumped him on the shoulder. "Delicate, are we, Johnson?"

The soldier scowled. "No, just smart, Taylor. And

don't be asking to borrow any like you did on our last sortie!" The hoots and laughter swelled.

Blake handed over the packages and added the money to the growing pile. The soldier shoved away from the counter, and another pushed into the void. "And for you, sir?" He tore off more paper.

The door opened. The bell jingled loud in a silence that spread over the joshing soldiers like a ripple in a pond. As if in cadence, they straightened and whipped their hats from their heads. He looked toward the door. *Audrey*. He glanced back at the cluster of staring soldiers and started toward the door, stopped as she swept a wide-eyed gaze over the crowded room then moved toward the open space behind the counter. She could make her way to the back room from there. He turned his attention back to the business at hand. "Did you want biscuits, Private?" No answer. "Private?" The soldier jerked, looked at him, his expression blank. "Did you want biscuits?"

A flush crept over the young man's face. "I'll take six. And some chew—" a callused forefinger jabbed at the glass display cabinet sitting on the counter "—and one of them straight razors. Some sneaking polecat helped hisself to mine."

He nodded and tore off a length of the brown paper. From the corner of his eye he saw Audrey near and pressed against the counter to give her space to pass between him and the wall of shelves at his back. Her long skirts brushed against his pant legs as she stepped into the narrow gap.

"Hurry it up, storekeep, or that train's gonna leave afore I kin git some of them biscuits!"

"Yeah, an' my stomach's fair tumblin' over itself at their smell!"

He glanced at the soldiers at the back of the massed group. "I'm doing my best, gentlemen." He reached for the biscuits, paused as Audrey's shoulder brushed against his arm.

"I'll wrap the biscuits for you." She set her lidded basket on the counter, then placed six biscuits on the paper, folded it and reached for the string.

He shook off his surprise and took a straight razor from the cabinet, slid it and the chewing tobacco into a small bag, handed it and the wrapped biscuits to the soldier and accepted payment. Another soldier moved forward, hat in hand.

"I'll have me a dozen of them biscuits. They smell just like my ma's. An' I'll take these gloves."

He made note of the sale and made change, handed the biscuits Audrey wrapped to the private and looked at the suddenly polite line. The next soldier slid a coin on the counter.

"I'll have a bar of Wright's soap, a bag of chew and as many biscuits as this will buy."

Audrey looked up at him. He did the calculations in his head and answered the question in her eyes. "Five biscuits."

He grabbed the soap and chewing tobacco, slid them into a bag and handed them to the soldier along with the wrapped biscuits.

"Blake." He glanced down. Audrey gestured toward the dishpan. "I didn't make enough. There are only—"

The door burst open.

"Train time, men! Move out!"

The soldiers pivoted and headed out the door.

A corporal shoved a bill at him. "I'll take the rest of them biscuits, storekeep. No time for wrappin', miss, jist drop 'em in my hat."

"On the double, Saunders!"

"Comin', Sarge!" The young soldier grabbed his change, clutched his hat full of biscuits close to his chest and ran out the door, the sergeant at his heels. The door banged shut. The bell jingled, faded away.

Blake looked from the empty dishpan to Audrey. She was rewinding the loose string on the cone. "What did you *do* at the station?"

"Only what you said." She laid the scissors by the cone, brushed a few crumbs off the counter and tossed them in the dishpan.

The concern for her rushed back. He frowned, shoved his fingers through his hair. "That was only my way of complimenting you on your baking, Audrey. I certainly didn't mean for you to go to the depot with all of those soldiers milling about."

"How else were they to smell the biscuits?" She lifted the lidded basket she'd carried off the counter, placed it in the dishpan and looked up at him. "Anyway, you were right. One whiff was all it took." She picked up the dishpan and started for the storage room.

His frown deepened to a scowl. "You walked around among that crowd of soldiers letting them smell the biscuits?"

She stopped, turned about. "Well, of course not! I'm a lady. I wouldn't do that."

"Then how—"

"I took the biscuits as a gesture of friendship to Mr.

Marsh and the train conductor." A soft laugh bubbled from her. "And when I opened the basket and placed the biscuits on the ticket window shelf, the soldiers standing nearby smelled them and asked if they were for sale. I, of course, explained they were a gift for Mr. Marsh, but that they could buy biscuits at your store. They, not I, told the other soldiers." She slanted a look up at him. "The conductor was most appreciative of the biscuits. He said he would certainly tell the passengers on his trains about your store."

"And Mr. Marsh?"

"Oh, Mr. Marsh appreciated the biscuits, also. Though he gave most of them to the engineer when I told him I would be back with another gift of biscuits for him when the next train comes." The gold flecks in her eyes flashed. "No sign indeed!" She turned and walked to the storage room, the empty dishpan clutched in front of her. "Oh! I almost forgot." She stopped, turned. "I need a few more supplies—flour and such. If it's all right?"

"Yes, of course. Take whatever you need. Just— No, wait…" He shoved aside his shock and ordered his thoughts. "Did you say you were going back to the station with more biscuits when the next train arrives?"

She nodded, halted with her hand still on the sack of flour she'd placed in the dishpan. "That's why I need more supplies. I used all that was in the kitchen."

"Replace what you used. But that's all." He stepped to her side and took the dishpan from her. "I'll carry this upstairs."

She shot him a measuring look. "I'm afraid merely replacing the supplies won't be enough. There are two more trains and—"

"No more baking for the trains—that's too much work for you."

"But it's not! And it's the only way to get the news of your store opening to the conductors. Mr. Marsh won't—"

"No more, Audrey." His tone left no room for argument.

Her chin lifted. "Have you a better plan?"

He stared, too astounded by this resourceful Audrey to speak. He'd thought her reserved and meek. The way she was when Linda— His stomach knotted. "No. But the work—"

"It's not hard to make biscuits, Blake. Please let me bake them for the trains. It's only for today. After that all of the conductors will know about your store, and there will be no need for me to continue."

He looked down at her standing before him with her head held high waiting for his answer. "I don't like you doing all that work." No response—no coaxing or coy behavior. Obviously, Audrey did not use womanly wiles to win her way. Linda would have— He thrust aside the thought, nodded. "All right, take what you need. But no more biscuit making after today."

"Agreed."

"Has anyone ever told you that you are a most persuasive young woman?"

Her lips curved. "No. Father's word was 'stubborn.'"

"Apropos." He growled the word.

She laughed, placed another sack of flour in the dishpan and reached for the canned milk.

The cot squeaked. Blake flopped onto his back, laced his hands behind his head and stared up at the ceiling. The image remained—Audrey, neat and trim in that gray dress with her red curls peeking from beneath that little black hat and her eyes shining while she stood beside him and wrapped biscuits. He tried, again, to picture Linda in Audrey's place and failed. Try as he might, he could not imagine Linda baking biscuits or standing beside him at the counter serving the customers who flocked into the store to buy them with the arrival of every train. Linda was too beautiful and coquettish for that. She would have been laughing and flirting with the soldiers, not wrapping biscuits for them. *Linda*. How he longed to hold her again.

He frowned, rose from the cot and went out onto the porch fighting the memories. Clouds had rolled in earlier, turning the night as dark as pitch. The waterfall was only a whisper blending with the wind. A storm was brewing. But it was nothing compared to the storm of emotions churning within him. How would he get through tomorrow?

Chapter Six

Sunshine streamed through the windows in the plastered walls, chasing the chill from the sanctuary and rendering the light from the oil lamp chandeliers in the church useless. But even the sunny warmth after last night's storm couldn't calm her nerves.

Audrey lifted her gaze from Mr. and Mrs. Ferndale sitting on the front bench, fixed it on Pastor Karl and pressed her hand against her roiling stomach. Every time she looked at the pastor she was assailed by memories of the marriage ceremony. *Do you, Audrey Prescott, take Blake Latherop...* Her pulse raced, beat so loudly in her ears she couldn't hear the man's sermon. And that meant more possible questions she would not be able to answer when they dined with the Ferndales this afternoon.

The board across the back of the wood bench that served as a pew pressed into her shoulders, some small protrusion causing discomfort. She desperately wanted to change her position but feared it would draw attention. Her mere presence did that—judging from the surreptitious glances directed her way from the few men in attendance. How had she ever thought she could get away with pretending to be Blake's bride? Mr. and Mrs. Ferndale were certain to see right through her act and— She couldn't remember the story they had rehearsed! A band closed around her chest, held her lungs in a viselike grip that refused her breath. She stiffened.

Warmth encased her hand. She looked down at Blake's hand covering hers and her panic ebbed, the constriction eased. His warm breath tickled her ear. "Steady, Audrey. Remember, we're in this together." His hand squeezed hers, lifted.

Together. Yes. Blake would help her. She drew a breath, focused on the agreed-upon story that came flooding back; she had come to Whisper Creek to tell Blake of Linda's betrayal in person. When they had seen each other again, they had realized they had fallen in love with each other while exchanging letters, and— The letters. Guilt struck. *Please help me, Lord. For Blake's sake. I know I was wrong, but I meant no harm—*

Blake shifted on the bench and stood. Her prayer ended on another wave of panic. Church had ended. Mr. and Mrs. Ferndale were rising... The constriction in her chest returned. A spasm clenched her stomach. She looked up, read sympathetic understanding in Blake's eyes and jerked her gaze away before it undermined what little self-control she had left.

There was a shuffling and scraping of boots. Pastor Karl strode up the aisle and opened the door. Sunshine flooded into the sanctuary. Blake offered his hand. She slipped her trembling hand into his, prayed her shaking legs would hold her and followed him out into the aisle. Quick footfalls and the soft rustle of silk caused a hitch in her breath. She glanced at the older couple coming toward them and another spasm hit her stomach. Blake pulled her close, tucked her hand through his arm. She looked up at him standing tall and steady and calm beside her, and she couldn't stop the wish that she had a fancier gown to make him proud of her. One with lots of lace and tiers of ruffles like Linda always wore, instead of this pathetic plain green silk whose only adornment was the narrow band of velvet that edged the collar, cuffs, waist and hem of the long skirt. She shifted her gaze back to the plump woman in the fashionable, ruffled gown and forced a smile.

"My dear Mrs. Latherop, I have been eagerly awaiting this day since your husband put the Open sign in his store window!"

The smile she'd pasted on her lips faltered.

"What a *lovely* bride you have, Mr. Latherop." Mrs. Ferndale beamed a smile at them. "I can quite see why she took your eye. She's so very pretty."

Oh, poor Blake! She tightened her hand on his arm, hoped he'd understand her silent message of sympathy.

His hand closed over hers. "I quite agree, Mrs. Ferndale."

He said it with such warmth she could almost believe him if she didn't know better. Linda was the beautiful one. She could never compare to her—especially in Blake's eyes.

"You'll have to forgive my wife's fervor, Mrs. Latherop." Mr. Ferndale sent an apologetic smile her direction. "It's been lonely for her with no other women here in

Whisper Creek. You have the unique distinction of being the first bride in our town."

"She knows that, John!" The older woman gave her husband a look of exasperation. "And you needn't apologize for me—I'm quite capable of doing so myself."

"There is no need for an apology, Mrs. Ferndale." She smiled, thankful for the change of subject. "I quite understand your situation."

"Nonetheless, John is right, Mrs. Latherop. I've let my loneliness override my manners. Please forgive me, my dear." A smile deepened the creases alongside the woman's mouth. "I promise not to overwhelm you with questions over dinner. Now, I must hurry home to tend to my meal." The woman shifted her gaze to Blake. "We will expect you and your lovely bride in one hour, Mr. Latherop."

"It will be our pleasure, Mrs. Ferndale."

"Everything is delicious, Mrs. Ferndale."

"Yes, it is." Blake glanced across the table at Audrey. She sounded relaxed, but the stiffness in her shoulders betrayed her nervousness. Still, that shouldn't make the Ferndales suspicious. It was natural for a new bride to be a little uneasy when meeting the important people in her husband's life.

"Thank you, both. I enjoy cooking." The older woman's round face creased in a smile. "But I guess that shows in both Mr. Ferndale and me."

"There's nothing wrong with that, Dora." John Ferndale patted his paunch. "Having a wife who is a good cook makes for a happy life, as Blake here will discover—if he hasn't already." The older man shifted his gaze to the other side of the table. "I understand you make an excellent biscuit, Mrs. Latherop."

Audrey went still, then lifted her chin in that little jut he was beginning to recognize as her defensive position. "I believe they are passable, Mr. Ferndale."

"They're more than 'passable' according to Asa Marsh."

"John, you stop teasing our guest!" Mrs. Ferndale reached out and patted Audrey's arm. "Pay him no mind, dear. He thought it was very clever."

"It *was* clever, Dora." A chuckle rose from the region of John Ferndale's potbelly. "Sending your wife to Asa with those biscuits was a good business move, Latherop. And having her give them to those conductors was sheer genius."

"I agree, sir. But you are giving credit to the wrong person." He looked across the table and smiled, spoke the truth. "It was Audrey who thought of taking the biscuits to the station."

"But only because you said the soldiers would come to buy them if they smelled them, Blake. I merely thought of a way to make that happen."

"Well, it seems you two make quite a team. But I'm confused." Mr. Ferndale looked up and impaled him with his gaze. "I thought your bride-to-be was named Linda, Latherop."

Linda. He finished cutting off a bite of beef, fought back the pain hearing her name spoken brought flashing through him. "And so she was, sir. But that…didn't work out." *She betrayed me.* He tamped down a surge of anger and looked up, held his voice steady. "Linda married another."

The older man's eyes narrowed, and he shoved his plate aside. "Now see here! What do you think you're pulling, Latherop? It was little more than two weeks ago you were talking about marrying this Linda!" The man's sharp gaze darted across the table. "Who are you, young lady? And how do you know Blake here? Or is this some sort of—"

"Audrey is Linda's sister! And I'll thank you to speak with respect to my wife, sir!" Blake shoved to his feet, moved around the table and placed his hand on Audrey's shoulder. She was as stiff as a board. He squeezed reassurance. "Audrey and I met and became friends when I was courting Linda. We…corresponded as such." *If you consider sending someone your regards correspondence.* He took a breath, swallowed back another surge of anger and glided over the half-truth. "As for how we came to marry—well, that was a surprise to both of us. Wasn't it, dearest?"

"Indeed it was."

Audrey's voice was soft, but steady and sure with truth. Her hand touched his; her fingers clung. He looked down, gave her what he hoped looked like a loving smile, then refocused his attention on John Ferndale. "When Linda ran off and married another, Audrey came to Whisper Creek to give me the news in person, rather than write it in a letter." The words spilled from his mouth, dragging shreds of his heart with them.

"Most considerate of you, dear."

He glanced at Mrs. Ferndale. *It was considerate. Amazingly so.* "Audrey's warm heart is one of the things I most…admire about her."

"I quite understand that." The older woman nod-ded, smiled.

"That doesn't explain how you came to marry her, Latherop."

Audrey's shoulder tensed beneath his hand. He gave her another calming squeeze and shifted his gaze back to the town founder sitting like a judge at the head of the table. There was suspicion in the man's eyes. "That was the surprise. When Audrey stepped off of the train, and I saw her again—" he blocked out the memory, concentrated on his story "—I realized I had fallen in love with the woman who wrote me those letters." *Misleading, but true. Linda...* He pushed her image aside and pressed on.

"I confessed my...feelings...to Audrey." That was the truth. "She admitted she felt much the same, and, conditions being what they are here in Whisper Creek, we married." He lifted Audrey's hand to his mouth, placed a kiss on her soft fingers and added the last bit of the story he had prepared. "There was no reason for delay. Audrey has no family but her sister."

Mrs. Ferndale sighed and rested a plump hand on her ample bosom. "That is quite the most romantic story I have ever heard. How fortunate for you both, that Audrey's sister married another."

The suppressed anger squeezed his chest and tight-ened his throat. He nodded and, again, pressed Au-drey's hand to his lips. It was the perfect excuse to not reply.

Mrs. Ferndale smiled and rang the bell by her plate, then swept her hand over the table as a Chinese man dressed in a white smock coat hurried into the room.

"Hung Wah, take these dishes away and bring in the cake, please. We have a wedding to celebrate!"

Audrey settled the bolero jacket of the red, white and blue narrow-striped cotton gown in place, then fluffed the closely gathered lace ruffles that formed the high bodice and sighed. The relief from having the Ferndale dinner over with made her feel like celebrating. And this dress was the most frivolous she owned. After all, it was red. And the color made her hair look lighter, more blond. She stepped closer and peered at her image in the mirror. Well, sort of. Mostly... The thin vertical stripes definitely made her look taller—like Linda.

You will never be as beautiful and attractive as Linda. The thought swept through her mind like a dark cloud. She turned her back to the mirror. What did her failure to compare to her sister's beauty matter? Why was she even thinking such thoughts? There were few men in Whisper Creek, and those who did live here were either married or betrothed, as Blake had been. And they all would know her as Blake's bride.

Blake. She drew a breath to settle a sudden flutter in her stomach. Blake had been wonderful at the Ferndales'. So steady and calm and...and husbandly. Of course! Blake had treated her as if he cared about her. That was why she was feeling this way. Foolish woman!

She shook her head and lifted her black hat off the shelf, then stared down at it, debating the wisdom of wearing it on their trip to the waterfall. Would it snag on the tree branches? She couldn't afford to have it ruined. It was the only hat she'd brought with her.

"Are you ready, Audrey?"

Her pulse leaped. "Coming!" She laid the hat back on the shelf, closed the wardrobe doors and hurried out into the U-shaped hall, her long skirts swishing around her button-up walking shoes. Her stomach flopped at the sight of Blake's face. "You're frowning. Is something wrong?"

"Is that the warmest outfit you have? It's cold by the waterfall."

"I'm afraid so. I didn't bring a large selection of gowns with me."

His frown deepened. "What about that gray one you wore yesterday?"

She shook her head. "That is for church and other occasions. I don't want it to get ruined walking through the woods. I'll be fine. See—" she held out her arms for his inspection "—long sleeves." He didn't look impressed. She took hold of the banister, lifted her skirts and started down the stairs before he changed his mind about the walk.

The path opposite the store's loading dock beckoned. She moved off of the steps, lifted her hems and followed Blake across the dirt road that ran behind the cluster of buildings.

"This part of the path is narrow. We'll have to go single file. I'll lead the way." He gave her a warning look. "Mind you don't trip on a clump of dirt."

She nodded and trailed him along the mixture of dead, trampled grass and dried mud. Cool air hovered in the shade beneath the branches of the towering pines on either side, defying the sunshine bathing her in its warmth. In the distance, the object of their foray roared a muted accompaniment to the crunch of their boots against the dirt, and the twitter of birds. A squirrel, disturbed by their presence, chased up a tree and out onto a branch, stopped and chattered his displeasure. She laughed and halted to look up at the furry creature. "Don't be so selfish! This is a vast forest. You can share this small bit of it with us." An imperious twitch of its tail was her answer.

"Do you talk to animals often?"

There was an amused glint in Blake's eyes that added to her pleasure in their excursion. She smiled and held herself from twirling about to release her exhilaration. "How else do you make friends of them?"

"I don't."

"More's the pity."

"Well, please don't try it with a grizzly bear or mountain lion." He headed back up the path.

A grizzly bear! Well, that took away her desire to whirl. Unless... She raised her hems and hurried after him. "You're teasing...right?"

"No." He glanced over his shoulder. "I don't want you to ever come into these woods alone."

He was serious. She stopped and looked into the shadows ahead that suddenly seemed darker, menacing. "Perhaps we should go back."

"No need. I'm armed."

"You have a *gun*?"

"A Smith & Wesson revolver. I bought it when I first came."

She ducked under a branch he held up out of her way, then lifted her gaze to his face. "Do you know how to shoot it?"

"Yes. I've practiced until I can hit what I aim at."

The idea of his skill with a pistol made her feel protected; something in his eyes made her feel safe. "All right." She dropped her voice to a whisper. "I'll be quiet."

"It's better to make noise. It lets them know you're coming, so they can slink away. I usually sing when I'm in the woods."

She played with that image, smiled and fell back into step behind him. "What songs do you sing?"

"Any that come to mind."

His words were curt, bitter. Only one thing made him sound like that; he was thinking of Linda. The happy image she'd conjured of him walking and singing in the woods vanished. She wished she hadn't asked the question.

He gestured ahead. "The path widens after it curves around that big boulder. Come up and walk beside me when it does. One of the men that hunts for the railroad told me to look as big as possible when I'm in bear country, and you're a little thing."

"I am not little!" She hated that description! All of her life she'd been Linda's *little* sister.

"All right then—slender. You're sure not big." He stepped around the boulder, looked back and motioned her forward.

She hurried toward him, rounded the bend and gasped. Tall ferns and plants she couldn't identify twined in and out and over stones and boulders that rimmed water with the surrounding mountains reflected on its surface. Sunshine danced on the ripples flowing down the center of the water to a stream that disappeared into the trees. "You didn't tell me there was a lake here."

"A drain-off pond really. There's another ahead— the one the waterfall drops into. It's beyond that gap. We'll start climbing these rocks now. Unless you would rather return to the store."

"Oh, no. I want to go on. I've never seen anything like this." She gazed at the boulders rising in a steady grade that led to a stone shelf along the break he called a gap. "I may need your help…" She let the words trail off to give him the opportunity to refuse.

"May?"

She looked up, thankful for the teasing tone in his voice. At least he'd stopped thinking about her sister. "All right… I *will* need your help." She lifted her chin a notch and threw his challenge back at him. "Unless *you* would rather return to the store."

He grinned.

She put the tremble in her stomach down to excitement over the trek ahead and scanned the rocks. "Where do we start?"

"Right here." He stepped up onto a boulder and offered her his hand.

Chapter Seven

Blake stopped at the beginning of the natural stone shelf that was the only way to traverse the break at the base of the mountain. The ledge was narrow, but safe. But the water was a different matter.

He looked at Audrey, holding her long skirts out of her way and gazing at the icy, white-capped water that swirled and boiled through the gap between the soaring mountain walls. She didn't look at all hesitant to continue on. He'd expected the hard climb among the boulders to defeat her, but she was a game little thing. And she *was* little, despite her protestation. Though not so much short as slender. His hands spanned her tiny waist when he lifted her to boulders too high for her to climb.

She looked up and smiled, said something he couldn't hear over the rush of the water and the roar of the waterfall ahead. He leaned down so his mouth was close to her ear. "We're almost there. The waterfall is just around that outcropping." He pointed to where the mountain wall jutted out onto the shelf. Her gaze followed then came back to meet his. She went up on tiptoes, curled her finger. He leaned down.

"It doesn't look as if there's much room for walking!"

"It's narrow but passable if you're careful. If you'd rather, we can turn back."

She shook her head, gripped her skirts and lifted the hems. "Lead on."

"Give me your hand. And don't let go!" She nodded and curled her fingers around his palm. He folded his over them in a firm grip. "Watch your footing." He faced forward, led her onto the shelf and walked ahead kicking small bits of stone out of the way and ignoring as best he could the clasp of their joined hands as she followed.

The wall of the mountain rose sheer and rugged beside them, meeting his left shoulder with unforgiving hardness when the shelf narrowed. Sunshine glinted on the gray stone and shadowed a few stunted pines that clung to the face, their roots snaking into cracks and fissures to find purchase and sustenance. Roiling water crashed against the shelf, hurled itself in frothy rage against the mountain wall on the other side of the narrow gap. Spume flew through the air, forming damp blotches on the legs of his pants. He stopped where the wall jutted out onto the ledge, pulled Audrey close and shouted, "Watch, and do what I do."

He turned his back and edged sideways along the stone to round the point of the protrusion. Her hand convulsed in his when he was lost to her sight. He splayed his legs to brace himself to hold her if she slipped and signaled her to come with a tug on her hand.

She came slowly, gripping his outstretched hand, his sleeve rubbing against the stone as she edged along the narrowest part of the shelf. *Almost there.* He stared at the rock, watching for her to round the protrusion into view. Her progress stopped. Her hand trembled. Had she become frightened and changed her mind? He leaned closer to the protrusion, hollered encouragement. "You're all right. You've almost made it. A couple more steps and—" Her hand squeezed, released, squeezed again. Her voice came, barely audible.

"My skirt is caught! I can't move."

He stiffened but bit back the suggestion that she turn and go back the other way. To accomplish that, he would have to let go of her, and she was at the narrowest point of the ledge; with her snagged skirt hampering her it would be too dangerous. He looked down at the turbulent water, too icy, deep and fast-moving to stand in. There was only one choice. "Hold on, I'm coming!" He pulled in a breath against the sudden knot of fear in his stomach. In order to help her, he would have to let go of her while he turned around. "Audrey, listen carefully!" He took another breath, shouted his instructions. "I have to let go of your hand so I can turn around. Press back against the mountain and stay there! *Don't move!* Do you hear me? *Don't move!* Squeeze my hand if you heard me!"

Her hand tightened. He released his grip and her hand slipped out of his. Air squeezed from his lungs. *Lord, hold her on that ledge! Keep her safe!* He turned and hugged the mountain, edged back around the protrusion, saw a bit of red dress and started breathing again. He moved close, slid his foot beneath her skirt and found solid footing. She grabbed hold of his shirt and gave him a smile at once so frightened and brave he lost his breath again.

"I'll hold you. See if you can tug your skirt free." He reached his arm across in front of her and slipped his hand between her back and the mountain. She tightened her hold on his shirt and stretched her right hand down to her side. Her shoulder pressed into him; her body tensed beneath his arm. Her right arm jerked, relaxed, jerked again, and again. Her teeth caught at her lower lip. She pulled again, harder, turned her head and met his gaze, her eyes clouded, worried.

"It won't come free."

"You're not strong enough. I'll do it." *But how?* He'd have to step in front of her to get a hold on that side of her skirt and there wasn't enough shelf there for a solid purchase for his foot. If he fell into that icy turbulence… "Let go of me."

"What?" Her gaze locked on his, protesting, fearful. "Why?"

He smiled to put her at ease. "Because that water is cold and if I slip there's no sense in both of us taking a bath in it."

She slid her other hand beneath his jacket and grabbed another fistful of his shirt. "I'll hold you."

He looked into her eyes, so close he could see the gold flecks darken with determination, and shook his head. "Don't do that. I have to be able to move freely. Put your hands down to your sides and press back against the stone as tight as you can."

"Blake—"

"It's the only way to do this."

She snagged her lower lip with her teeth again then let go of his shirt. He slid his foot to the left. The toe of his boot touched hers—there was nothing but air beneath his heel. "Can you slide your foot back at all?"

"No. My heel is against the stone."

He held back a frown, wiggled the toe of his boot into as solid a position as possible and shifted his weight to that foot. Audrey stood as still as a statue, the soft warmth of her body squeezed between him and the cold mountain wall. He murmured, "It's all right to breathe," took his own advice, then leaned to the side. There was a splintered section of a small broken-off tree trunk visible at the edge of her hem. He gripped her skirt as close to the snag as he could reach and shook it. It stayed caught. He shook it harder, straightened and placed his mouth by her ear. A curl at her temple brushed against his cheek. It smelled like roses. "I'm going to have to tear your skirt free." Her face turned toward his. His gut clenched.

"No matter."

Her warm breath touched his cold skin, light and soft as a feather. He sucked in a breath, locked his gaze on the mountain wall and slid his right hand over the surface seeking something to grip. The cold, flat stone defeated him. No handhold. Nothing beneath his boot heel. If he lost his balance— No, that couldn't happen. If he were injured…or worse, she would be alone and helpless out here. *Help me, Lord!*

He leaned as far toward the mountain as possible and yanked. There was a tearing sound. Her skirt hem flew upward clutched in his fist. The impetus of his strong pull rocked him backward and his heel dropped.

He let go of her skirt and grabbed for the mountain, his fingers scraping over the hard stone. The toe of his boot slipped, slid backward… He threw his weight onto his right foot, let his body sag forward. The edge of the shelf pressed into the sole of his boot beneath his curled toes. The slide stopped. He pulled his dangling foot back to the shelf until his toe found a purchase, closed his eyes and sucked in air. *Thank You, Lord!*

Cold, hard stone chilled his hands and the side of his face pressed hard against it. There was warmth, a soft pressure against his ribs at his sides—fingers holding on to his shirt. When had she taken hold of him again? Anger, hot and immediate, surged. He drew a breath filled with the smell of stone, fresh water and roses, pulled his head back and glared down at her squashed between him and the protruding stone. "I told you to let go of me!"

"And I told you I would hold you."

The fear for her rose again, urgent and overwhelming. "You're not *big enough* to hold me!" The words exploded against the mountain inches from his face. "If my foot had slid another inch I would have fallen in that water and *you with me*! What would you have done then!"

"Swim!" Her raised chin bumped against his breastbone. "Father taught me."

He stared down at her, fought a compelling urge to bury his fingers in her mussed-up red hair and press his lips against that sassy little mouth of hers. "Not in *that* water." He growled the words and inched to the side—to safety. He grabbed her hand and edged back around the protrusion to where the shelf widened and they could turn around. The roar of the tumbling, cascading water echoed off the encompassing mountain walls and crashed against his eardrums. Air cold and wet with overspray penetrated his shirtfront, replacing the warmth of her. She followed him around the jutting stone, stopped and stared.

"Oh, my!"

He read her lips, watched an expression of wonder sweep over her face at the fierce beauty of this small, God-made cul-de-sac. She wiped beading moisture from her face and swept her gaze over the sheer soaring mountain walls that encased a deep pool dark with shadow and freckled with bits of white froth from the tempestuous foaming where the waterfall splashed into it. Loosened curls tumbled free of her gathered hair and spilled down her back as she tilted her head to gaze up at the top of the mountain to where the gushing, roaring cataract began. She turned her face to him and mouthed, "It's amazing!"

He nodded and stepped closer to her side, ready to grab her and haul her back to safety should she slip on the wet surface. She pointed down at the water and held her hand out to him. He read her intention in her eyes, and something more—trust. He took her hand in his and she knelt down and dipped the fingers of her other hand in the water, yanked them out and rose. A shiver shook her. "It's freezing! Too cold for swimming!" Her lips curved then parted with laughter swallowed by the echoing roar. Moisture glittered on her hair and eyelashes, made damp spots on her gown.

He dragged his gaze from the sparkling gold flecks in her eyes, shrugged out of his jacket and draped it over her, pulling it forward on her shoulders. She looked down, curled her fingers around the lapels, then tilted her head back to look at him. His pulse kicked. He pulled his hands away and motioned toward the gap behind them.

She stood a moment looking at the waterfall, then met his gaze and nodded. He took her soft, cold hand in his and led her back onto the shelf.

"I've never seen anything like it." Audrey took another stitch and looked up at Blake, who was standing by the desk thumbing through the pages of a book. "Thank you, again, for taking me to the waterfall."

"For the third time—you're welcome."

There was an underlying tension in his teasing response and his smile looked forced. It had been that way since they had returned from their excursion. She glanced at the blue settee, wished there were some way to disguise it. But it wouldn't make any difference. Linda's presence permeated the entire house. She pressed on with the safe subject, hoping it might take Blake's mind off his lost love. "I know I thanked you before, but it was just so wonderful!"

"In spite of your ruined gown?"

She stopped sewing, looked up at him and smiled. "Seeing that waterfall would be worth the cost of a gown, but it's not ruined." She resumed her work, poked the needle through the fabric, pulled the stitch taut and took another. "When I finish, you won't even be able to see that it was torn—unless you search out the spot and look directly at it."

"So you are a good seamstress?"

"Yes—if I do say so myself. Have you any mending that needs to be done?" The words fell on her ears, domestic...*wifely*. Her cheeks warmed. She lowered her head over her work to hide their color.

"No. Ah Cheng takes care of that. He will pick up the laundry tomorrow. I should have told you. It would have spared you that work." He dipped his head toward the gown she was mending, put down the book and turned to look out the window. "At least you won't have to wash your gown."

There was an undertone in his voice that kept her from replying. Anger toward her sister swelled. At first it was Linda's casual attitude toward breaking her promise to Blake and putting his inheritance in jeopardy that irritated her. Now, witnessing Blake's pain made her ache for him. She pressed her lips together to keep from commenting on her sister's betrayal, aligned the edges of the tear and took another stitch.

"I've been thinking about selling the store." He lifted his hand and scrubbed it across the back of his neck. "Trying to come up with a workable plan."

Her stomach flopped. She'd been so taken up with baking biscuits and helping in the store yesterday and with the dinner with the Ferndales and the walk to the waterfall today she hadn't even thought about it all ending. But, of course, it must. And the sooner it happened the better it would be for Blake. "Have you settled on one?"

"Not yet. There are details I have to consider. John Ferndale is a shrewd businessman." He shoved his hands in his pockets and leaned his shoulder against the window frame.

She nodded, looking down at the dress in her lap to erase the memory of him leaning over her on the ledge—putting himself in jeopardy to protect her. Her throat constricted.

"I just wanted you to know that I'm keeping my word and working on solving the problem. Making you stay here is unfair—not to mention selfish. I will get you home as soon as possible."

To never see him again... Tears threatened. She forced her voice past the lump in her throat, held it steady. "It's a house that awaits me, Blake—not a home." She knotted the thread, snipped it free and stuck the needle in the pincushion he'd brought up from the store. "A home is a place that is shared with someone you love." *The way you love Linda.* She rose and gathered her dress and sewing supplies while she got her emotions under control. "I feel like a hot cup of tea. Would you like one?"

"Maybe later."

Later. She would be going back to New York later. How long would that be? A month? Two? The tightness spread to her chest. The tears welled. She hurried from the room lest Blake notice and ask her what was wrong. She had no answer beyond this sudden hollow feeling at the thought of leaving.

Blake read the reversion clause a second time, shoved the contract in his desk drawer and leaned back in his chair. His plan to sell the store should work. He could see no reason why John Ferndale would hold him to that clause if the person he sold the store to was a married man. That was what Ferndale wanted—married men who would become solid citizens and raise their families here in Whisper Creek. He'd thought he would be one of those men. But that hope was dead.

The ache he did his best to bury twisted his gut, made him fight to fill his lungs. How could he have been so wrong about Linda? He could understand how he could have been...distracted from the truth by her coquettish ways and her physical charms, but her letters... Pain flashed through him. That was when he'd really fallen deeply in love with her, when he'd read her letters. They were lively with humor, rife with interest in him and his store and Whisper Creek, and filled with warmth and love. The woman who wrote those letters was the woman he'd wanted to share his life—to mother his children. And it had all been a lie.

He surged to his feet, twisted the knob to smother the flame in the oil lamp and strode from the room. His office was too small to contain his anger. So was his bedroom. He yanked open the porch door and stepped out into the darkness, drew his lungs full of cold air laced with the scent of the pines.

Roses. Audrey's hair smelled like roses. He scowled, replaced the thought with a memory of Linda in his arms.

The moon slipped out from behind a cloud, its silver light glinting on the patches of water that showed between the high branches of the towering pines. *The waterfall. Audrey.* He jerked his gaze from the sparkling water, but the image had taken form: red curls in disarray, hazel eyes dark with determination, small chin lifted and— He shook his head, scrubbed his hand over the muscles at the back of his neck to rid himself of the memory—but he knew he would never forget how she looked in that moment on the ledge. Or the blended scent of stone, water and roses. Disgust curdled his stomach. What sort of man was he to have felt such a compelling urge to kiss Audrey when he loved Linda? His betrayer.

The word stabbed deep. Was that it? Was that what caused that intense urge to kiss Audrey? Was he so mean-natured he wanted revenge? He cringed, sickened by the thought. Audrey did not deserve that. No matter what he felt, or how strongly he felt it, he must never demean her in that way—never.

He leaned against the porch post and stared out into the darkness, listened to the muted whisper of the waterfall and tried to hold his mind blank, seeking to quiet the turmoil within. It was impossible. Thoughts and images tumbled and roiled in his head, crashing against obstacles and shooting off in a dozen different directions like the water forcing its way through the gap that afternoon. He tried to bring them under control, but they refused to be disciplined. The images played against the darkness: Audrey smiling up at him as he helped her climb over the boulders…holding his shirt while he tried to free her skirt…the wonder on her face as she gazed up at the waterfall…standing looking up at him with his jacket draped around her shoulders…

He frowned, tried to slip Linda into Audrey's place and failed. He couldn't imagine Linda doing any of those things. Or baking biscuits to bring him customers… Or helping him in the store…

The wind rose. He scrubbed a hand through his hair and scowled into the darkness. He may not be able to sort out his emotions, but one thing was certain—he would never eat another biscuit without picturing Audrey, neat and determined in her gray gown, walking out of his store carrying that basket of biscuits for Asa Marsh and the conductors. It was another smell he would forever associate with her—biscuits. Roses and biscuits...

Chapter Eight

The train whistle echoed down the valley. Audrey's pulse quickened. Would her efforts bear fruit today? Would the conductor tell the passengers about the store?

She glanced from the mound of bread dough on the table to the window, pushed a curl off her forehead with the back of her hand and resumed her kneading. Fold, push, turn. Fold, push turn. Fold, push, done! She placed the dough in the bowl, turned it so the greased side was up, tossed a towel over the bowl and slid it in the warming oven. Now for the rolls.

She sprinkled more flour on the table, kneaded the next lump of dough, pressed it into a rectangle and smeared it with soft butter. A liberal sprinkling of sugar, another of cinnamon and she was finished. She rolled the rectangle into a log, sealed the edge with a bit of milk, sliced the roll into even pieces and placed them in a baking pan.

Two quick blasts of the whistle rattled the window-panes. The train was at the station! The conductor

would be swinging down, pulling the steps in place…
She threw a towel over the rolls, slid them into the
warming oven to rise and hurried to the sink to wash
her hands. Cleaning the worktable could wait.

She dipped her fingers in the hand cream, rubbed it
on her hands and ran to the window. A woman, garbed
in green, appeared in the passenger car door, took the
conductor's hand and descended. A man, woman and
child followed. Soldiers filed out and gathered on the
platform, their blue uniforms unmistakable even over
the distance.

Her plan didn't work. And she'd been so certain it
would after the way the conductors had received her
gifts of biscuits. She breathed a long sigh, swallowed
her disappointment and went back to clean the worktable. Perhaps she could think of another way to— No.
She had interfered in Blake's life enough. She would
simply play her part as a stand-in bride until he found
the solution to saving the store and his inheritance.
And he would. Blake was a very intelligent, resourceful man. And thoughtful…and kind…and strong…
and— *Audrey Elizabeth Prescott, you stop thinking
about yesterday!*

She carried the dirty utensils to the sink, grabbed
the sharp knife and scraped the stuck-on dough and
flour loose from the worktable and into the slop pail.
Was that a bell? She paused, listened, then shrugged
and wiped the table clean, thinking about dinner. She'd
been avoiding the deer meat Blake told her was in one
of the packages in the refrigerator. She wasn't familiar with deer meat—had no idea of how best to cook
it. Perhaps she could call on Mrs. Ferndale for advice.

She played with the idea, thinking of the benefits and drawbacks of an unscheduled visit. She didn't want to appear rude. On the other hand, she didn't want the meat to spoil, and Mrs. Ferndale had invited her to come anytime. She would go. But first, she needed to tell Blake what she was going to do and get his approval. She had forged ahead on her own too much since arriving.

She brushed the clinging flour from her apron and started down the stairs, paused at the sound of the bell on the door. Was a customer coming or leaving? She didn't want to interrupt Blake when he was doing business. She walked through the storage room to the connecting door, stopped and stared. Blake was behind the counter waiting on the family she had seen getting off the train. Soldiers roamed the store or stood in line waiting for service. The woman in green was choosing notions from the dry goods section. It had worked! The conductor had told the passengers about Blake's store. She caught her breath to keep from laughing and crying and shouting, pivoted to go back upstairs.

"Excuse me, miss. Do you have this needlepoint yarn in a lighter blue?"

She turned. The woman in green was coming toward her clutching a handful of yarn spools. "I'm sorry, madam, but I don't—"

"Audrey..."

She shot a glance at Blake.

"If you wouldn't mind—there's a small box of yarn there in the storage room. It's on the shelf to your left." He went back to tallying the family's order.

She looked at the woman and smiled to hide her inexperience. "One moment, madam…" She found the wood box, pulled out a spool of blue wool the color of a summer sky and took it to her. "Will this suit?"

"That is exactly the color I need. Thank you, dear."

She smiled and turned back toward the storage room.

"Do you have peaches in a tin, miss? And tooth powder? I'm partial to cherry flavor if you have it."

She glanced at Blake, now busy writing up the woman's order, then back to the soldier waiting for her to answer. She took a breath and plunged in to help as best she could. "Yes, of course. The peaches are there on that shelf. I'll get the tooth powder for you." She slipped behind the counter, found a tin of cherry toothpaste and offered it for the soldier's inspection. "There is no cherry-flavored tooth powder. Will this do?"

The soldier nodded, fished coins out of his pocket. "How much will that be?"

She smiled and indicated the short line in front of the counter. "Mr. Latherop will take care of your payment."

"Please, Papa…"

Ah, she recognized that coaxing tone. She smiled at the memory of the anticipation of getting some candy when she went to the store with her father, glanced over the counter at a young girl of perhaps five years of age, then shifted her gaze to the father. Oh, dear, he looked unyielding.

"Please let her have some candy, Tobias. It helps to keep her stomach settled on the train." The mother looked down at the daughter, gave a conspiratorial wink.

"Very well. For her stomach, Penelope. But you

will ration them out to her. You're spoiling the child with your largesse!" The father noticed her behind the counter and waved an imperious hand toward the jars of candy. "Give me a nickel's worth of candy in a mix of lemon, peppermint and horehound."

She bit back a desire to remind him of his manners, tore off a small piece of paper, twisted and tied one end and smiled at the little girl. "Do you prefer one flavor over another?"

"Lemon, please. It makes my tummy feel better."

"I gave you your instructions, miss. Mix the candy as I ordered. And be quick about it!"

She kept her gaze down, lest the father read her opinion of his arrogant attitude in her eyes, and pressed her lips together to keep from responding. She took candy from the jars, adding extra lemon ones as a gift for the child, twisted the open end closed and tied it with string. "Would you like to carry it?" She leaned over the counter and held it down to the little girl.

"My wife will take the candy." The father scowled, slapped a nickel on the counter. The man's imperiousness was too much. She gave him a polite smile. "If you will step into line, Mr. Latherop will take your payment, sir."

"Now, see here, miss—"

She jutted her chin, gritted her teeth behind her polite smile. "I am only helping Mr. Latherop serve his customers, sir. I do not accept payment." She caught sight of Blake's raised eyebrow from the corner of her eye. He'd overheard. Her stomach sank. She handed the paper twist to the woman and smiled down at the little girl. "Enjoy your candy."

"Thank you for your service, miss." The woman glanced at her scowling husband waiting to pay, leaned close and whispered, "He's not used to being made to wait in line." The woman smiled and placed a nickel on the counter. "For the extra lemon drops."

She shook her head. "Those are a gift—"

The woman pursed her lips, touching a finger to them. "I know, dear, but your kindness in adding those extra lemon drops is worth much more than that coin. And so is that!" She glanced in her husband's direction, smiled again and took hold of her daughter's hand. "Come along, Susan. Father still has to pay, and we don't want to miss our train."

She watched the mother and child walk away then looked down at the nickel. It was too much money. She caught her lower lip with her teeth and slid the coin toward Blake.

"We'd like to buy some biscuits, miss."

"Yeah, we heard they were powerful good, not like those rocks they give us at mess."

Two soldiers stood at the end of the counter, hats in their hands, a hopeful look in their eyes. "I'm sorry, but—" Disappointment clouded their eyes. Guilt smote her. "It will take a moment for me to get them. Wait here, gentlemen."

She whirled and ran upstairs to the kitchen. The biscuits in the bowl were from dinner last night, but they were still good. She hurried back to the store, slipped behind the counter and tore off a piece of paper. "There are six biscuits. How many—"

The train whistle blasted its warning of departure. The few people browsing about left the store.

"We'll take all six, miss. No need to wrap 'em. Grab 'em, Jonsey." The soldier with a stripe on his sleeve dug in his pocket and pulled out a coin, slapped it on the counter and ran for the door on his buddy's heels.

"Wait!" Blake grabbed a coin, started after them. "You've paid too much!"

"Give me more biscuits my next time through!"

The door slammed behind them. The bell jingled. Footsteps pounded across the porch and down the steps, faded into silence. She took a breath then looked up at Blake.

"I'm sorry—" Their words collided.

"Ladies first." Blake stepped back behind the counter, made a notation in his ledger and slipped it on the shelf. "What's this?" He picked up the nickel.

"It's the reason I need to apologize. That man—"

"The arrogant one reluctant to buy candy for his daughter? The one you handled in such a cool, polite manner?"

So he had noticed. "Yes. I know I should have been more patient, but— Why are you laughing?"

"I thought you were going to choke! Or he was."

"That's not funny, Blake! He was your customer and I—"

"Handled the matter exactly right. You never have to accept rude treatment from one of my customers, Audrey. You send them to me, and I'll take care of them. I'll put this nickel right here by the cash box to remind you."

He'd been pleased with her work. Pleasure spurted through her. "Are you saying you may want me to help you in the store again?"

He nodded, stepped close. "Would you be willing to

help me when the trains come? I wouldn't ask, but there is no one else in town I can hire. And if this morning was any example, I will not be able to handle all of the customers from the trains by myself. Twenty minutes is too short a time for me to take care of everyone. I'll pay you, of course."

So he wasn't pleased with her work. It was only that there was no one else. And he thought so little of her he offered payment for her help—as if she were a stranger. She swallowed hard against the sudden lump in her throat, lowered her head and smoothed the front of her apron so she didn't have to meet his gaze. "I will help you whenever you need me, Blake. But without pay."

"No, Audrey. I insist on paying you a fair wage."

The constriction in her throat swelled. She took a breath, drew back her shoulders and looked up at him. "I'm well aware that I am only a *pretend* wife, Blake. But you would not pay your *real* wife to help you, and you will not pay me. If you insist on doing so, I will not help you."

He frowned and shook his head. "That's not fair to you, Audrey."

Neither is what Linda did to you with my help. "It is our arrangement. A deal is a deal."

He stared down at her, scrubbed his hand across the back of his neck. "You are the most frustrating, *stubborn* woman I've ever known."

Silence.

"All right, I yield. I'm in no position to argue. But I also have a condition as to your employment as my clerk."

"And what is that?"

He lifted his hand, gently brushed it over the curls at her forehead. "No more waiting on customers with flour in your hair."

Heat flowed into her cheeks but didn't compare to the warmth that spread through her when his fingers touched her face. She caught her breath, pulled her gaze from his and hid from the sensation with conjured anger. "I was setting bread dough before I came downstairs. You might have told me sooner!" She lifted her hems and hurried toward the safety of upstairs.

"Audrey, wait!" His hand wrapped around her upper arm, brought her to a halt. "I didn't notice the flour in your hair until just now when we were talking. It was barely visible. Truly. I was only teasing."

He was so close she could feel his warmth on her back. She glanced at his hand holding her arm, so strong yet gentle, and held her breath against the quivering in her stomach, the ache in her throat. *Please make him let go of me, Lord.* She blinked to ease the pressure of tears stinging her eyes and cleared her throat. "I know. I was only having a…a 'redhead' moment."

"Then I'm forgiven?"

The bell on the door jingled. "Of course. Now, I have bread waiting to be baked, and you have a customer…" She stood quietly, waited for him to release her arm. Boot heels struck the plank flooring in the store, drew closer.

"You back here, Latherop?" Garret Stevenson strode through the doorway, came to an abrupt halt. "Oh, sorry, Mrs. Latherop, I didn't mean to intrude."

Blake's hand fell away from her arm. She felt him take a step back—no doubt embarrassed to be seen by his friend in what could be interpreted as an intimate moment with her. She turned to rescue him. "Not at all, Mr. Stevenson." *The only thing you intruded upon is my foolishness.* "I was on my way upstairs to bake some cinnamon rolls—perhaps you would like some when they are done?"

A grin spread across the young man's face. "Mrs. Latherop, I'd trade you my hotel for some of them! I haven't had any fresh-baked bread or rolls or such since I came to Whisper Creek."

She managed a small laugh. "That won't be necessary, Mr. Stevenson. And, since you are Blake's friend, please feel free to use my given name of Audrey." *I'm not Mrs. Latherop. I'm only a pretense.*

He dipped his head. "It will be my pleasure, Audrey."

Not for long. "If you'll excuse me, gentlemen, those rolls are waiting…"

"Of course, dearest." Blake placed his hand over hers on the banister. "I'll join you upstairs when I've taken care of Garret and sent him on his way."

Her heart skipped at the warmth in his voice, the look in his eyes. *Stop it! It's only an act.* She nodded, lifted her hems and started up the stairs, watched Blake stride over to Garret Stevenson.

"I forgot about your bride, Blake. I'll confine myself to the store from now on."

"No need, Garret. Now, what can I do for you?"

No need. None, indeed. What if— No. No silly imaginings. Blake loved Linda, and that was the end of it. This pretend marriage was simply that—pretend. And she knew, as well as anyone, that reality was never like foolish dreams.

* * *

Two doorknobs… Two sets of door hinges… Four pounds, six-penny nails… Blake listed the purchased items in his ledger and looked up. "Anything else, Garret?"

"Your wife, *Audrey*…" Garret Stevenson popped a peppermint drop in his mouth and leaned his elbows on the counter, his eyes alight with curiosity.

He gave Garret a mock scowl. "She's not for sale."

"Funny." Garret's eyes narrowed. "I thought your betrothed's name was Linda."

"That's right." He gestured with his pen toward the items on the counter. "Is that it for today? Or have you other purchases?"

"Knobs and hinges for six cupboards."

"Any preference?" He stepped from behind the counter and strode to the hardware display to get the needed items.

"The ones on the left. So what happened?" Garret turned and leaned against the counter. "Where is Linda?"

"In San Francisco with her husband." The bitterness was in his voice, but it didn't burn in his gut—not like before. He must be getting used to the idea of Linda's betrayal. He carried the knobs and hinges to the counter, placed them beside the other items and picked up his pen.

"Sorry, Blake. I'm not meaning to pry into things that are none of my business. I was surprised over Audrey's name is all."

"You and John Ferndale."

Garret stopped loading his purchases into his pail.

"Ferndale had a problem with your bride being Audrey instead of Linda?"

"At first. But he came around when I explained—"

"Why should Ferndale care who your bride is?" A scowl knit Garret's dark brows together. "The contract I signed only says we have to be married and then live here in Whisper Creek with our wife or family for five years. Ferndale has no say as to *whom* we marry! Or why! We owe him no explanation for our choice of bride!" Garret shoved the remaining items in his pail, lifted it from the counter and strode out the door.

Blake stared after him, the words ringing in his head drowning out the slam of the door and the jangle of the bell. He dropped his pen onto the counter, shoved his fingers through his hair and glanced up toward the ceiling. In all the turmoil, he'd forgotten about that living-in-Whisper-Creek-for-five-years part. Now how was he going to free himself and Audrey from this sham of a marriage?

Chapter Nine

Audrey leaned toward the mirror and peered closely at her hair. No trace of flour remained. She closed her mind to the memory of Blake's fingers against her face, secured her brushed hair into a loose figure eight at the nape of her neck, then pinned her hat in place and stepped back to examine her appearance. A quick tug on the bolero jacket of her gray wool dress and she was ready.

She strolled into the kitchen, grabbed the plate of cinnamon rolls she had waiting and hurried down the stairs. Light streamed into the storage room through the open door. Wheels rolled over wood planks on the loading dock. Blake, his shirt straining across his shoulders, backed through the doorway dragging a handcart laden with various-size crates. The muscles in his forearms below his rolled-up sleeves corded against his effort and the cart bumped over the sill.

"What is all of that?"

He placed the toe of his boot against the wheel and eased the cart erect. "Supplies for the store that came in on the train." He unrolled his sleeves, turned to face her. "I'm glad you're still here. I forgot to tell you not to leave until I returned from the station."

"I was waiting for the cinnamon rolls to finish baking."

"Is that what you have there?"

She followed his gaze to the covered plate she held. "Yes. I'm taking them to the Ferndales as a thank-you for their hospitality."

"That's a good idea…" He came to stand in front of her and lifted the towel. "A *very* good idea. They look delicious. And that smell makes my mouth water." He took a deep sniff, gave her a hopeful look. "Are there any left?"

Gratification shot through her. Linda may surpass her in appearance and coquettish behavior, but not at baking or housekeeping—though Blake would never know. The thought brought a spasm of guilt. Shame on her for taking pleasure in besting her sister—even if she would never say it aloud. "There are plenty. I left some on a covered plate on the table for Mr. Stevenson, should he come again before I return."

"If I share them with him."

She looked up. He grinned. Her stomach started that foolish fluttering again. She headed for the front door. "Your rolls are in the dish on the cupboard. I'll return before the next train is due."

"Wait until I get my jacket. I'll walk with you."

"But, you're working—"

"It can wait. I don't want you to come to harm."

"Harm?" She paused, watched him close the door

to the loading dock. "You said I was safe from the Indians as long as I stayed in the town."

"It's not the Indians I'm concerned about." He lifted his jacket off a nail driven in a board by the door and shrugged into it. "I don't want you coming upon a rattlesnake unaware."

"A *rattlesnake*!" She stiffened, staring at him through the dimmed light. "There are rattlesnakes on the path?"

"Could be. They like the water and the rocky outcroppings at the bottom of the mountains. And they hunt rodents and such in the deep grass." He came back to her side. "Ready?"

"Yes…" She wrinkled her nose. "But I'm nowhere near as eager to walk to the Ferndales' as I was a moment ago."

He chuckled and walked with her to the front of the store, hung the Closed sign on the door and escorted her across the porch and down the steps. "You really don't have to worry. Most of the time the snakes slither out of your way. And, if one should strike at you, your long skirts will protect you—unless you happen to step over one."

She halted, stared at the long path through the tall grasses. "Why didn't you tell me about the snakes on Sunday?" She gave him an assessing look. "You're only teasing me!"

He shook his head. "Not about rattlesnakes. There was no need to tell you about them on Sunday because I was with you. But you need to know about them. I don't want you to come to harm."

That was the second time he'd said that. She looked

down, smoothed a wrinkle from the towel covering the plate and reminded herself that it meant nothing beyond his general concern for anyone. He was simply a nice man—a *very* nice man. She needed to stop looking for signs that Blake...*approved* of her. And she needed to stifle her growing pleasure in his presence. It made no difference one way or the other, beyond the fact that it made her situation more tenable.

"I'll carry those." He took the plate of rolls then bent his left elbow in invitation.

She slipped her hand through and rested it on his arm, remembered the muscles beneath her fingers cording in strength when he'd tugged the loaded cart over the threshold. The soft thud of a horse's hoofs sounded on the station road behind them.

"Morning, Blake..."

"Morning, Mitch. May I present my bride?" Blake looked down at her. "Dearest, this is Mr. Mitchel Todd. He's the man who has built this town—including my store."

The man dipped his head her direction and smiled. "Your husband is too modest, Mrs. Latherop. He did more than a little of the work on the store and your home himself. And, may I say, I now understand his eagerness to get the work finished."

No, that was for Linda, Mr. Todd. Her growing ease evaporated like the mist over the pond in the morning sunshine. "You're too kind, Mr. Todd. And a man of talent. Blake's store and the living quarters are much nicer than I expected to find here in the wilds of Wyoming." *Please, Lord, let him stop talking about Blake's eagerness to marry Linda.* His face blurred. She looked down and smoothed the front of her gown, blinked the tears away.

He chuckled. "I imagine you expected to find one-room log cabins and soddys."

"Something like that. They certainly do not tell us back East that there are towns like Whisper Creek to be found in the newly opened territory." She forced a smile to her lips and looked toward the wagon bed loaded with sawn boards. "I see you are working on another project."

"Several. But this wood is for the apothecary's house. He wants it finished so he can live here and oversee the finishing of the inside of the store himself. He needs special-made counters and tables and such."

"And a special-made house as well. Have you ever built an octagonal house before, Mr. Todd?"

"No, that's the first. It's been interesting." The man looked that direction then drew his gaze back to Blake. "If you're headed for the Ferndales', you're welcome to ride. You can fill this order when you return." He handed a slip of paper down to Blake, then slapped his hand to the seat beside him. "It's not a buggy, but it will keep your wife's dress out of the dirt."

"Thank you for the offer, Mitch, but—"

"If it's no trouble, Mr. Todd..." *Blake will be free of me for a little while.* She blinked her vision clear and looked up at Blake. "I will be safe on the wagon, and you can fill Mr. Todd's order and then go back to your work."

He studied her for a moment, then nodded. "If that's what you want, Audrey. Take the rolls." He handed them to her, and, before she knew what he was about, grasped her waist and lifted her to the seat. "I'll come for you in an hour. Don't walk that path by yourself." He lifted a hand to Mitchel Todd, placed it briefly over hers, then climbed the steps to the store.

She settled the plate of rolls on her lap and gazed out over the valley to the encircling mountains, trying to ignore the quiver in her stomach from the touch of his hand.

"What a lovely surprise!" Mrs. Ferndale stepped back and pulled the door wide. "Come in, my dear Mrs. Latherop, come in!"

"Thank you, Mrs. Ferndale." She stepped into the entrance and held out the plate. "I—that is, Mr. Latherop and I wanted to express our gratitude for your kind hospitality on Sunday. These rolls are a small thank-you."

"Why, what a thoughtful gesture. Thank you, my dear. I'm sure John and I will enjoy them. They smell wonderful!"

"I hope I haven't come at an inconvenient time."

"*Inconvenient?* My dear, you have no idea of what a blessing your call is to me." The older woman reached out and squeezed her hand. "I have been so lonely for our daughters, and for my women friends back home. But I'm forgetting my manners. Come along, we'll visit in the turret room."

She followed in Mrs. Ferndale's wake, stepped through an archway and stopped. "Oh, how lovely…" Sunshine streamed in through six small-paned, floral-draped windows that circled the round room. Outside two of the windows, the crystal clear water of Whisper Creek flowed by, magnifying the room's brightness. A chair and a needle-point easel sat in front of one of the windows, a basket of colorful yarns ready-to-hand on the deep windowsill. And in the room's center, a small round piecrust-edged table and two hoop-back Windsor chairs sat on a round oriental rug.

"Come in, dear. We'll have tea." The older woman pulled a cord hanging by the archway, then led the way to the table. "I've been thinking about you since we heard your story—about how you and Mr. Latherop fell in love through your letters to each other."

The letters. Her stomach sank. The letters she'd exchanged with Blake were the last thing she wanted to talk about. It had been a mistake to come here. "Not entirely, Mrs. Ferndale. Blake and I were friends before he came to Whisper Creek." She smiled and walked over to study the unfinished needlepoint—towering pines, a creek flowing through tall grasses—a faithful depiction of the scene outside the window. "You do lovely work." *Please let her accept the change of subject, Lord. If I make a mistake...*

There was a soft pad of footsteps and the Ferndales' Chinese manservant appeared.

She grasped the opportunity to rehearse the story Blake had prepared to explain their sudden marriage.

"Missus, call?"

"Yes. Please take these rolls to the kitchen and then bring us some tea, Hung Wah."

Footsteps padded against the floor, faded away. She braced herself to answer any questions.

"I'm going to send the needlepoint to our daughter Jeanne in Philadelphia." Mrs. Ferndale sighed and came to stand beside her. "I miss our daughters. It's so wonderful to have a woman to talk to again! John has tried to keep me from being lonely, but he has his work overseeing the birth of the town, and, in truth, he's a very poor substitute for a woman. Now, as I was saying…"

"Please forgive me for interrupting, Mrs. Ferndale, but—"

"Call me Dora, dear—the way my friends back home did."

Mrs. Ferndale smiled, but there was sadness in her eyes. How long had she been the only woman in Whisper Creek? A pang of sympathy swept through her for the woman. "It will be my pleasure, Dora." She smiled and turned back to the table. "As I said earlier, I came to visit you today because I wanted to thank you. But I had a second purpose for coming—venison. Blake has a roast in his refrigerator, and I don't want it to spoil, but I know nothing about cooking game." She gave a helpless little shrug. "I thought, perhaps, you could help me?"

"Oh, of course, my dear!" Dora Ferndale beamed. "The secret to tasty venison is to soak it in a mixture of vinegar and water and spices…black peppercorns and such…before roasting it. I place mine in a crock, pour the liquid over it and put it in the refrigerator to soak. The night before you're going to cook it is best."

"So I should set it to soak in vinegar water tonight and roast it tomorrow?"

"That would be best, but even a few hours will help to take away the 'gamy' taste."

"How much vinegar should I use?"

"A good robust splash or two, depending on the amount of water it takes to cover the roast. And I find apple cider vinegar to be the best for the purpose. Oh, here's our tea. Just set it on the table, Hung Wah. I'll pour."

"What a lovely view of the creek." She walked to a window, peered out at the water flowing swiftly by at the base of the towering pines behind the Ferndales' house. There was no part of the waterfall visible. She thought of the view from the porch over the loading dock, the muted sound of the waterfall.

"The tea is poured, dear. Do you care for cream or honey? Perhaps a cookie?"

She went to her chair, stirred cream into her tea.

The older woman slid the plate of cookies toward her. "As I was saying earlier… I've been thinking of your story about the letters."

Her stomach knotted. She stared down at her cup, forced to listen. She couldn't interrupt a second time.

"My grandmother had a similar story. It seems my grandfather had come to America, found employment on a farm, and, after a few years, became the manager of the owner's various properties."

She looked up, intrigued by the story in spite of her apprehension.

Dora Ferndale stirred two spoonsful of sugar into her cup, placed the spoon on her saucer and reached for a cookie. "But Grandfather was lonely. He wrote home to his favorite sister asking her to come to America and tend house for him. But his sister was to be married. She told her best friend about her brother's plight, and the friend wrote him out of sympathy. He was drawn to her warmth and concern, and wrote back, offering marriage to his sister's friend. She took the next ship to America."

She watched Dora break off a bite of cookie and pop it into her mouth, wanting to hear the end of the story despite the tightening in her chest at the mention of a sister. "Obviously, they married…"

"They did. And they lived happily together until the Lord called them home."

"That's a lovely story." *And it has nothing to do with Blake's and my situation.* She took a sip of her tea to ease the tightness.

"Yes, and your story made me remember it, because both started with a letter." Dora took a sip of tea, put her cup down and smiled. "My mother—she was the only daughter out of their five living children—used to tell me how Grandfather would look at Grandmother, shake his head and murmur, *What if Grace*—that was his sister—*had never shown her my letter? God works in mysterious ways.*" Dora fastened her gaze on hers. "I've always found it odd that Grandfather never considered that perhaps he, too, was walking in God's mysterious ways when he *wrote* the letter."

Blake slid his ledger on the shelf, grabbed his pricing book and looked over at Audrey. She'd been unusually quiet since he'd called for her after her visit with Dora Ferndale. Of course, they'd been busy in the store caring for the customers from the late morning train since her return. She was probably tired, though she hadn't mentioned it. She'd just started straightening the rows and stacks of canned goods that had been set askew, her movements quick and efficient.

He tried to imagine Linda working at his side in the store, building the life they'd—he'd—dreamed of together. But he couldn't place her there. Had she ever shared his dream for their future of a life together raising children and enjoying the fruits of their labor? Or had she simply been toying with his affections… laughing at his devotion? No, that wasn't possible— her letters were too caring.

His stomach knotted. His grip tightened on the pricing book. He tossed it onto the counter and walked over to his grocery section. "I'll straighten the shelves, Audrey. You've been working hard. Why don't you rest before the next train comes?"

She glanced over her shoulder at him. "I'm not tired."

He looked beyond her to the shelves. "You've changed things around."

She snagged her lower lip with her teeth, glanced from him to the shelf and lowered her hands to her sides. "I'm sorry. I'm not that familiar yet with—"

"Why did you place the canned meats there?"

She rubbed her hands down the front of her apron. "I don't know. I guess when I started straightening the shelves I simply put the meat so it would be first when you come to the grocery section. That's the way a woman plans a meal. We start with the meat and then decide which vegetables and fruits and baked goods we will serve with it. I just did it without thought. But I certainly have no business rearranging your shelves.

I'll put them back. Where did you have the meat? After the vegetables?" She turned and reached for the cans.

He caught hold of her wrist. "Leave them this way. What you said makes sense—not that there are many women planning meals in Whisper Creek at present. But there will be. And men buy more meat than vegetables. I hadn't considered that in the placement."

"Very well. If you're certain."

The words were soft, breathless. She gave a little tug of her arm and looked up. The gold flecks in her hazel eyes shone through her long, dark brown lashes; a faint rose blush colored her cheekbones. Her pulse raced beneath his fingers. His heart lurched.

He jerked his gaze from Audrey, let go of her wrist and stepped back. "You have an aptitude for this business, Audrey. If you would like—you're in no way obligated, as it is I who owe you—I will show you the pricing book and how to enter purchases in the ledger. That way, you can take care of customers if I am busy elsewhere." Which might be an excellent idea judging from his fickle, physical reaction to her beauty and appeal. "I want to paint the store."

A smile trembled onto her lips. "I'll be happy to help in any way I can, Blake. It's why I came." She drew her shoulders back, lifted her chin and started for the counter. "Shall we begin? I have a lot to learn before the next train arrives."

Chapter Ten

"In this ledger I have listed every item for sale in the store."

Audrey stared at the large black leather book on the counter and wished she could think of an excuse to move away. Blake was so close that when he lowered his head over the book, she could smell a faint trace of the Swiss Violet shaving cream he used. She'd never known violets could smell so...*manly.*

"—is the price per shipping container. The second column is the price per item or pound or ounce. That's the way I do it. If you keep this book open beside the till box you will know how much to charge the customer. Though with your keen mind you will soon have the cost of things memorized."

"I'll do my best." She took a deep breath she immediately regretted and stared down at the book. *With your keen mind...* She'd rather he thought she was beautiful... like Linda. As if that could ever be. She held back a sigh, wishing she had not gone to visit Mrs. Ferndale. The woman's story about her grandfather and grandmother meeting by letter had put foolish, romantic thoughts in her head. Now, every time she looked at Blake she wondered *What if?* And that was pure foolishness.

"And this is my sales ledger." He pulled another large black leather book off the shelf beneath the counter and opened it. "As you can see, I write every purchase in it—that way I know when I'm about to run out of the item and I order more."

"I understand. I'll be careful to record every sale." She tugged at her jacket and used the movement as an excuse to edge a short distance away from him.

"Is something wrong, Audrey?"

"What?" She glanced up, shook her head. "No. I'm just a little...distracted. I was thinking of...dinner." *Sort of.* "I want to start it before the next train arrives." She tucked a curl beneath her hat. "I had thought to have the venison roast, but Mrs. Ferndale said it would be better to soak it and have it tomorrow. So..." *Stop babbling!* She looked down at the ledger. *Smoked ham...* "Do you like ham?"

"Yes. Listen, Audrey, if there is not time enough, or if you've decided it's too much work and have changed your mind about helping in the store—"

"Not at all. I want to help. I enjoy working in the store. It's only..." She focused her scattered thoughts to come up with an excuse. She couldn't tell him the truth. "I can't reach the hams. Or the other items hanging from the ceiling." She tipped her head and looked up. "Is there a ladder in the back room?"

"Not for you to use. It's not safe with your long skirts."

"Then how shall I help the customer who wants a ham?"

"I'll hang them from a shelf in the back room where you can reach them."

"And the saws and other tools?"

"Have the man who wants to buy one take it down."

"But—"

"Must you always argue? *No ladder!*" He scowled, walked to the hams and lifted one down. "Is there anything else?"

The words were growled. Why was he so out of sorts all of a sudden? "Some cloves…and a can of pineapple chunks." She went to get the pineapple, came back and reached for the ham.

"I'll carry that. It's heavy. You take the cloves."

His tone of voice dared her to disagree. She picked up the small folded paper package and led the way to the stairs, climbed to the top and crossed the hall into the kitchen. He followed her to the worktable and plunked down the ham. "I think we need to set some rules."

"Rules? About what?" She set down the can of pineapple, placed the package of cloves on top of it and looked up at him. "If it's the ladder—"

"Our marriage."

"Our *marriage*?" She gaped up at him, trying to follow the leap in subject.

"Yes. It may be in-name-only, but I am still your husband, Audrey." His eyes darkened, captured hers. "It is my job to provide for you, to protect you and keep you safe. I would appreciate it if, from now on, you would act like my wife and let me do my job— especially in front of others."

Where had that accusation come from? "In front of others? Who—"

"Mitch."

"Mr. Todd?"

"Don't sound so shocked." He scowled, braced his hands on the worktable and leaned toward her. "I told you I would escort you to the Ferndale house, but you overrode my wishes and accepted Mitch Todd's offer of a ride."

"Because I thought you would like to be rid of me for a while!"

"Be *rid* of you?"

"Yes." She lifted her chin, cleared a lump from her throat and spoke out the truth. "I know how you feel about me being here in Linda's place."

He straightened, shoved his hands in his pockets. "Linda has no place here."

"That's not true, Blake. She's everywhere. She's in the kitchen when we eat…in the sitting room when we relax… She's behind all of our careful conversations…" Tears welled. She fisted her hands and blinked them away. She had no right to cry over a situation she had caused.

"That *was* true, Audrey. It's not true now. Not for me." His voice, deep and quiet, banished her tears. She looked up at him, saw something she couldn't identify in his eyes. "I can't imagine Linda in this kitchen—not now. Not after—" He sucked in a breath, turned away from her and lifted the towel to pick up a cinnamon roll. "I'll need this for strength while I'm painting the store."

She grabbed the apron off its hook and tied it on,

joined him in the change of topic. "Have you selected a color?"

"White." He leaned against the cupboard, his eyes dark, inscrutable, and took a bite of the roll.

Her heart sank. Why didn't he leave? She needed to be alone to think—to try to make sense of what he had said. Perhaps if she started preparing the vegetables. She gathered potatoes, carrots and a rutabaga and carried them to the table.

"You don't approve of my choice?"

"I didn't say that." She went to the sink, filled a bowl with water. *Please make him leave, Lord.*

"You didn't have to. Your silence spoke for you." He popped the last of the roll in his mouth, lifted the towel and picked up another one.

"Aren't you afraid you'll spoil your dinner?" It came out on a bit of a huff. She wanted him to go, not stand there eating rolls.

"Not the way you cook. So what is wrong with white?"

She was too confused by what he had said to take pleasure in his compliment of her cooking. "Nothing at all. White is fine." He looked at her. She caught her breath, took a paring knife from the drawer. "It's your store, Blake. The color you choose to paint it is none of my business."

"I asked you, Audrey. That makes it your business. Besides, I've learned to trust your instincts. Now, what color would you suggest?"

She took a firm grip on the knife and began scraping a carrot. "Very well, if you insist. I would paint the store the mustard-gold color of an autumn leaf and trim it with other autumn colors…perhaps dark pine green and rusty red. Those colors would make the store stand out against the gray stone of the mountains behind it. And they would draw the eyes of the passengers on the trains."

"That sounds much better than white." He finished the second roll, licked the end of his thumb and forefinger and started for the kitchen door. "If you need me, I'll be on the loading dock mixing paint." He stopped in the doorway, glanced back at her. "Dark pine green for the fascia and soffit?"

"I don't know—"

"The boards that run around the building under the roof eaves."

"Oh. Yes, dark pine green."

She listened to his footsteps fade away on the stairs, her throat constricted, her chest tight.

I can't imagine Linda in this kitchen—not now. Not after—

She blinked away a rush of tears and began cutting the rind from the rutabaga. Blake was too polite and kind to say so, but what he had started to say was clear. Her presence there had ruined his dream. Not that she hadn't known that. But, for some reason, it hurt terribly to hear him say it.

It looked too bright to him. More like a leaf than a pine needle. Blake checked again to be sure he'd added the right amount of pigments to the bucket of linseed oil, then mixed in the turpentine. Maybe it looked different after it was painted on the wood. He'd soon know.

He brushed his hand over the bristles on the round

brush to be sure they were free of dust then jammed the handle in his pants pocket. The bucket swung from his hand when he scaled the ladder. The thought of Audrey climbing one in a long skirt made him sick. It would be so easy for her to step on her hems and fall. The woman had no sense!

The hook he yanked from his pocket thunked against the handle when he suspended the bucket from a rung. Another stir with the stick and the paint was ready. He dabbed the brush in it and swept the bristles across the fascia board and soffit where the roof peaked. It looked even lighter green. Maybe the second coat would look darker. He painted as far as he could reach, climbed down, moved the ladder to his right and started up again, jerking himself from rung to rung with his free hand. Audrey was stubborn—even if she did support her viewpoint with good sense. He had a perfect right to be angry. He was her husband and— No, he wasn't. Not for real, anyway. He was a *sham* husband in a *sham* marriage!

He clenched his jaw, stretched out his arm and swept the brush along the fascia far to the right. The ladder slid. He threw his weight forward and grabbed the edge of the roof, closed his eye when the brush collided with the side of his face. A drip hit his cheek and slid down. *Botheration!* He dare not open his eye. He used his legs and feet to square the ladder against the house, let go of the roof edge then grabbed the bucket and climbed down.

He snatched up a rag, then thought better of wiping at the paint for fear of making the damage worse. He covered the bucket with a board, stomped across the porch and through the storage room to the stairs. "Audrey…" No answer. *"Audrey…"* Hurried footsteps approached the stairs.

"Do you need something, Blake?"

"I need your help—quick! Grab a couple of towels and come down to the loading dock right away!"

She spun out of sight. He heard her running to the bathroom, turned and went back outside. He sloshed a rag in a bucket of water and scrubbed linseed oil soap on it.

The door burst open. Audrey rushed toward him, stopped and stared. Her lips twitched.

"It's not funny!"

She shook her head and pushed the towels she clutched against her mouth, her hazel eyes sparkling up at him. Muffled laughter escaped the towels.

He glared…grinned…tasted paint and closed his mouth.

She tossed the towels over her shoulder and took the rag from his hand. "Close your other eye, Blake, and whatever you do, keep both of your eyes closed. There is paint in your eyebrow and on your lashes that must be cleaned away and then they have to be washed. Don't open either of them again until I tell you it's all right to do so. Now, I need you to sit down on the railing so I can reach your face."

Her hand folded around his, guided it backward until it touched wood. He resisted the urge to wrap his fingers around the warm softness of her hand, grasped the railing and sat.

"I'm going to start cleaning away the paint from around your eye. Tip your head back…" Her fingers touched his forehead, gave a gentle push. "I don't know if the soap will sting…"

"Doesn't matter. Just do it."

"It will take a while because I only want to dampen the cloth. If it's saturated the soapy water might seep into your eye."

The rag touched his eyelid, moved downward, brushed against his eyelashes and onto his cheek. Her touch was gentle, deft. He sat perfectly still as she repeated the procedure again and again, trying to ignore the warmth from her hand holding his face, the brush of her arm against his shoulder. He clenched his hands on the railing to keep from reaching for her, pulling her close, telling himself it was only natural to think of doing such a thing under the circumstances. The temptation to open his eyes and look at her leaning over him with her face so close to his was unbearable.

He pulled up a vision of Linda and concentrated on the memory of her silky blond curls against his cheek, her lips yielding willingly to his. It didn't work. The memory had no strength against the touch of Audrey's hand. He frowned.

"Don't move!"

Her breath, warm and sweet, touched his face, took his breath captive. He dug his fingernails into the underside of the wood railing and commanded his lungs to work. This growing attraction to Audrey was simply rebound emotion. And she deserved better.

"I've got the paint off of your eye, but I need to wash the residue and linseed oil soap away. You stay here and keep your eyes closed while I get some clean warm water. I'll be right back."

Her hand lifted off his face. He listened to her footsteps running across the loading dock and into the storage room. He sat on the railing, the sun warm on his back, the coolness of the shadow under the roof on his face. They couldn't go on this way. Audrey should have her chance at finding true love and happiness. He had to think of some way of saving his investment in the store. He'd read over that contract again tonight.

"I'm back."

A pan clunked against wood. A washrag was squeezed out. The English garden fragrance of Pears' soap reached him…grew stronger.

"I'm going to wash your face now. Remember, don't open your eyes until I tell you."

A warm soapy rag touched his face, but it was the softness of her hand urging his chin up that sent an answering ripple of warmth through him. He held his breath…endured the sweetness. There was nothing sweet in Linda's touch; it had been more…enticing. He focused on the thought. Held to it as Audrey rinsed off the soap and patted his face with a towel.

"Turn your face to the sun so I can see if I got all of the paint off of your eyelashes." Her fingertips pressed against the left side of his face. He shifted his weight to the right, bumped against the firm softness of her… remembered her standing between him and the mountain on the ledge and gritted his teeth.

"I think it's all right. Dear Blessed Lord, please let Blake's eye be all right." There was a quick intake of breath. "All right…open your eyes. But be ready to shut them again if—"

He looked up. The gold flecks glowed through the

sheen of tears in her eyes. "I opened them while you were praying. They're fine, Audrey. A bit blurry, but that's going away already. Thank you for your help."

She nodded, spun away from him and grabbed the rag and linseed oil soap. "There's still paint in your hair and on your ear..."

He rose, reached around her and took the rag from her. "That soap is harsh for your hands. I'll manage now."

"Very well." She reached for the pan and Pears' soap.

He clasped her wrist, shook his head. "I'll bring them in when I finish here."

"Of course." She started for the storage room, stopped in the doorway and glanced over her shoulder. "I forgot to mention, I like the green color."

He might have believed her smile, if her voice hadn't trembled.

Audrey tied her long, still damp hair with a ribbon at the nape of her neck, fastened the buttons that divided the embroidered panel on the front of her dressing gown and stepped into her slippers. She had hoped a hot bath would relax her enough to sleep, but the story Mrs. Ferndale had told of her grandmother and grandfather meeting through letters haunted her. She felt so guilty for writing to Blake in Linda's name. But now she wasn't sure what to think.

I've always found it odd that Grandfather never considered that perhaps he, too, was walking in God's mysterious ways when he wrote *the letter.*

Was it possible that something similar had happened with her?

The muted whisper of the waterfall called to her, but she turned her back on the door to the porch and went to look out the window facing the hotel. She didn't want to look at the waterfall tonight—didn't want to remember her trip there with Blake. Not that she could ever forget. But for now the emotions the memory stirred were too new. Or were they?

A disturbing thought. She frowned and wrapped her arms about herself. She'd been drawn to Blake's honesty and sincerity when he was courting Linda. But now his quiet strength and quick flashes of humor, the way he tried to protect her from harm, his voice, his eyes all stole her breath and made her stomach flutter. Was she falling in love with him? Had she been a little in love with him while he was courting her sister?

Guilt swept over her. Her stomach churned. Was that the real reason she had acquiesced when Linda told her to answer Blake's letters as her? Had she thought of her plan to save Blake's store because it was an acceptable way to come West and be with him?

She lifted her gaze to the stars glittering in the night sky, her thoughts swirling, her heart aching. Had she been blind to the truth all of this time? Or was it all a part of God's mysterious ways?

Chapter Eleven

"Whoa…" The horse stomped her front hoofs, and the squeak of the wagon stopped. "Morning, Mrs. Latherop, Blake. The store's looking good."

Audrey turned from examining the display of new laces and trims she had arranged in the window. Mitchel Todd was stepping down from his wagon, a piece of paper in his hand. "Good morning, Mr. Todd. I agree with you. Blake is doing a wonderful job with the painting." She smiled and gestured toward his hand. "It looks as if you have a list of things you need."

"Some nails and such."

"I'll be right with you, Mitch." Blake glanced over his shoulder. "A couple more boards and I'll have this section of wall painted. I wanted to have it finished before the next train arrives and the customers start coming."

The carpenter tossed the reins over the hitching rail and climbed the steps. "No need for you to stop your work. I just need some nails right now. *You* need to get that spot of paint off your face before it dries." Mitch chuckled and reached for the door. "I'll get the nails and leave the list on the counter. You can set the stuff out on the loading dock, and I'll stop by and pick it up this afternoon."

"I'll do that." Blake bent and reached for the rag on the porch floor.

"Here, Blake, use this." Audrey held out her handkerchief. "That rag is so dirty you'll get more paint on you than you'll take off."

"I don't want to ruin your handkerchief." He scowled, turned his head a bit. "I can't see my face in this window anyway. I'll just—"

"Let me." She dipped her handkerchief in linseed oil and stepped close. "Bend down." She went up on tiptoe, turned his face toward the light and dabbed at the paint. "I don't want to wipe it and smear it all over your cheek."

"At least it's not dark green."

She looked into his eyes, warm with a teasing light, and lost her balance, fell against him. He caught her with his free hand. Her pulse jumped, raced. Heat spread across her cheeks. She pushed herself erect, tugged at her bodice. "I'm sorry. That was clumsy of me."

"I'll steady you." He clasped her about the waist.

She told herself not to think of the warmth and strength in his arm, or how it would be to have the right to rest her head against his shoulder. She willed her hand to stop shaking and reached for his face again.

"Good thing I didn't grab you with the hand I've got this brush in." He frowned, cleared his throat. "I should put it down, before I get paint on your gown."

"No need, I'm finished." She settled back on her

heels, wished she could have stayed in his clasp, and immediately chastised herself for the thought. She grabbed hold of the broom she'd leaned against the railing and swept the pile of dust from the porch down the steps and into the road. The horse snorted, tossed her head. She leaned the broom against the porch and stepped over to the mare, stroking the velvet-soft muzzle and crooning tender words.

"I didn't know you liked horses."

She looked up and watched Blake come down the steps, paint bucket in hand. Her pulse stuttered when he stopped beside her. She nodded, focused her watery gaze on the mare. "I've loved horses since I was a little girl. I used to beg to be taken for carriage rides in the park. Father always promised we would get a horse, but we never did." She combed through the mare's forelock with her fingers, smoothed it down. "You don't need a horse living in the city. But I thought living out here a horse would be a necessity."

"It would—if I'd turned cowboy instead of store-keeper."

She glanced up. Her stomach fluttered at his teasing grin.

"What's this about turning cowboy?" Mitch Todd strode out of the store balancing a small keg of nails on each shoulder. The door swung closed behind him, the bell jangling.

Blake laughed. "I was just joking. I'm not cowboy material. I've seen the way they ride." He set down the bucket of paint and lifted a keg from Mitch's shoulder to the wagon. "This another load of wood for the apothecary's house? I thought that was almost finished."

"It is." Mitch set the other keg on the seat and freed the reins. "You're looking at the parsonage. John Ferndale told me to start building it. We hauled in a load of stone from the mountain and finished laying up the foundation walls yesterday. In case you don't know—this is your last keg of four-pennys."

"I've got them on order. They could be in today."

The words brought a tingle of pride in Blake's success with the store. She smiled and looked down the road at the stone-framed hole in the ground beside the church. "Pastor Karl must be excited. He will soon be reunited with his family."

"It will be a little while, but I've got three men working on the parsonage." Mitch stepped up into the wagon, clicked his tongue and grinned. "We want to keep our pastor happy."

"I can't think of anything that would do that better than having his wife and children with him."

Something in Blake's voice made her heart ache with the wish that it could be so for him. She wouldn't allow her thoughts to go further than that. She glanced up at him, her breath catching at his handsome profile as he stood beside her watching the wagon lumber down the rutted road toward the church, and couldn't resist the need to know. "Do you want children, Blake?" He looked down and heat flowed across her cheeks. "I mean...when—"

"I know what you meant, Audrey." The muscle along his jaw jumped. He leaned down and grabbed the handle on the bucket of paint. "Yes. I want children someday. Every man does." He stopped, looked at the bucket in his hand. "I'll take this around to the loading dock and clean things up before the next train comes." He strode off around the corner.

She stared after him, his figure blurred by the film of tears in her eyes. "Forgive me, Lord. I've caused so much hurt. Please let Blake find true love with a woman who will make him happy. A woman who will bear him the children he hopes to have one day. Please, Lord, it's my fault he's in this position. Please help him to find the answer he needs to save his inheritance so he can be free of our pretend marriage and find the woman who will answer the longing of his heart." Would any woman be able to do that after his love for Linda?

"Good morning, Mrs. Latherop. How are you keeping this lovely day?"

Oh, no! She blinked her vision clear, spun about to face Pastor Karl. Had he overheard her prayer? "I'm fine. It is a lovely day, isn't it? And an exciting one for you. Mr. Todd told us that they are going to start building the parsonage today." *Stop blabbering!* She gripped her broom handle and forced a smile. "May I help you?"

"Indeed. I believe you are the very person I need to help me."

"Then I shall be pleased to do so." She lifted her hems with her free hand and climbed the steps, entered the door he opened for her and set the broom in the corner out of the way. The pastor started talking before the bell stopped jingling.

"I have a problem." He removed his hat, held it at his side. "Mr. Todd told me yesterday that the parsonage will be ready to occupy within two weeks' time. I was so excited I sent Ivy—that's my wife—a telegram with the good news. Her reply came this morning. I just received it from Asa Marsh." He lifted his right hand, the telegram gripped in it. "She's bought the tickets for her and the children. They will be here in two weeks!"

The man looked completely undone. She hastened to calm him. "And how is it you wish me to help?"

"Any number of ways!" The pastor paced back and forth in front of the counter, the telegram flapping in his hand. "Mrs. Karl and I have always moved into parsonages that have been occupied by a previous pastor and his family. Moving into an unfurnished parsonage is a new experience for me, and, well, I'm feeling quite inadequate." He stopped pacing, shoved the telegram into his coat pocket and pulled out a piece of paper. "I have been writing down everything Mrs. Karl mentions in her letters that she will need at the parsonage. But the list is nowhere near complete. Even I can tell she will need much more than what she mentions. And, well…" He gave her a pleading look.

"You would like me to go over the list with you?"

"To start."

"To *start*?" She stared.

"Mrs. Latherop, I know you're a new bride, and that you spend a good deal of your time helping your husband in the store. And I feel terrible for asking, but there is no other woman in Whisper Creek but Mrs. Ferndale, and while I appreciate her good heart and giving nature, she's just not capable of doing what I need."

"And what is that, Pastor Karl?"

He handed her the paper. "If you would go over this list and add any necessities that Ivy has not mentioned.

Mr. Ferndale and the church will be paying, so no luxuries, of course. And please set aside for us the items already here in the store that we will need, and have your husband order the rest—along with the necessary furniture. Only the bare minimum, of course. We can do without any carpets or runners or such things. And then—"

"Yes?"

"If you would come to the parsonage and put all of the furnishings in order—the way a woman likes them." His eyes pleaded with her. "I will understand if you do not wish to—"

"I will be happy to do whatever I can, Pastor Karl. I will go over the list today and have Mr. Latherop order the necessary items." She glanced down at the paper. "I believe you mentioned children. And children have specific needs, depending on their ages…"

"Of course—how remiss of me!" His face flushed. "Mrs. Karl always takes care of the things concerning the children."

"Mothers usually do." She smiled, moved behind the counter and picked up a pen. "What are your children's ages?"

"Edward is nine years old, Minna is seven years old and Nixie is four years old." The pastor's face softened; a smile curved his lips. "They write me notes at the end of their mother's letters. Even Nixie has learned to write 'I love you, Papa'—though I'm certain it's with her mother's help." The pastor straightened and slapped his palm against the counter.

She jerked, making an ink blotch on the paper.

"It has just occurred to me, Mrs. Latherop, that

letters are *wonderful* things. They are uplifting and strengthening and…" The pastor laughed and stepped back from the counter. "And I think there is a sermon in there somewhere. I shall save it for church." He dipped his head in a small, polite bow. "Thank you, Mrs. Lath-erop, for your kindness in helping me to prepare for my family's arrival. Now, I must get back to the church and help as best I can. Good day. And may God bless your marriage with happiness and healthy children as He has Ivy's and mine." He walked to the door, pulled it open. "I will return later in case there is some infor-mation you need."

"There is one thing more. You didn't mention if Mrs. Karl is shipping any of your personal furniture or household equipment."

"No, nothing but clothes and personal items. When you live in a parsonage, the furnishings all belong to the church."

The door closed behind him, the bell jangling. She looked at the list and sighed. It was a short list. It seemed the Karls were accustomed to living with very little in the way of comfort. She heard the sound of footsteps and looked up. Blake stood in the storage room door-way, his shirtsleeves rolled up to his elbows, a towel in his hands. A faint smell of linseed oil and turpentine wafted into the room. "I was washing up and couldn't help but overhear." He tossed the towel to the side and stepped into the room. "It sounds as if you have quite a task ahead of you."

Did he approve? "And you, also. There is a lot of furniture and other household items that will need to be ordered. I only hope they will arrive before Mrs. Karl and the children."

"Then we had best start. You tell me what is needed, and I will make out the orders. That will save time as I am familiar with the various companies with which I do business. And I know the products they sell, and which are of the best quality." He joined her behind the counter and reached for paper and pen. "Let's begin with the furniture as there are most likely to be shipping problems or delays with large items. What is first?"

"I haven't gone over the list as yet. But we can do this room by room. We'll start with the bedrooms as they require the least fussing. They will need beds, of course."

"How many of what size?" He looked up and their gazes met. Her heart skipped. He cleared his throat.

"I don't know." She pulled her thoughts together. "There are three children—two daughters and a son. I suppose the girls share a bed."

"That makes sense. So, two double beds and a single." He frowned, lifted his pen from the paper. "Perhaps we should make that three double beds to allow for an…er…addition to the family."

"And if the…addition is another daughter?"

"There is that. Though it hardly seems fair to the boy." His grin set her pulse skipping again. "All right. Two double beds and one single. What's next? Dressers? Three of them?"

"Three will be sufficient if there are wardrobes in the rooms. And three nightstands to hold oil lamps. Will they need washstands?"

"No. There will be a dressing room like ours, with a bathing tub and hot water."

Ours. He didn't mean it the way it sounded, of course. But the word stole her breath just the same.

Blake glanced at the page number and set his book aside. It was too comfortable sitting and reading while Audrey sat on the settee and sewed. And too easy to remember things that were better forgotten—like the way the light had edged her red curls with gold when she bent her head over that list. Or the way the look in her eyes had softened when they talked about the Karl children. He bit back a growl, went to the window and looked down the moonlit road toward the train depot, fixing his thoughts on the mundane. "The store did a good business today."

"And well it should. You have worked hard to make the store a success."

He glanced over his shoulder at her. "As have you."

She looked up from her sewing, shook her head. "I only help when things are busy. It is your skill and ability that have enabled you to attain your goal."

He frowned, irritated by her niceness. He was itching for something to break this…this *hominess.* "Don't you ever accept credit for the things you do?"

Her eyes widened. She gazed up at him for a moment then lowered her head. "I gobble it up like candy when it's deserved."

"Well, that judgment should be left to others."

"Perhaps you're right. I guess I've never thought about it that way." She shifted the green dress in her lap, lined up the lace she was attaching to the collar.

The stove crackled, poured warmth into the room. He shoved his hands in his pockets and leaned against the window frame. "The nights are cooling fast. I've been wondering what winter will be like here in Wyoming. I've asked a few people, but they are all from back East and no one knows. At least we don't have to worry about being cold. Not with the coal being mined close by, and the train hauling it east."

"And with this wonderfully comfortable home you've built." She rested her hands in her lap, looked at him and smiled. The gold flecks in her eyes warmed to a dreamy glow. "I can't wait to see how beautiful the mountains will be with the pine trees having a white covering like frosting on a cake. And the trains chugging through the valley when it's all covered with snow."

"If we're here."

The glow in her eyes faded. "Yes. There is that to consider." She lifted the dress and took another stitch.

Guilt pierced him. Audrey didn't deserve to suffer for his foul mood. He yanked a hand from his pocket and scrubbed the back of his neck, searching his mind for a topic that would put that happy lilt back in her voice. "I haven't had a chance to ask about your visit with Mrs. Ferndale the other day. Did everything go all right?"

"Yes. It was very pleasant."

"Then she didn't ask you any difficult-to-answer questions?"

"No. I was worried about that—unnecessarily so." She set her sewing aside and rose, ran her palms down the front of her skirt. "Would you care for a cup of tea?"

What had caused that abrupt change of subject?

"Sounds good." Surprise flashed in her eyes. If she hadn't expected him to agree, why had she offered? Curiosity rose. He followed her into the kitchen and adjusted the draft to make the coal burn hot while she filled the teapot with water. "What did you and Mrs. Ferndale talk about?"

"Oh, this and that—a lot of woman things." She spooned tea into the china teapot, went to the dresser for cups and saucers.

She was avoiding looking at him. His curiosity deepened. "Such as…"

"Her needlepoint—she does lovely work. And her daughters. And letters. And cooking." She took biscuits from a cupboard, put them on a plate with marmalade and honey.

He split one of the biscuits and drizzled honey on it, mentally discarding the topics of needlepoint and cooking. "What kind of letters?"

She bit at her lip, brushed a few biscuit crumbs off the worktable and threw them away. "Homesick ones."

"To her daughters?"

"No. They're not her letters. That is, she didn't write them."

He held his silence.

She poked at the curls on her forehead, smoothed the front of her gown. "It was a story she told about her grandmother and grandfather. Do you want butter for your biscuits?"

"No, thank you." He went to the refrigerator for the milk, then leaned against the worktable and watched her. She was nervous. And it seemed to have something to do with the story about those letters. "What was the story?"

"Something about her grandfather being lonely when he came to America." She picked up the plate of biscuits and carried them to the table, arranged the cups and saucers and flatware, smoothed the tablecloth.

"So he wrote letters home to his wife?"

"No. He wasn't married…then." She went to the stove and poured the steaming water into the china teapot, then turned to face him. "He wrote back home to his sister, asking her to come to America and offering her a home with him."

He picked up the tea tray and carried it to the table, heard her sigh. She had no choice but to follow. "So his sister came to America…" He used his tone to urge her to continue.

"No." She poured their tea and slipped onto the chair across from him. "His sister was to be married. She told a friend about her brother's letter, and the sympathetic friend wrote him a letter…to help keep him from being lonely. He was attracted to her…kindness and wrote her in return."

"I should think so." She glanced up but looked away before he could read the expression in her eyes. "And this is the young woman who became Mrs. Ferndale's grandmother."

"Yes."

The tension left her. He watched her shoulders relax, her nervous stirring of her tea stop. He took another biscuit onto his plate and drizzled honey on it. "And what was the moral of the story?" Her head jerked up.

"The moral?"

"Yes. People usually have a reason for telling a personal story. What was Mrs. Ferndale's reason?"

She stared at him a moment, then looked down, started swirling her spoon through her tea again. "She said the story of our…marriage made her think of her grandparents' because it all started with a letter. She said her grandfather always said what if his sister had never shown her friend his letter—that God works in mysterious ways."

Her words hung in the air. He watched her stirring her tea, a tightness growing in his chest. Was that why Audrey had read his letter to Linda? Was it God's will?

Chapter Twelve

"God moves in a mysterious way... His wonders to perform..." The hymn bubbled inside her, poured from her throat in a soft, lyrical celebration of God's grace. Audrey swiped the rag over the last of the shelves in the kitchen, leaving a faint scent of the lemon juice she'd mixed with linseed oil. "He plants his footsteps in the sea... And rides upon the storm..."

"Whoa!"

A horse snorted outside. They were here! And just in time. She hung the dusting rag over the top of the tin of linseed oil on the floor of the pantry cupboard and hurried through the small entrance hall to the front door.

"Are you ready for this furniture?" Blake squinted down at her from the front seat of Mitchel Todd's wagon, his blue shirt bright in the sunshine.

Her heart jolted at the sight of him. "I am." She moved across the porch to the top of the steps and gave her long apron a vigorous shake. "The parsonage is all clean and ready. There isn't a speck of sawdust to be found inside this house!" Blake's smile set her stomach quivering. She shielded her eyes from the brightness and gave the loaded wagon a sweeping glance. "Did the dressers come in on the train?"

"Two of them. There's a delay on the small one." He wrapped the reins over the hitching rail, picked up one of the crates stacked on the seat and hefted it to his shoulder. "I have to hurry and get all of this unloaded— Mitch needs his wagon back. Garret is coming to help."

"And I'm here." Pastor Karl came hurrying from the church. "Forgive my shirtsleeves, Mrs. Latherop, but I can't chance damaging my suit coat." He hurried to the wagon, picked up a crate and followed Blake to the porch. "Where do you want me to put this?"

"Here on the porch. I thought you men could take all the crates apart out here to keep the house clean. I'll carry the dishes and such in."

"A good idea." Blake set his crate down and went back to the wagon. "Garret and I loaded the furniture by rooms, according to your list. The bedroom furniture is at the back. So, Pastor Karl, while you work on these crates, I'll start putting the beds together." He grabbed hold of a headboard and carried it up the porch steps. "There's a hammer and pry you can use on the floor in front of the seat, Pastor."

"Thanks, I'll get them."

"Looks like I'm just in time." Garret marched up to the wagon, stuck the footboard under one arm and tucked the bundle of rails under the other. He clomped up the steps, paused on the porch and looked down at her. "Blake bribed me to do this. He said you'd give me a piece of the apple pie you made for supper."

"Don't believe him, Audrey. He's a blackguard! That

pie is mine!" Blake's growled words were accompanied by what sounded like the thud of the headboard hitting against the bedroom floor.

Garret grinned and shrugged. "I thought he was far enough inside he wouldn't hear me. It was worth a try." He shot a teasing look over his shoulder. "You don't think the Lord will hold that little lie against me, do you, Pastor?"

"I'm quite certain the Lord understands the extreme temptation that burdens a man when he smells a fresh-baked apple pie, and will extend you forgiveness, Garret." The pastor jammed the claws of the hammer between the boards of a crate and yanked. The board splintered and fell away. The pastor looked up and grinned. "When you have exhibited the appropriate amount of remorse, of course."

"I'll do that. After I eat a piece of that pie."

She gave a phony gasp and clasped her hand to her heart. "Well, if it will become that great a matter, you shall each have a half of the pie, and I will bake Blake another!"

"You can't do that, Audrey." Garret spoke in a somber tone. "The pastor can't eat that pie—it would be ill-gotten gains. You will have to give the whole of it to me."

"I'll thank you to let me see to my own conscience, Garret." The pastor laughed and jammed the claws under the board again. "I must taste the pie for the sake of fair judgment."

Garret laughed and edged through the door into the house.

Another board cracked. "Ah, that's got it! Here are the dishes, Mrs. Latherop."

She lifted out plates and bowls and cups and saucers from the crate and carried them to the kitchen.

Grunts and thumps accompanied the footsteps in and out of the other rooms. The pound of a hammer and the splinter of wood sounded outside. Sunlight streamed through the window, gleamed on the red-and-white-patterned dishes as she washed and dried them, the words of the hymn humming through her mind.

"Deep in unfathomable mines of never-failing skill, he treasures up his bright designs and works his sovereign will." She sang softly, stood the platter on its edge behind the stack of plates and admired the way they looked against the whitewashed wall. "You fearful saints, fresh courage take; the clouds you so much dread… Are big with mercy and shall break in blessings on your head."

She lifted her long apron to wipe her warm face and turned toward the door. "His purposes will ripen fast, unfolding every hour— Oh!"

She collided with a hard, solid body, bounced back. Strong hands caught hold of her arms and steadied her, held her. She looked up, met Blake's gaze and forgot about breathing.

His eyes darkened. "The bud may have a bitter taste, but sweet will be the flower." His deep voice finished the verse as his gaze held hers. Heat crawled into her cheeks.

"What'd she say, Blake?"

She jumped at Garret's shout.

Blake's hands tightened, then released their grasp

on her. He stepped back, cleared his throat. "Are you ready for us to bring in the table?"

"Yes. That would be...helpful..."

He nodded and strode toward the porch.

She covered her burning cheeks with her hands and sagged against the wall, shaking like a leaf in a windstorm. The thunk of a hammer and the splintering of wood sent her scurrying back to the task at hand. There wasn't any time to waste. Mrs. Karl and the children would be here tomorrow.

"I'm ready."

Blake's heart jolted. Audrey was wearing the red dress she'd had on the day he took her to the waterfall. Memories crashed against his will to deny them. He turned his attention to the covered basket she held and curved his mouth in a teasing smile. "Looks as if there's enough food in there to feed a family."

Her answering smile settled in his heart. "I hope so." She looked down, caught at her lower lip with her teeth. "I made a shepherd's pie, cabbage salad and a molasses cake. Oh, and snickerdoodle cookies for the children. Do you think that's enough?"

"Enough? I think it's a feast." He reached into the crate and folded back the brown paper protecting the tissue-paper flowers he'd ordered for the store to avoid those hazel eyes that played havoc with his self-control. "My first meal here was a can of sardines and two stale slices of bread."

"I wish—"

"Yes?"

She shook her head, looked away, but there was a

tinge of pink across her cheekbones. He studied her a moment wondering what she'd been about to say, then stepped from behind the counter and reached for the basket.

"Oh, my! Those flowers are beautiful, Blake! Mrs. Ferndale will buy the lot of them when she sees them."

Not the ones I meant for you.

She glanced up at him. "Would it be all right if we included one of them for Mrs. Karl? I know you've only just unwrapped them, but —well, it seems a nice gesture."

"A very nice gesture. Pick the one you want." He set the basket on the counter and lifted the lid.

"A yellow rose." She lifted one of the buttery flowers out of the crate, laid it on top of the dishes in the basket and smiled. "It will remind her of summer sunshine during winter."

"Do you think we should include a few pieces of candy for the children?"

"What a wonderful idea!"

The gold flecks in her eyes sparkled up at him, and her mouth curved into a happy smile. His heart lurched. He stepped behind the counter and packaged the candy. "Let's go." He grabbed the basket and headed for the door, more aware of her walking beside him than he wanted to be.

"I'll get the sign."

He waited, offered her his arm. It felt natural now walking with her.

"I can't believe how quickly Mr. Todd and his men built the parsonage."

"It's not that large. We'll—the town—will add on to

it as soon as the church can support it." *And we won't be here to be part of it.*

"It's big enough for the family to be together. That's what matters."

Her soft voice broke. He glanced down at her, but she'd lowered her head, and he couldn't see her eyes.

Sun bathed the surrounding mountains in light, causing deep shadows in the crevices and caves. A slight breeze stirred the grasses, carried the sounds of hammer blows and the rasp of saws across the valley. Her long skirts whispered against the rutted path and his boots struck the hard packed dirt. Anger rose in him, growing with their every step. How ironic for them to be welcoming Pastor Karl's family to a community they would soon leave.

Blake was upset over something. He hadn't said anything at supper, but she could feel it. Audrey dried the cup, added it to the stacked dishes and carried them to the dresser to put away. The dishes were high-quality china and made a lovely display on the open shelves, but she wished the pattern were any color but blue and white. She was so tired of blue!

She sighed, turned her thoughts back to Blake. Perhaps there was something wrong at the store, though she'd found nothing amiss while working there earlier. Or perhaps it was Linda. It was always Linda.

She pushed a curl back off her forehead and looked out the window toward the train station. Linda must be settled in San Francisco by now. Was she happy with her husband? Would she ever see her again? Perhaps there would be a letter from her waiting when she returned home. Her chest tightened. Tears welled, blurred the view out of the window. It was getting harder and harder to think of leaving Whisper Creek. It had become home. And to never see Blake again—

She whirled from the window, hurried to the sink and scrubbed at the pan she had left soaking while she dried the dishes. She should make plans. She couldn't bear the thought of simply sitting in an empty house all day with no one to—to— A tear fell on her bared wrist. She blinked hard, took a deep breath and held it to gain control.

The faint sound of a bell, the closing of a door and muted footsteps rose from downstairs. "Blake… Blake, are you up there?"

Pastor Karl! What was he doing here? Had something gone wrong with his family's arrival? She pulled the pan from the soapy water, rinsed and dried it, then wiped any trace of tears from her cheeks.

"I'm here, Pastor!"

She listened to Blake's footsteps hurrying from his office as he pounded down the stairs.

"Do you need something?"

The pastor's reply was lost in the gurgle of the dishwater she poured down the drain. She rinsed the dishpan and dry sink, took off her apron and rubbed cream into her hands. *Please don't let anything have gone wrong for Pastor Karl or his wife and children, Lord. He's been so eager to have them with him again after so many months alone.* She crossed to the window, looked toward the new parsonage.

"Audrey…"

She turned, looked at Blake standing in the doorway and hurried toward him. "What's wrong?"

He raised the telegram in his hand. "Asa asked Pastor Karl to give me this." He pulled in a breath, swallowed hard. "It's from my father's attorney. My father is ill and not expected to live. He advises that I come immediately."

"Oh, Blake, I'm so sorry..." Tears filled her eyes. She reached for his hand holding the telegram, wishing she could go into his arms and take some of his hurt for her own. "Is there anything I can do to help you prepare for your journey home?"

"No. I'll pack my valise tonight and take the first train east in the morning." He gave his head a shake, ran his fingers through his hair and began to pace. "I don't know how long I will be gone. How can I close the store? Mitch has to have building supplies. And—"

"I can tend the store."

He halted, shook his head. "No, Audrey. Helping me is one thing. Taking on the entire task is something else again. I can't ask you to do all of that work."

"You didn't. I offered. With you gone, I will have time on my hands." She lifted her chin, ready to do battle. This was too important for her to lose the argument.

"Are you going all redhead on me?"

"If I must."

His gaze locked on hers, and her knees went weak. She grabbed for a chair. "The town needs the store open, Blake. You have no choice."

For a moment that felt like forever he stared at her. She was about to collapse onto the chair when he raked his fingers through his hair, blew out a breath and dipped his head. Her heart thudded an accompaniment to his footsteps as he strode from the room.

The train whistle sounded up the valley, echoed off of the mountains. The lamp from the engine beamed out of the dim early morning light and gleamed on the rails that would carry him away.

"All aboard!"

"You didn't have to get up this early to see me off, Audrey."

Blake's words were gruff, brusque. She swallowed the tears clogging her throat and raised her chin. "You're forgetting we are newly married. Of course I would want to be with you every moment until you leave."

"I suppose."

He sounded downright surly—not that she blamed him. He was worried about his father's failing health, and, no doubt, worried about his store. She stopped at the edge of the platform, put her hand on his arm. "I'll do my best with the store, Blake. Please don't worry about it. I know all of the prices now. And if I have any doubts about anything I will make a note of it, and you can straighten it out when you return." The tears closed her throat again. She stepped back.

He shifted his valise into his left hand, muttered, "Asa is watching," and swept her tight against him. He lowered his head and claimed her lips.

Her knees gave out. He released her, jumped off the platform and strode to the train. She sagged, caught hold of the railing.

"I'll send word of what happens with my father and

when I'll return." Blake growled the words over his shoulder and swung aboard.

She clung to the platform railing and tried to breathe.

Blake scowled at the mountains outside the soot-grimed window, wished there were room in the passenger car for him to pace. What a fool he was! He shouldn't have done it. He never should have kissed Audrey. He'd been fighting the urge to do so ever since he'd taken her to see the waterfall; he should have held out those few minutes longer. But the worry in her eyes, the tears she'd tried to hide as she said goodbye had snapped his resistance. Asa had been the excuse. But what had been the reason? He'd loved Linda, and the residue of that love lingered. So why this driving need to kiss Audrey? Was it the anger at Linda's betrayal?

He shoved his valise to the end of the seat, stood and strode to the door at the front of the car, grabbing hold of the backs of seats to steady himself against the swaying. The door opened at his tug and he stepped out onto the small platform, grabbed a post against the rocking and let the wind rush over him.

He shouldn't have let her come to the station to say goodbye. He'd known the moment they started up the road to the station he would kiss her. Had fought it to the last moment. But the thought of leaving her alone in Whisper Creek with all of those young single men Mitch hired from the railroad workers brought forth an emotion he hadn't known was in him. It had started when she chose Mitchel Todd over him to escort her to the Ferndales'. Not that he thought Audrey fickle. She was no flirt like Linda. But still, she was beautiful and innocent and when she looked at you with those eyes—

He let out a growl and clenched the iron railing that enclosed the small platform. He'd wanted to "brand" her. That was what that kiss was about. He'd wanted to mark her as his own, so every man in Whisper Creek would stay their distance from her. Their marriage was a pretense, but she had made his house into a home. She was everything a man could want in a wife—skilled in cooking and housekeeping for certain, but also talented and inventive. The way she had fixed the bedding on his cot so it would stay in place was ingenious. And she was funny and smart and stubborn and frustrating and caring…and…and he was afraid of losing her. How selfish he was! His heart was too wounded to invite anyone in, but he still wanted her fidelity.

He splayed his legs, let go of the railing and rubbed his hands together to get rid of the indentations across his palms. He was concerned for his father, but, the truth was, this trip east couldn't have come at a better time. It would give him a chance to come to grips with Linda's desertion, and the separation would put an end to his rebound attraction to Audrey. And it would give him time to figure out a workable plan to recoup his investment in the store. When he returned he would have a talk with Mitch Todd. It had been months since Mitch had opened his business and Mitch was still unmarried. He hated to pry into the man's private affairs, but he needed to find an answer to his dilemma.

He looked down at the railroad ties flashing by beneath the train and listened to the clack of the wheels against the rails carrying him farther and farther from his store. Odd that he wasn't at all concerned about it. But it was safe in Audrey's care. She had an aptitude for the business, a real talent for doing the right thing to bring in customers and increase sales—like baking biscuits. A smile tugged at his mouth, died aborning. All those soldiers...

His stomach knotted. He blew out a breath and stared down the rails ahead, let the thought that had been nagging at him form. Now that he had held Audrey close and tasted of the sweetness of her lips, how was he to forget?

Audrey swept the porch, dusted the windowsills and front door and wiped down the storefront windowpanes. She tried to stay focused on her tasks, but her gaze kept turning to the train station, her pulse racing at the memory of Blake's kiss. It hadn't meant anything. Blake had kissed her because Asa Marsh was watching them and it was expected. She'd told herself that a dozen times, but her heart just didn't listen.

She went inside, hung the Closed sign on the door and swept the floor. She had straightened and dusted the shelves to stay busy in between the rush of customers from the trains. Her work was done.

The crate of tissue-paper flowers waited on the shelf. She carried them to the counter, took out a few of each flower in the different colors—white or tan, yellow and pink. A white crockery milk pitcher made a perfect holder. She chose a pink rose and a white carnation, carried them to the front window and placed them on the bolt of green fabric, letting the stems hang off of the edge of the material.

She worked with slow deliberation, the stems of the flowers tapping against the pitcher as she put them in place. The quiet settled, a heavy pressure on her chest. She finished the arrangement, placed the pitcher on the counter by the till where the colorful flowers would draw the eye of the customers and looked around. There was nothing more to do.

The sound of her footsteps followed her into the storage room. She took off the apron she wore for sweeping, hung it on a nail by the door and walked to the stairs. The pressure in her chest grew with every step she climbed.

I'd forgotten how optimistic you are...

Not now. Not in this situation. She stood in the hall at the top of the stairs in the dim light of the oil lamp sconce and faced the truth. His kiss had erased all doubt. She was in love with Blake—always had been. It was not some mysterious act of God that had brought her to Whisper Creek—it was her budding love for him. That budding love had made the possibility of his losing his store unacceptable to her. Her guilt over deceiving him by answering his letters in Linda's name was an obfuscation of what was hidden in her heart.

The heart is deceitful above all things...

"Your word is true, Lord." She swallowed back a rush of tears, walked by the kitchen sickened by the thought of food and prepared for bed. Blake must never know the truth. She couldn't bear his pity. She had come to Whisper Creek to stand in for Linda as Blake's bride and save his store, and that is what she would do.

She settled the thought in her mind, pulled on her dressing gown and stepped out onto the porch. It had been painful when John had broken his promise to her and wed another, but it was nothing compared to the unbearable ache in her heart now.

A rising wind blotted out the whisper of the distant waterfall. Storm clouds blocked all light. But the agony of baring her heart and facing her love for Blake was too raw for sleep. She stepped back inside, wrapped the blanket at the foot of the bed around her shoulders and went back out onto the porch to wait for the rain.

Chapter Thirteen

"Have you anything for nausea?"

Audrey noted the last sale in the ledger, put down her pen and looked at the woman across the counter. Her face was pale with a clammy sheen on her forehead. And she kept swallowing.

"One moment!" She grabbed a cup from the display of dishes on the shelf behind her, ran to the storage room, splashed in some of the vinegar she used for cleaning the windows and filled the cup with water. "Here, sit down on this keg and sip this. It's a remedy my mother always gave us when we were ill. I'm certain it will help. Apple cider vinegar is very effective at calming a queasy stomach. Now, you rest here. I have to take care of the other customers."

"Thank you, you're very kind." The woman swallowed hard, took a sip of the vinegar water and closed her eyes.

Please don't let her faint, Lord. She hurried back to the counter and smiled at a family waiting to pay for their purchases. She noted the items in the ledger, placed them in two bags and accepted payment. A soldier stepped forward, set his items on the counter. She glanced at the woman, drew her gaze back and looked from the items grouped on the counter to the soldier waiting to pay. "Will that be all, sir?"

"Unless you have some of the biscuits I've heard about for sale. I didn't see any."

"I'm sorry. There are no biscuits today."

The train whistle blasted its warning of pending departure. The few remaining customers drifted out of the door. She tallied the soldier's purchases, snagged her lower lip with her teeth and glanced up at him. Another quick look at the woman made up her mind. "Sir, the woman seated on the keg over there is ill. Will you be so kind as to escort her back to the train?"

The soldier shot a look the direction she indicated, glanced back at her and nodded. "I'll be happy to help, ma'am."

"Thank you, sir. If you'll wait here..."

She hurried to the woman, touched her shoulder. "Miss, the train is about to leave. The soldier at the counter has offered to escort you back to the station."

"How kind of him..." The woman's lips trembled into a smile. "Thank you for your help. I am feeling a bit better. I'd like some of the cider vinegar, please. Will this be enough?" She drew a coin from her purse and handed it to her, tried to stand and sank back down. She blotted her forehead with a lace-edged handkerchief.

Boots thudded against the floor. The soldier reached down and took hold of the woman's arm with his gloved hand. "You just lean on me, ma'am."

Audrey gave him a grateful smile and hurried to the shelf for the vinegar. She slid it into a bag along with the woman's change and carried it and the soldier's bag of purchases to the door. "I hope you feel better soon." She smiled at the woman and handed the bags to the soldier after he helped the woman down the porch steps. "Thank you, sir. May the Lord bless you for your kindness."

She stood watching the soldier half carry the woman up the station road, then turned and went inside. She hoped the vinegar would help the sick woman; it was all she knew to do. She straightened the baskets of notions on the dry goods table that had been sifted through, smoothed a wrinkle from the top bolt of fabric. It would be good when the apothecary came to town. He would likely have some remedy for the nausea that struck some of the passengers on the trains, and she could send them next door to him. If she were still here. Tears clogged her throat, stung her eyes.

The bell on the door jingled. She drew a steadying breath and blinked the tears from her eyes.

"Mrs. Latherop?"

The name brought the tears welling again. She brushed them away with her fingertips, pasted a smile on her face and turned. A short matronly woman with dark blond hair and friendly blue eyes stood by the door holding baking dishes. Three young children clustered in front of her. The oldest, a dark-haired boy with blue-gray eyes, grinned, showing a gap where a front tooth was missing. Except for the missing tooth he was the image of Pastor Karl.

Her lips curved in answer to his infectious grin. "And who might you be?"

"I'm Eddie. Are you the lady that made them cookies?"

"Edward! Mind your manners." The woman placed a hand on the boy's shoulder and smiled up at her. "I'm sorry, Mrs. Latherop. I'm afraid Eddie has become a little bold without his father to restrain him these past few months. I'm Mrs. Karl—" her smile warmed "—Ivy, if it would please you. And this is Minna—" her free hand touched the head of a young girl who looked like a sober edition of her mother, then moved on to rest on a little towhead "—and this is Nixie."

"I'm pleased to meet you all." She smiled down at the children. "Welcome to Whisper Creek, Edward… and Minna…and Nixie." Bright blue eyes gazed up at her a moment before the toddler turned and buried her face in her mother's skirt. Adorable. She lifted her gaze to the mother. "I'm so pleased to meet you, Mrs. Karl—Ivy. Welcome to Whisper Creek." She cleared her throat, steered away from shaky ground. "May I help you?"

"I came to thank you for your kindness in providing our dinner last night." Ivy Karl's smile was as warm as a hearth fire. "It was a true blessing not to have to cook when we arrived so late. And with so little by way of provisions in the house." The woman's laugh was as infectious as her son's grin. "That's the other reason I'm here. My Konrad thinks meals simply appear on the table." She reached into the top baking dish and pulled out small pieces of paper. "I have lists."

To her surprise, Mrs. Karl handed the pieces of paper to Eddie and Minna. The children looked up at her. "The grocery section is over there." The children hurried off, their lists clutched in their hands.

"Your shepherd's pie was delicious, Mrs. Latherop. But then, everything was. It's delightful to eat someone else's cooking."

"Thank you, and please call me Audrey." She stretched out her hands. "Let me take those dishes."

Ivy Karl nodded and urged her toddler forward into the depths of the store. "I know it is customary to return dishes full, but Konrad told me your husband has been called out of town due to his father's illness. I thought I would wait until his return to send over a meal."

"That's very thoughtful of you, Mrs. Karl. But it's not necessary." She set the dishes on the counter and smoothed a curl off of her forehead. "I don't know when Mr. Latherop will return." *Or how long I will be here.* She smiled at the boy and changed the subject. "Gracious, that is quite a load you're carrying, Eddie. Let me help you."

The doctor held out little hope. Blake sat beside the bed, waiting...praying. He wasn't ready to let go of his father. He wanted him to come to Whisper Creek and see the store and home he had built with the small inheritance he'd received from his mother.

His father blinked, coughed and opened his eyes. "Do you need something, Dad?" He leaned forward and covered his father's hand resting on top of the covers.

"Besides a…new…body?"

He pushed down the fear and smiled. "Yes, besides that."

"Water."

"Let me help you." He grabbed the glass and slid his arm beneath his father's shoulders, trying not to notice how bony they were.

"Thank…you."

He nodded, set the glass back on the nightstand. "I'm eager for you to come to Whisper Creek, Dad. I want you to see the country. It's rugged, but beautiful."

"Tell me…about…your wife…"

He took a breath, looked into his father's eyes. He'd never lied to his father. And thanks to Audrey's plan he wouldn't have to now. "You'll like her, Dad." He thought about Audrey, let the images and memories he'd been holding at bay since leaving Whisper Creek flood his mind. A smile tugged at his lips. "She reads Major Jack Downing's adventures."

"Ah… I do…like her." His father chuckled, a shadow of what his laugh used to be, but the first laugh he'd heard from him since he'd come home. "Pretty?"

"She's beautiful. She's neat and trim, slender but… womanly. She comes up to my shoulder and has this red-gold hair that curls around her face. It smells like roses. And she has hazel-colored eyes with gold flecks that talk to you. They sparkle when she's happy or amused and turn dark when she's upset or angry. And freckles—five of them right across the bridge of her nose. But they're so pale you can only see them when she blushes."

"Mother blushed." His father gave him one of those looks that men share. "Blushes are...danger...ous..."

"Yes. She has this innocence that—well, it's... appealing."

"Appealing, hmm." His father's smile almost turned into a grin. "Good...cook?"

"The best since Mom. And she's smart and stubborn and caring." He stopped, looked down at his father's hand gripping his. He lifted his gaze to his father's face, saw peace in his eyes.

"Glad you're...happy, son. It's...in your...eyes." His father smiled and closed his eyes. "I'll...tell... Mother. She'll be...glad..." There was a soft sigh. His father's hand fell away.

"Dad? *Dad!*" His throat constricted. He tried for a breath, managed a small one against the tightness in his chest and took his father's limp hand in his strong ones. "Goodbye, Dad. Tell Mother—" he swallowed hard, blinked tears from his eyes "—tell her I miss her."

What was that thumping? Audrey dropped her dusting rag on the counter and hurried to the storage room. A quick look out of the back window answered her question. Garret Stevenson stood in the rutted road lifting kegs and crates from Blake's cart onto the plank floor of the dock. She pulled open the door, shivered at the rush of cool air. "Good evening, Mr. Stevenson. What is all this?"

"Supplies Blake ordered for the store." He heaved a

large keg onto the dock, dragged his sleeve across his forehead and peered up at her through the fading light of day. "I signed the consignment sheet and brought them along. I figured that was all right since I'll probably be buying most of them."

"Oh." Her stomach flopped. She hadn't thought about supplies coming in on the trains. "I'm sure Blake will be grateful."

"Well, gratitude is always nice, but—" his teeth flashed white against the growing darkness "—I'd prefer more of those cinnamon rolls. After Blake gets back, of course. Which reminds me…" He dug in his pocket, held up a folded piece of paper. "Mr. Marsh gave me this telegram to give to you. It came in while I was signing for the supplies."

Her breath caught. She leaned down and took hold of the paper, her fingers tingling to open it. "Thank you, Mr. Stevenson."

He nodded, grabbed hold of a crate and added it to the growing pile on the dock. "Night's closing in, and Blake will shoot me with that pistol of his if I let you walk around alone in the dark. I'll be pleased to escort you to the station if there's a reply."

"That's very kind of you. I'll go in to the light and read this in case…" She hurried inside to the oil lamp hanging on its hook by the stairs. The paper crackled in her eager fingers.

THE WESTERN UNION TELEGRAPH COMPANY
Dated, New York City 29 Aug. 1868
Received at Whisper Creek, Wyoming
To Mrs. Blake Latherop

Father passed late afternoon. Must stay and settle
estate. Know store is in capable hands. Will send
word of date of my return.
Regards, Blake

She read the message a second time hoping for some
hint that Blake missed her, then remembered her sense
of loss and betrayal when her father had gone home
to be with the Lord and chided herself for being selfish. Blake had his grief on top of legal matters to take
care of. He had no time to pander to her feelings—
even if he knew about them. Still, she wished she were
in New York City to comfort him. But would he want
her comfort?

Know store is in capable hands. The words cut deep.
She pushed her wishes aside and faced reality. She was
of the most help to him right here. He didn't want her
for anything more. Tears welled, but she refused to let
them fall. This false marriage was her fault, and the
hurt it brought her was hers to bear.

She squared her shoulders and walked back to the
door. "There will be no reply, Mr. Stevenson. I'm to
await another telegram. Thank you again for your
help." She forced a smile to her lips. "You shall have
your cinnamon rolls when Blake returns."

He nodded, grabbed the jacket draped over the handle of the cart and slung it over his shoulder. "It's getting late. I'll drop by in the morning to cart these things
into the storage room."

"At your convenience, Mr. Stevenson." She watched
him disappear into the darkness and returned to the oil
lamp, glanced down at the telegram. *Mrs. Blake Lath-*

erop. In spite of her determination, her vision blurred. It was the first time she'd seen her name written. And it *was* her name—for now. How had Blake felt when he spoke it to the telegraph operator? Angry? Upset? Resentful? He was too fine a person to ever let her know. But it was certain the message would have been different if Linda were his wife. Imagined words imposed themselves on the telegram. *Close store. Come first available train. I need you.*

If only…

She closed her eyes against the ache.

A double blast of a train whistle sounded. The last train of the day had pulled into the station. She tucked the telegram in her dress pocket, walked through the store to the front windows and turned up the wick on the oil lamp she'd set on an empty keg she'd found in the storage room. It was unlikely she would have any customers from among the passengers this late at night. They tended to stay in the train after dusk fell. Still, someone might have a need—like that poor sick woman this afternoon. And the light from the lamp could be seen from the station.

She gazed out at the beam of light streaming through the darkness from the engine, reached into her pocket and fingered the telegram nestled there. How long would Blake be gone? Would he miss her while he was away? Her heart caught hold of the hope, refused to let it go. Perhaps this was one of God's mysterious ways. Perhaps Blake's heart would grow hungry for the life they had shared, short as it had been, and he would come to love her—

Movement caught her eye. A shadowy form passed

in front of the light from the engine, appeared to be coming toward the store, but the light from the oil lamp kept her from seeing clearly. She took a breath and hurried to the counter, tucked her dusting rag out of sight. Shoes tapped against the porch floor. The door opened, and the bell jingled. She smoothed back her hair, looked toward the door and gasped.

Chapter Fourteen

"Linda!"

"Audrey?"

"Yes!" Audrey ran to her sister and threw her arms around her, laughing and crying. "You're all right! Oh, Linda, I've been so worried. I didn't know if you would find me—"

"You always worry about me, Audrey." Linda straightened, patted her back. "But I'm quite able to take care of myself—with the help of a few servants. Or a little sister."

Linda's laughter sounded to her like crystal bells ringing. It always had. "I'm so relieved to see you well and happy, Linda. I—" She stopped, looked toward the door. "Where is your husband? Is he still at the station? There's no—"

"Nigel isn't here."

"He's not *here*? But—" She stared at her sister, noted the way Linda turned away.

"So this is Blake's store..."

Why was she changing the subject? "Yes. Linda, what is wr—"

"Then where is he?" Linda stepped around her and glided toward the door at the back of the room. "Blake, darling…"

Her stomach sank. Her joy at seeing her sister again flattened, turned into a vague uneasiness. Why had Linda come to Whisper Creek without her husband? She took a breath, pressed her hand against her stomach and waited. Linda would make her request in her own time. "Blake is not here, Linda."

"Not here? But I need—" Her sister turned, looked at her. Her delicately arched brows peaked, her lovely features hardened. The act was over. "What are *you* doing here, Audrey?"

But I need—Linda was exactly the same. And her sister wanted something. She snuffed the flame in the oil lamp and hung the Closed sign in the window, found strength in doing so. "I came to save Blake's store. Surely you remember?" She snuffed the chandeliers and led the way into the storage room, thought about following Blake to the stairs on the night they were wed and remembered his pain. The unease turned to anger. "You broke your betrothal, married Nigel and left Blake in danger of losing the store and all of his inheritance. And when I challenged you on your duplicity, you told me if I was so worried about Blake losing his store *I* should marry him."

"Poof!" Linda dismissed the indictment with a wave of her lace-gloved hand. "Blake is too smart to lose his—" Linda stopped, stared at her in the light of the oil lamp by the stairs. "You married him."

It was an accusation. She lifted her chin. "Yes."

"You little fool! Why would you do such a thing?" Linda's eyes turned dark—a sure sign of a storm to come. "Blake loves *me*."

The words stuck like knives in her heart. She couldn't deny it—but she wouldn't affirm it. And she wouldn't let Linda hurt Blake. Not again. She would give her whatever she had come after, so she would leave before Blake's return. "And you're married to Nigel." She gripped the banister, lifted her hems and climbed the stairs, focused on the mundane to control the churning in her stomach. "It's supper time. Have you eaten?"

"I haven't had a decent meal since I left St. Louis."

She jerked to a halt, turned. The light from the sconce fell on her sister's beautiful face, shone on the creamy skin revealed by the low-cut neckline of her fashionable satin gown. "St. Louis? I thought you went to collect your husband's inheritance from his family in San Francisco."

Linda's blue eyes flashed, her mouth tightened. "Do not call that gambling *liar* my husband!"

"Linda." She rushed to her sister, took hold of her lace-gloved hands. "Oh, Linda, what happened?"

Her sister stiffened, tugged her hands free and pushed at the golden curls resting on her forehead. "Nigel lied to me about everything. There *was* no inheritance! No *family*! He only told me those things because I had told him I was planning on using my inheritance from Father to go to San Francisco and become an actress."

A memory flashed. *I've only come home to collect a*

bank draft for my share of our inheritance from Father, get my jewelry and say goodbye. Dread settled like a rock in her stomach. "Your inheritance…"

"It's gone. Along with my jewelry. Nigel gambled it all away on a Mississippi riverboat. I had to sell a few of my best gowns to purchase my train ticket here."

"Oh, Linda, I'm so sorry. Why didn't you write—" *What are you doing here, Audrey?* Everything in her went still. Linda hadn't known she was here. She locked her gaze on her sister's eyes. "Why did you buy a ticket to Whisper Creek, Linda? Why didn't you go home?"

Linda tossed her head, glanced around. "To what purpose? There's nothing for me there."

You thought I was there. She pushed aside the hurt. At least Linda hadn't lied. Her chest tightened. Whatever her sister wanted had to do with Blake. Money. What else could it be? She spun and walked into the kitchen, lit the oil lamps, pulled food from the refrigerator and arranged it on a platter. Cabbage slaw, pickled beets and carrots, boiled eggs and cold ham, a few olives… "I'm afraid this is all I have to offer." She set the platter on the table along with a pitcher of lemonade and walked to the dresser for dishes and flatware. "I haven't been cooking or baking since Blake left."

"Where is he?"

"In New York." She put the dishes on the table and slid onto a chair, prayed for the food and hoped she'd be able to eat. If she didn't, Linda would know she was upset and—

"How long will he be gone?"

She looked at her sister sitting and eating at Blake's

table and squared her shoulders. She would resolve whatever problem had brought Linda to Whisper Creek and have her sister out of town before Blake returned. She couldn't—*wouldn't*—let Linda hurt him again. Not if it cost her every cent she possessed. "The date of his return is indefinite. His father passed away."

"His *father* died!" Linda lifted her head, put down her fork. "Blake is an only child…"

"Yes." There was a disturbing, speculative gleam in Linda's eyes that made her stomach churn. She stopped all pretense of eating. "What about Blake's being an only child?"

"Oh, nothing." Linda picked up her knife and fork, cut a piece of ham. "I simply recall him mentioning once that he had no living family but his father."

"I didn't know." Tears sprang to her eyes. "How awful for him to have to bear his grief and sorrow alone."

"Why, Audrey, you're in love with him!"

Another truth she couldn't deny—but she couldn't bear to have Linda know of her feelings for Blake. She would be merciless in using them as a weapon to get her way. "It's necessary for the people of Whisper Creek to believe that's so."

"Oh, yes. Because of that foolish contract Blake signed."

Because of you! She reached for her lemonade, swallowed the words along with the cool sweetened liquid and turned the conversation away from Blake. "Do you think your husband will follow—"

"Nigel is not my husband."

The glass slipped from her hand. She grabbed for

her napkin and sopped up the spilled lemonade, carried the napkin to the dry sink and rinsed it. "I don't understand. You told me you were married."

"I thought I was."

Her stomach clenched tighter than the wrung-out napkin. She shook out the cloth, hung it over the hot water pipe to dry. "What do you mean, you *thought* you were married? Either you are, or you aren't." *Unless you're only a pretend bride.*

"I'm not. When Nigel deserted me, he left a note saying that our marriage was bogus. The ceremony had been performed by his friend."

"Linda, that's terrible!" Indignation on her sister's behalf swept away all thought of her own troubles. "You must have been devastated! No wonder you came—" Linda wasn't married. And neither was Blake. Not in his heart. The room tilted, righted itself. She clutched the edge of the sink while her hope seeped away like the water swirling down the drain. *Please, Lord...*

She drew a breath, turned to face her sister. "Why did you come here, Linda?"

"Why, to marry Blake, of course."

The clop of horses' hoofs and rumble of carriage wheels faded away. The last of the mourners had gone. Blake pulled up the collar of his coat, turned his back to the wind whipping through the cemetery and stared at the headstone with his father's name newly engraved beside his mother's. *Robert Sydney Latherop. Born, June 11, 1809—Departed this world, August 29, 1868.* He jammed his hands in his coat pockets, tried to catch a full breath. The platitudes about time spoken by his father's colleagues were well intended, but he doubted the ache in his heart would ever heal.

The wind gusted. He staggered forward. He looked up at the dark clouds that rolled and boiled above the nearby trees whose branches were thrashing about in a wild frenzy. He should leave before the storm broke and the rain started. He closed his eyes and searched inside for the strength to walk away. When he did, he would be alone. *Help me, Lord.*

The wind plastered a leaf against the side of his face. He snatched it away, opened his eyes and stared. All around him dried autumn leaves were lifted from the ground, rode the wind in a swirling eddy around the headstone and fell. A thin layer of them already covered the mound of raw earth—a blanket of mustard-gold and rusty-red leaves with a few green ones that hadn't yet dried mixed in. *Audrey.* The need to see her struck with the swiftness of a lightning bolt. The pressure in his chest eased. She was waiting for him in Whisper Creek.

Glad you're...happy, son. I'll...tell... Mother.

He tugged his hat down, lifted his gaze to the darkening sky. His father wasn't in that grave. He was with Mother in Heaven. And one day he'd see them both again. Meanwhile, he had a life to live. And he'd learned one thing since being home in New York; he wanted to live it in Whisper Creek—with Audrey, if she would agree to continue their arrangement. And why wouldn't she? They had worked out a pleasant relationship. The only difficulty was his attraction to her. But that was only rebound emotion and would fade. Meantime, he could control his instincts.

Was that what his father had seen in his eyes—his pleasure with life in Whisper Creek? Whatever it was, his father had understood. He would miss his wisdom. He took another breath, pushed words through the tightness in his throat. "Thanks, Dad, for all you taught me. I'll try to live up to the examples of honesty and fidelity with Audrey that you and Mother set. Perhaps love will follow."

That was an intriguing thought. He bent down and picked up one of the gold autumn leaves, put it in his pocket and walked to his father's carriage. He would keep the leaf as a symbol of this moment when he'd decided on the course he should take. He had found an honest, faithful woman in Audrey. Or, rather, she had found him.

I came to marry you.

He shook his head, still amazed by her proclamation. And her tenacity when he'd challenged her. She'd always been quiet and obsequious around Linda—sort of faded away when her sister came into the room. But not that night. She'd never hesitated a moment in her plan to save his store. And what a sense of honor she had, to offer herself in her sister's stead in order to uphold Linda's word—to a point.

Rain spattered on his hat and shoulders, bounced on the carriage roof. He picked up the ground tie, set it on the floor, climbed in and took the reins in his hand. "Let's go home, T-T." The bay leaned into the harness and the carriage rolled forward. He smiled, urged the mare to a faster pace. He needed a horse. He would keep the bay when he settled his father's estate and take her home with him. He had a hunch Audrey would like the name his mother had given the mare—Twinkle-toes. His dad had hated it—said it embarrassed him saying "Get up, Twinkle-toes" in front of his business cohorts—and shortened it to T-T.

He chuckled at the memory, wiped a splatter of blowing rain off his cheek. Now, he had a decision to make. Should he tell Audrey the mare's name and face the embarrassment of owning a horse named Twinkle-toes in the wilds of Wyoming Territory—or simply call the horse T-T?

"This sitting room is very small. However do you entertain?"

Linda's voice floated into the kitchen, cool, patronizing. Audrey stiffened, put the beets and carrots back in the crocks and set them in the refrigerator. "We're newlyweds." *Pretend ones.* "We're not expected to entertain until a suitable amount of time has passed."

"Oh, yes. I forgot that boring rule. I notice the settee and chairs are blue."

She clenched her teeth, crossed to the sink cupboard and turned on the spigot. Linda knew full well Blake had chosen everything in this house for her! Hot water splashed into the dishpan. She swished the soap through it and slipped in the dirty dishes, thankful, for once, that her sister didn't deign to perform household tasks. It gave her an excuse to hide from Linda's probing gaze until she gained control of her emotions. She took a breath to steady her voice. Perhaps acknowledging the truth would stop Linda's taunting. "Yes. Blake bought them before you broke your betrothal to him and married Nigel."

"Must you take every opportunity to remind me of my mistake, Audrey? You're not usually that unkind."

Mistake? Her stomach churned.

"What is this room?" A door opened. "Oh, it's Blake's office." The door closed.

Linda was exploring. *No!* She yanked her hands from the water and ran for the hall. *Lord, don't let her—*

"Oh, a bedroom."

Too late. She stopped, watched Linda make a slow turn in the center of Blake's bedroom. Her heart pounded. Her stomach knotted.

Linda looked at Blake's boots sitting on the floor beside the cot, turned to her and smiled. "And where do you sleep, Audrey dear?"

Linda had guessed the truth. The knowledge of it was in her eyes, in the smug smile curling her lips.

Bile surged and burned into her throat. She swallowed hard, took a breath to calm the churning in her stomach and lifted her chin. "Come with me. I'll show you."

Chapter Fifteen

"This is it. You will sleep here tonight." Audrey stopped in the doorway, forced the words from her aching throat. It had to be, but she could not bear to see Linda sleeping in that bedroom.

Linda brushed by her, the short ruffled train on her gown floating across the floor. She stopped, removed her flower-bedecked hat, tossed it onto the dressing table and fluffed her blond curls. "Well, at least there is a bed. And a wardrobe where I can hang my gowns when I get my trunks from the station. How shall I do that without Blake here to fetch them for me?"

She looked into Linda's eyes, read the determination in them. Her sister was staying. Linda intended to marry Blake, and she wouldn't let a little thing like their marriage stand in her way. And there was nothing to be done about it. Linda would be Blake's choice. "I'll have your trunks brought here in the morning. It's too late now."

"Morning will be fine. I'll manage without them tonight." Linda opened the doors on the dress cupboard, glanced her way and smiled.

She stiffened. Linda smelled victory. The lack of any male garments or accessories in the wardrobe gave mute testimony to her in-name-only marriage to Blake. And though Linda may not know exactly what it was, she was certain that something was not right. That small superior smile meant that her sister would not rest until she learned what was amiss.

"I've so much to tell you about what happened to me while we've been apart, Audrey. And, of course, I want to hear the story of your marriage to Blake." Linda gave her another smile, came and touched her arm. "Shall we have a cup of tea while we talk?"

There was no way to escape it; the conversation would happen sooner or later. She fisted her hands, hid them in the folds of her long skirt and nodded. She would not be able to hide the truth. And she did not have the right to do so. Blake loved Linda. She couldn't protect him from his own heart. "I'll put the water on." She turned and headed for the kitchen, her heart aching for the love she had recognized too late—a love that must now stay hidden for the days and weeks and months and years to come.

Tears stung her eyes. She hurried to the stove, added a scoop of coal, closed the door and adjusted the draft. She would have to teach Linda how to use the stove. She ran her fingers along the oven handle, swallowed hard. She'd come to think of the stove as hers. But it was Linda's stove. Blake had bought it and everything else in the house for her sister. He loved Linda. She had to remember that. It was the only way she would get through this.

"How sweet of Blake! The stove is blue. And the dishes, too." Linda carried two cups and saucers to the table, set them down and frowned. "The lack of a proper dining room certainly limits the entertaining possibilities, doesn't it?"

Linda was making plans. A band of steel squeezed her heart and lungs. She braced herself against the worktable, tried to breathe. She had to get out of here! Go home to New York and— She couldn't leave. Not until Blake returned. She had to tend the store. And how would Blake explain Linda's appearance and her abrupt departure to Mr. Ferndale? She couldn't do that to him. What a mess she had created. And she had thought her letters to Blake on Linda's behalf might have been God working in a mysterious way. Tears and laughter bubbled into her throat. She bit down on her lower lip to stop the hysteria. *Blessed Lord, help me. Please give me strength to see this through for Blake's sake.*

"The lack of people limits the entertaining possibilities." She opened the tea, spooned it into the blue-and-white-china teapot, then placed it on the matching tray beside the sugar bowl and creamer.

"What do you mean lack of people? There have to be people in a town."

Linda stared at her, a gleam of suspicion in her eyes. Hope sprang up in her heart. Linda liked fun and entertainment and excitement. Perhaps she could discourage her about marrying Blake. "Whisper Creek is a growing town, Linda. Blake's store is the only business that is open—other than the railroad station and saw-mill and church. There are two—no, *three*—women in town. Mrs. Ferndale, a kind, motherly sort of woman—she's the wife of John Ferndale, the town founder. And Mrs. Karl, the pastor's wife…" She snatched up a towel, lifted the steaming cast-iron teapot and filled the china one with the hot water.

"And you are the third woman?"

"No. I wasn't counting myself." She carried the tea tray to the table and went to the refrigerator for the milk. "The third woman is Yan Cheng, a laundress."

"A *laundress*! That is not amusing, Audrey."

"It wasn't meant to be." She returned the milk to the refrigerator and took her seat. "I'm merely telling you the way it is here."

Linda stopped stirring sugar into her tea and slanted a look at her. "What do you do for pleasure?"

"Well…we attend church. And go for walks." *The waterfall.* She ducked her head and added milk to her tea to hide the tears flowing into her eyes. "And the Ferndales invited us to dinner one Sunday. And I help Blake in the store." She blinked her eyes and took a sip of tea to clear the lump from her throat.

"How charming."

She lifted her chin, stared across the table. "It's how he makes his living, Linda."

"Well, that won't be necessary now."

Something cold touched her spine. She knew that tone. She tightened her grip on her cup handle to steady her hand. "What do you mean?"

Linda waved the question away. "Tell me about you

and Blake." Linda's eyes narrowed on her. "Are you truly married?"

So that was the conclusion Linda had drawn. Her back stiffened. "Of *course* we're married! Pastor Karl performed the ceremony." She put offense in her voice. "You should know I would not live here with Blake if we were not."

"But you aren't living as man and wife, are you, Audrey?" Linda's blue eyes focused on her. "You are in one bedroom, and Blake is in another. That is not a marriage."

She jutted her chin. "It's a marriage in all but that one respect."

Linda nodded, looked down at her cup. "And mine was a marriage in that one respect only." There was bitterness in her voice.

"I'm sorry, Linda."

"Well, it was what I deserved, running off with a man I barely knew in search of fun and excitement." Linda sighed, circled her cup on its saucer. "I have learned my lesson, Audrey. It's folly chasing after fun. I realize now that I love Blake. That's why I came to Whisper Creek. To ask him to forgive me and to marry him if he still loves me. I didn't know you had married him." Linda dabbed at her eyes with her napkin. "How did that come about?"

Was Linda sincere? She looked at the tears shimmering in her sister's blue eyes and her heart softened. She took a breath, rose and went to the window to look out into the darkness. "It was as I told you. When I opened Blake's letter after you left I learned that he had signed the contract because of your promise to marry him. He asked you to come quickly as he had only thirty days or he would lose the store. The letter had been on your dresser unopened before you came home that day and there was not enough time to write Blake. And that wouldn't have helped. So, I did what you suggested. I came to Whisper Creek and married him in your place. It was the only way I could think of to save his store." She stared out into the night, her heart awash with pain. "It's a marriage in-name-only."

"Time to board, T-T, but this will be the last time." Blake walked the mare around the paddock, took a firm grip on the halter and led her up the ramp to the livestock car.

"Whoa there, fella." A burly soldier with sergeant's stripes on his dusty, faded uniform stepped into the center of the doorway. "This here car is for army mounts."

"Yes, I know, Sergeant." Blake reached into his pocket and pulled out a paper. "I have permission for my mare to ride in the car as far as Whisper Creek."

The soldier scowled and held the paper to the oil lamp hanging by the door. A grin slanted across his mouth. "Yo, wranglers! This here mare is to be given the best of care by order of General G. R. Otterman. Bigsby, front and center! Twinkle-toes is your charge."

"Twinkle-toes?"

Hoots and guffaws, the sound of knee and back slapping burst from the dark interior of the car. A private, grinning from ear to ear, stepped to the doorway and took hold of the mare's halter. "Come along, girl."

"If it suits you better, I call her T-T, Private."

"I shouldn't wonder." The private stroked the silky muzzle, gave a tug on the halter and disappeared into the center of the car, the clack of his boot heels swallowed by the clop of the mare's hoofs.

Blake hurried back to the Laramie station, picked up his valise and boarded the passenger car. It wouldn't be long now. He grinned, surprised by his eagerness to be home. He'd been growing more impatient to be in Whisper Creek again with every mile.

He chose a seat with a window clean enough to see through, set his valise beside him and leaned back to relax. The blast of the whistle brought him upright again. Smoke huffed by outside the pane of glass, the train lurched, rolled forward and picked up speed.

It would be good to get back to the store. He missed tending the customers. And he needed to finish painting it. Memories flashed. The corners of his lips twitched, broke into a grin. He'd never heard Audrey laugh the way she had when he'd slapped himself in the face with that paintbrush. It was like music. And her *eyes*—those gold flecks sparkling up at him, then warming with concern. And her touch…

The sun streamed in the window, warmed his left side. A nice day. Perhaps he'd get back to the painting, check over the books after dark. The sign would be there in a few days. He pulled his shoulders back to stretch his travel-cramped muscles and grinned. He couldn't wait to see Audrey's face when Mitch or one of his men hung the sign. He'd ordered it made with a pine-green background, rusty-red border and Latherop's General Store in mustard-gold lettering.

Latherop's General Store. His grin died. He'd taken

a chance, having his name put on the sign. He wasn't at all sure he would have the store much longer. That would be up to Audrey. He was content with their arrangement. For now.

He stiffened, scowled and scrubbed his hand across the nape of his neck. Where had that *for now* come from? He thought he had this all settled. That he had his plans made, his arguments for Audrey prepared. But, if he were honest, would he truly be content to have an in-name-only marriage for the next five years with Audrey for his wife? Could he maintain the friendship-only relationship with Audrey's sweetness, beauty and caring heart right there before him, tempting him every day? He'd already yielded to the temptation to kiss her!

He let out a low snarl, shoved from his seat and headed for the door at the front of the car. He had to get this situation settled in his own mind before he could approach Audrey with the idea of remaining married. He had to know what he was proposing and be sure he could uphold his end of the arrangement. He yanked the door open, stepped out onto the small platform and got a face full of smoke. He coughed, blinked his smarting eyes and moved to the other side.

He splayed his legs and braced himself as they rounded a bend, shoved his hands through his hair and laced his fingers behind his neck. Could he ask Audrey to become his wife in truth? No. Of that he was certain. He liked and respected Audrey too much to offer her less than she deserved. Linda's betrayal had left him uncertain of his emotions, and he couldn't ask Audrey to take Linda's… leavings.

The train lurched. He caught hold of the upright

post, watched the breaking sunlight play on the pines and the mountains and wished the train would slow down. He'd been so certain in New York that he knew what he wanted. But the closer they came to Whisper Creek the stronger his doubt and indecision grew.

I'll try to live up to the examples of honesty and fidelity with Audrey that you and Mother set.

Honesty...fidelity...honesty...fidelity... The words ran through his mind in cadence with the clack of the wheels on the rails. Linda and Audrey. He was caught in an impossible situation. He'd loved one sister he couldn't have, and respected and liked the other he shouldn't have married. The only solution was to sell the store as he'd promised Audrey so she would be free to find the love she so deserved. He gritted his teeth against the thought of losing her. Audrey had made his house a home. She worked beside him in the store like a true helpmate would. He wouldn't even *have* a store or a home to sell if it weren't for Audrey. It would all have been lost when Linda betrayed him. It was settled. He owed Audrey the chance to find love. He'd work out some sort of a plan to sell the store.

He gripped the edge of the roof overhead, hung his head between his upstretched arms and watched his hope of a life in Whisper Creek disappear like the railroad ties flashing by.

Audrey blinked her dry, tired eyes, hung her damp towel over the rod to dry, pinned her hair into its loose figure eight at the nape of her neck and went back to the sitting room to fold the blanket she used for a cover during her long, sleepless nights.

Dawn lightened the eastern sky, sent gold and rose streaks probing into the fleeing darkness. The first train would soon be pulling into the station. It was time to start Linda's breakfast. She tucked the blanket out of sight in the chest that sat along the sitting room wall, walked down the hall and knocked on the bedroom door. "Linda…" She knocked harder, raised her voice. "Linda!"

"Go away, Audrey."

"Not this morning, Linda. It's been four days. You have got to come to the kitchen and watch me or you will never learn how to use the stove and the water heater."

Footsteps padded across the floor. The door opened. Linda blinked, pushed her blond curls out of her eyes. "I've told you that I don't have to learn to cook or to do any other household chore. When we are married, Blake and I will leave this boring place where there is *nothing* to do and move back to his father's house in New York. All I have to do is ask him. Now, go *away*, *Audrey*!"

She lifted her chin, buried her clenched hands in her skirt. She couldn't protect Blake from Linda's selfishness, but she could at least make her cook! "Very well, Linda. I will do as you ask. But I am *not* going to fix your breakfast, or your dinner, or your supper. If you want to eat, you cook." She spun on her heel and stalked toward the stairs.

"Audrey, wait! I didn't mean to upset you." Linda caught her by the arm, whirled in front of her and put on her pouty face. "I'm just a grouch when I wake up.

You know that. And I'm out of sorts from having to hide in this house all day and night."

"I'm sorry you can't go out, Linda, but you can't be seen—it would ruin everything for Blake. It could mean he would lose the store to Mr. Ferndale, and—"

"What does that matter?" Linda walked back to the bed and slid beneath the covers. "Blake can afford to lose the store now."

Blake is an only child.

The memory of Linda's words stole her breath. She stared at her sister, fighting the suspicion that had taken root in her mind. Surely, she was wrong. Surely, Linda wasn't that grasping, that…conniving. "Is that when you decided to marry Blake, Linda? When I told you his father had died, and you realized that as his father's only child he would inherit everything?"

"Of *course* not!" Linda gasped, sat up. "Do you honestly think I would do such a thing, Audrey?" Linda's lower lip trembled, and she wiped at her eyes. "When Nigel treated me so badly, I realized what a *wonderful* man Blake is, and that I loved him. That's why I came to Whisper Creek. I didn't know you were here or that you had married him in my stead." Linda pressed her hand to her chest, gave a little sob. "I thank you for that, Audrey. But, the way things are, I think it would be best for us all if you went home before Blake returns. Don't you?"

She swallowed hard, waited for the painful constriction of her throat to ease so she could speak. "You may be right, but I can't do that, Linda. I have to tend the store." Tears flowed beyond her control. She choked out the rest of what she had to say. "But, I will leave as soon as Blake returns. You have my word."

"You always do the right thing, Audrey. You are such an inspiration to me." Linda gave her a sweet smile. "I want to make this as easy for you as possible. I'll pack your trunks for you this morning so you will be ready."

It *would* be easier if she left as soon as Blake returned. She couldn't bear the thought of seeing him, knowing— She forced air into her aching chest and nodded. "I won't need my trunks, only a valise with what is necessary for the trip home so I can leave quickly. You can send the trunks later." Sobs clawed at her throat, demanding release. She whirled toward the kitchen. "I'll cook your breakfast."

The train whistle echoed down the valley. Audrey's stomach knotted again. Was this the train that would bring Bake home? The wire had said he would arrive today or tomorrow.

Home.

Not for her. Not anymore.

She sealed the letter she'd written, fought down the denial in her heart and walked out of the kitchen. Sounds of a drawer opening and shutting came from Linda's bedroom. Her sister had started packing for her as soon as she finished her breakfast. And she hadn't stopped with a valise. Linda was packing all of her clothes. Her sister wanted every trace of her gone as quickly as possible.

Bile burned into her throat. Her temples throbbed. She stiffened her spine and forced her legs to move, made her fingers grasp Blake's bedroom doorknob and twist. She crossed to the dresser and placed the letter on the top, trying not to think about the day they had moved his things into the room, or of him moving them back to the other bedroom when he began a true marriage with Linda.

The whistle shrilled its message of the train's arrival into the morning air. She stepped into the hall, closed the door and walked to the dressing room to check her appearance, frowned at her reflection in the mirror. She had a store to take care of and customers to tend to no matter how her heart ached. She wet a cloth with the freezing glacier water and held it to her eyes hoping it would take away the red puffiness. There was nothing she could do about the loose way her gown fit. She had no appetite for food.

The faint sound of a bell jingled. She brushed the red curls off her forehead, pasted a smile on her face and hurried downstairs. Soldiers swarmed in the door, their blue uniforms a familiar sight to her now. She was even learning how to tell their ranks—not that she would need that knowledge anymore. She pushed away the thought and stepped behind the counter, pulled out the ledger and smiled at the corporal with a can of fruit in each hand. "Will that be all today, soldier?"

"No, ma'am. I'd like some of that cherry toothpaste. And a handful of that peppermint candy." He looked at her and grinned. "No offense, ma'am. But, I'll get the candy—you got sort of small hands."

"No offense taken, Corporal." She tore off a piece of paper, twisted and tied the end and held it out to him.

One after another the soldiers lined up at the counter paying for their purchases. They all raced out the door when the train's whistle blew. The twenty minutes were a painful blur. She entered the last purchases in the ledger, slipped it onto the shelf beneath the counter, walked through the storage room and climbed the stairs. Perhaps a cold cloth on her forehead—

The door to the loading dock opened, closed. Her heart sank. Mr. Stevenson must have brought more supplies from the train. She would have to take care of them.

"Audrey... *Audrey*..." Footsteps pounded up the stairs.

Blake! Her heart lurched, pounded in her ears. She whirled around, grabbed the railing for support, blinked to clear a rush of tears from her eyes.

"There you are." He pivoted at the top of the stairs and came toward her. "It's good to be home, Audrey. I tried to finish with Twinkle-toes in time to help you with the rush in the store, but it took longer than I thought to get her watered and the bedding spread."

It's good to be home, Audrey. Her heart seized on the words, stored them away for the empty tomorrows. She gazed up at him, memorizing every feature of his handsome face, the way his short brown hair curled toward his temples, the smile in his eyes.

"Audrey?" He frowned, set his satchel down and reached for her. "Are you all right?"

"Blake darling!"

Shock froze his features. He spun about, stared. *"Linda?"*

"Yes! Oh, yes, darling!" Linda ran down the hall and threw herself into Blake's arms. "I've been waiting for you!"

Blake turned his head, looked at her, his shock apparent.

The sight of Linda in his arms was more than she could bear. She lifted her hands, rubbed at her temples and closed her eyes. "If you'll excuse me... I'm not feeling well, and you two have a lot to discuss. I'll just rest for a while..."

"Audrey, wait. What's wrong with you?"

"Let her go. She's only tired, Blake darling." Linda cooed the words, smiled at Blake and rested her hand against the front of his shirt. "Let's go into the sitting room, darling. I have so much to tell you." Linda shot her a smug look, took Blake's arm and walked with him into the sitting room.

She started toward the dressing room, kicked something and looked down. Her packed valise was sitting by the railing, her blue Zouave jacket draped over it, her purse resting on the top.

"Oh, Blake darling, it's so good to be in your arms again."

Linda's words floated out of the sitting room. It was too much. She could not stay here with the two of them another minute. She pulled on her jacket, picked up her purse and the valise and crept down the stairs and out onto the loading dock. There was no one in sight. She blinked her vision clear, hurried across the road and into the trees to wait for the next train.

The air was warm but with that special autumn briskness to it. Audrey put her valise down close to the rutted road, wiped the tears from her face and took a deep breath. It was cowardly to run and hide, but the thought of Linda and Blake together was devastating. To *see* them in each other's arms was shattering.

She followed the path of trampled grass that led to the pool that fed Whisper Creek, her heart aching with a pain she didn't think she could survive. But somehow she had to get through these next couple of hours until her train came. The distant, staccato beat of hammers played a steady accompaniment to the murmur of the waterfall. She rounded the curve, stopped and let the beauty of the wilderness pool soak in, folded the image within her heart. She examined the wild ferns and plants that meandered between the surrounding stones and boulders, then sat and watched the mist rise from the frigid water and form a cloud against the backdrop of the mountains.

A lump formed in her throat. Her heart splintered in a thousand pieces. She rose and picked a yellow flower and a small purple one. She would press them in her Bible and keep this much of Whisper Creek with her always.

Chapter Sixteen

Linda.

Blake looked down at the woman in his arms, shock warring with reality. Her hands slid over his shoulders and her fingers toyed with the hair at the nape of his neck, just as they had so many times in his memories.

"You haven't said you're glad to see me, Blake darling." Linda looked at him through her lashes and gave him a pouty smile. "You *are* glad to see me, aren't you?"

"I'm—surprised." He raised his hands, grasped her wrists and lifted her hands away, took a step back. "What are you doing here, Linda? Visiting your sister?" Bitterness sharpened his voice. He didn't bother to curb it. Anger was his best defense against the sudden flare of his remembered love for her. "Where's your husband?"

"Blake dearest, I don't blame you for being angry. But don't be cruel." The pout deepened.

"Save the endearments for the man you love."

"But, darling, I love *you*!" Linda reached out, rested her hands on the front of his shirt.

"Stop it." He pulled her hands away, stepped back out of her reach. "I'm not interested in playing your games, Linda."

"It's not a game. It's the truth. I love you. That's why I had my marriage annulled." She blinked her eyes; her lower lip quivered.

His whirling thoughts jolted to a halt. "You had your marriage annulled?"

"Yes. Oh, Blake darling, I made a terrible mistake! But you were gone, and I missed you so!" She rushed to him, laid her head on his shoulder. "With every letter you wrote me, my loneliness for you grew worse, until I just couldn't bear it. And then—" her voice shook, broke "—and then Nigel came to visit my friend, and he was so kind and attentive and—well, I simply lost my wits and married him. But I soon came to realize it was only my longing for you, for your love, that drove me to marry Nigel, and I left him. I came here to you, as soon as my marriage was annulled. I've missed you so, darling." She lifted her head off his shoulder.

The invitation to kiss her was there in her eyes, in her slightly tilted head and parted lips. How many times had he wished to have her in his arms? But not now. It was too late. He took hold of her upper arms and set her away from him. "You made the journey here in vain, Linda. I'm married to Audrey." Where was she? Was she all right? "I'm surprised she didn't tell you."

"She did, darling. And that your marriage isn't a true…union."

He stiffened. "Audrey told you that?"

"Of course. She wanted me to understand, so I wouldn't leave before you returned. She knows how much we love each other." She gave him a coquettish look. "And she wants us to be happy together."

Audrey…mothering Linda and protecting him. Well, he didn't want her protection! Or her mothering! He wanted—he wanted to *see* her. To talk to her. He glanced toward the hall, frowned. "She said she was going to rest because she wasn't feeling well. Perhaps you should go and see if she's all right." He didn't have the right to go into her bedroom. The thought rankled.

"Audrey's not ill, Blake. She only said that for an excuse to leave us alone so we could talk."

There was a trace of exasperation in Linda's voice. He ignored it. This situation involved the three of them. "Well, I want to hear what she has to say. I'll get her." He pivoted, strode out into the hall. Linda ran after him, grabbed his arm.

"She's not here."

There was something in Linda's voice… He turned, looked at her. "What do you mean she's not here? Where is she?"

Linda stepped close, shrugged her bare shoulders. "I don't know, dearest. Perhaps the train station. She had me pack her valise so she would be ready to leave when you came home. She would have left before, but she said she couldn't leave until you were here to tend to the store. I put her valise, jacket and purse there by the stair railing." Linda smiled, touched his arm. "I'm sure she left because she didn't want to intrude on our first meeting after being so long apart."

He glanced at the floor, strode to the bedroom and

rapped his knuckles against the door. "Audrey…" He knocked louder. "Audrey, are you in there?"

Silence.

He twisted the knob and shoved the door open, glanced around the empty room, pivoted and hurried to the kitchen window and looked down the road to the train station. There was no one on the platform. Where was she? Was she saying goodbye to Mrs. Karl or— No, she wouldn't do that. Audrey would not do something that might cast him in a bad light and cause him to lose the store.

The store. Of course.

"Stay here, Linda."

He trotted down the stairs, strode to the door that led to the store. "Audrey…" The store was empty. Where—

He pivoted, stalked to the loading dock, glanced up at the ceiling. The porch. No, she would have heard him calling for her.

She would stay out of sight.

He looked toward the trampled path across the rutted road. A brown leather valise sat at the base of a tree. A chill chased down his spine. He put his hand on the railing, leaped from the dock and ran.

"Audrey… *Audrey!*"

Blake! She squelched the instinct to hide, took a deep breath and gathered every ounce of inner strength she possessed. "I'm here, by the pool!"

Boots thudded against the dirt. He burst into sight, ran to her and grabbed her upper arms. "You little fool! What do you think you're doing?" He glared down at her, sucked in air. "I told you never to come out into these woods alone!"

There was fear mixed with the anger in his voice and eyes. Her heart leaped with hope. She took firm control of her emotions. If she allowed herself to think the fear meant he cared for her in any special way, she *was* a fool. His love was waiting for him in the house. She lifted her chin. "I was careful. I watched for rattlesnakes."

"And what about the *Indians*?"

She caught her lower lip with her teeth, looked down and kept silent. She couldn't tell him she was so undone she hadn't thought about the Indians. His fingers worked against her arms. He sucked in another breath, lowered his hands to his sides.

"What are you doing out here anyway?"

She held up the flowers, willed her hands not to tremble. "Gathering memories to take back to New York with me."

A whistle shrilled up the valley, giving notice of a train's approach. An eastbound train. Her stomach knotted. "It's time for me to go." She swallowed hard, turned and started back down the path, fought not to be ill with every step.

"Listen, Audrey, Linda—"

She shook her head. "Please don't say anything more, Blake." She cleared her throat, plunged ahead before she broke down. "I've been thinking about this new…situation ever since Linda came. And, I think, I've thought of an acceptable solution." She paused, reached for her valise. Blake was faster.

"I need that."

"And the three of us need to talk, Audrey." His gaze fastened on hers. "You and Linda have had time to discuss this situation—to think about it. I'm not over the shock of seeing—"

"Your true love waiting for you." She choked out the words, forced a smile. "I'm happy for you, Blake. Truly, I am. Now, give me my valise, or I'll miss my train."

"You can catch the next one if you insist. I have no right to stop you. But first—"

She shook her head, raised her chin. "I do not intend to spend another moment here in Whisper Creek. Surely, you can see how...untenable that would be." *Help me, Lord. Please keep me strong.* She held out her hand. "Please don't make me board that train without my valise."

The muscle along his jaw twitched. "You are the most stubborn, frustrating—"

She turned and started for the train station, paused when he fell into step beside her. "I think it would be best if you stay here." Her throat closed.

His gaze fastened on hers. "You're my wife. It's strange enough that you are leaving for New York as soon as I return. Since you will not yield to my wishes, I'll see you off. It would be expected."

He had turned her argument against her. She nodded, lifted her hems and started walking again. "It's not a matter of stubbornness, Blake. It's a solution. It's not perfect—" she tried to laugh, failed "—I'm not sure there is such a thing for this...unique circumstance. But it's the only thing I can think of that may allow us all to escape unscathed—and enable you to keep your store." *Unless Linda has her way.* "I have to leave in a way that will seem appropriate and satisfy Mr. Ferndale—not to mention everyone else in town."

"Appropriate!" The word hissed from between Blake's teeth.

She hurried up the platform steps, reached for the purse dangling from her wrist and headed for the ticket window. Blake's fingers closed around her arm, halted her.

"At least allow me a husband's right to buy his wife's ticket."

"All right." She focused on explaining the solution to control her tears. "I told you I haven't been feeling well, Blake. And that is the truth." She pushed out the words, not giving him a chance to speak. "You can tell Mr. Ferndale that my illness has become extremely painful the last few days, and that I have gone back to New York to try to find an…answer. After all, there is no doctor here to treat sickness." *There is no doctor anywhere who can help me.* "And you can tell him that…that my sister, Linda—who has been visiting me these last few days—has stayed on to…to take my place." The words pierced to the depth of her being. "And that, also, is the truth. You don't have to lie."

"Good of you to be concerned with my honor." His eyes locked on hers, dark, clouded. "I told you before, I don't need you to protect me!"

The whistle sounded the all aboard.

He brushed by her to the window. "I need a ticket to New York City, Asa."

"You just come back. Something wrong?"

The words floated out the window. *Everything is wrong!* She pressed her lips together, dug her fingernails into her palms to stop the sobs clawing at her throat.

"The ticket is for my wife. She's ill."

"Sorry to hear that, Blake. Mayhap one of them New York doctors can fix her up."

"Yes." He took the ticket, turned and handed it to her, that small muscle along his jaw jumping.

Her heart pounded. Tears threatened. She tucked the ticket in her purse.

"All aboard!"

Her legs were like sticks of wood, refused to work right. She started up the boarding steps, reached deep inside, found the strength to smile and held out her hand for the valise. "Goodbye, Blake. I wish you and Linda every happiness."

"You're forgetting about Asa." He tossed her valise through the open door, grabbed her hand and pulled her into his arms. Their strength crushed her against him, held her. His lips covered hers, claimed them; their searing heat branded what was left of her heart his forever. He stepped back, pivoted on his heel and strode away.

She pressed her fingers to her lips and collapsed against the railing, unable to control her tears.

"Let me help you, ma'am."

The conductor took hold of her elbow, helped her up the steps and to a seat. The whistle blew. "I've got to tend to my duties, ma'am. And I don't suppose it will help much—but I want you to know those biscuits you gave me were the best I've ever eaten." He put her va-lise on the seat beside her and walked away.

The biscuits. Memories washed over her. A fresh spate of tears flowed into her eyes. She opened her hand, put the stem-crushed flowers in her valise, leaned back against the seat and fought down the impulse to sob out her broken heart.

Blake stepped into the hotel and followed the sound of hammering. "I need to talk to you, Garret."

Garret Stevenson glanced at him, nodded and mo-tioned him back out into the hallway. "When did you get back?"

"The afternoon train from Laramie."

"I'll bet that beautiful bride of yours was happy to see you. She's been working hard tending the store and shelving the supplies that came in while you were gone. Come on in to my office. It's quieter there."

"Actually, I want to see one of your finished rooms."

"You mean my *only* finished room. All right. This way."

He ignored Garret's curious look and followed him down a bisecting hallway lined with closed doors. "There's been a lot done since I was last in here."

"It looks that way with the doors hung. But it is com-ing along. These rooms are being plastered. Here's the finished one."

He stepped into a small, unfurnished room with a varnished wood floor, plastered walls and ceiling. The dusky light of evening shone in through a small-paned window set in the side wall. A wardrobe stood open against the end wall. An oil lamp sat on a wall shelf to the left of the door. "It looks good, Garret."

"It will look a lot better once it's painted and the window has some sort of covering. And, of course, there will be a rug and good furnishings. And dressing rooms with hot water and bathing tubs down the hall. When it's finished this hotel will be so classy and comfortable, my customers will tell people about it all up and down the Union Pacific Line."

He closed the door, scrubbed his hand over the back of his neck. "Garret, I have a problem."

"I've been waiting for you to tell me what's wrong."

"Linda's here." He absorbed Garret's stare.

"Linda? Your betrothed who married another man Linda?"

"Exactly. She's been staying at the house with Audrey the last few days—they're sisters. But Audrey just left to go home to New York City and—" He stopped at Garret's long, low whistle, shoved his fingers through his hair and took a deep breath. "I can't have Linda staying at the house with me. Will you rent me the room?"

"I'd like to help you, Blake, but there's no bed. Or necessary, or…"

"I'll take care of all of that."

"Then…sure. You can use the room. When—"

"Right now. I'll bring the things she'll need over when it turns full dark." He blew out a breath, stuck out his hand. "Thank you, Garret. I didn't know what I would do if you said no."

Garret shook his offered hand, thumped his shoulder and grinned. "You could always take the next train out of town."

With the mess his life was in, the idea didn't sound half-bad.

Chapter Seventeen

"This is the last of it." Blake set the dressing table on the end wall beside the wardrobe, placed the bench seat he'd brought over earlier in front of it and looked around the room. The oil lamps sitting on the shelf by the door poured a warm golden light over the furnishings. He had brought everything but his dresser from his bedroom and added a blue-flowered washbasin, pitcher and necessary from the store. The lamp table served as a washstand.

"Well, that dressing table adds some class." Garret lifted one of the oil lamps Blake had brought over from the store and set it on the dressing table. "I guess that does it."

"One more thing." Blake stepped to the cot, lifted the head of it and tucked the ends of the sheet under the legs.

"What are you doing?"

He straightened, looked at Garret. "It's a trick I learned from Audrey." *The day she moved me into my bedroom.* "It keeps the bed linens in place." The muscle along his jaw twitched. He closed his mind to the memory, dropped the head of the cot and moved to the end.

"Well, I'll be…" Garret stepped closer, watched him trap the corners of the sheets and blankets under the legs at the foot of the bed. "That's clever! Why'd you leave the quilt corners free?"

Because she did. The muscle in his jaw twitched again. "No need to trap them as long as the other blankets stay put." He headed for the door, turned. "I truly appreciate this, Garret. I'll make it up to you."

"I'm not doing anything but letting you use the room. It's not costing me anything as long as Ferndale doesn't count it as my hotel opening and start the counting days until—"

The words stopped. Garret stared.

Blake met his astounded gaze, watched him working through unspoken thoughts—putting two and two together, realizing their concerns were the same.

"So that's what happened. I wondered…" His friend shook his head and gave him a look he could only read as admiration. "It's none of my business, Blake, but how did you get Audrey to agree to marry you?"

"I didn't. It was her idea. She found out about the contract, that I had signed it on the strength of Linda's promise to marry me, and that I was in danger of losing the store." Bitterness soured his stomach, sharpened his voice. "She felt guilty about Linda's part in my dilemma, so she came to Whisper Creek and proposed that she marry me in Linda's place—to save my investment."

"Audrey did that? That's…amazing. I'd almost consider getting married if I found a woman like that."

He straightened, eyed his friend. "What do you mean *almost*? Are you saying you're not planning on marrying? If you're not betrothed, how will you—"

"Haven't figured that out, yet." Garret frowned, tugged at his ear. "So you and Audrey married without Linda knowing. And now Linda's come—uninvited?"

"And unmarried. She got an annulment."

"So *that's* why Audrey left so suddenly." Garret let out a long, low whistle. "What are you going to do?"

He blew out a breath and shook his head. "I don't know."

Darkness hid the scenery outside the window. The conductor moved through the car, dimming the light of the oil lamps that flickered with every bump. Silence settled over the passenger car. Snores, low murmured conversations and the rustle of people changing to more comfortable sleeping positions vied with the clack of the wheels against the rails.

Audrey leaned back and closed her eyes, tried not to think. The past was too painful, the future too empty for contemplation. Every clack of the train wheels carried her farther from Blake and the home she'd come to love at Whisper Creek and closer to the empty house awaiting her in New York City. Her heart ached. Her eyes burned. Her temples throbbed. She rose, grabbed for the back of the seat ahead of her when things went out of kilter. Her legs threatened to give way.

A few deep breaths cleared away the light-headedness. She made her way to the washroom at the front of the passenger car, managing to evade the long legs and booted feet stretched out into the aisle. Nausea washed over her, made worse by the swaying of the train. She leaned against the wall and took deep breaths, fighting the urge to purge an already empty stomach. A splash of cold water made her eyes feel better. She dampened her handkerchief, made her way back to her seat and sank down onto it, held the wet cloth to her forehead. The coolness of the handkerchief soothed some of the pain.

The thoughts returned despite her effort to hold them at bay. Had Blake and Linda enjoyed their first meal together? Had Linda found the beef soup she'd left simmering on the stove? Had she kept the fire going? Blake liked his food hot. Tears welled. It was not her place to worry about Blake's meals. It was Linda's responsibility now. Still, she should have insisted Linda learn how to work that stove.

I've told you that I don't have to learn to cook or to do any other household chore. When we are married, Blake and I will leave this boring place where there is nothing *to do and move back to his father's house in New York.*

Linda had her plans made. And she knew her sister well enough to know that she could coax Blake into giving her exactly what she wanted. Men always did what Linda wanted—except Nigel. How terrible for Linda to be cast aside once her money was gone. To find out that she'd never been married, only used. But that was what Linda was doing to Blake. The only difference was, Blake's love for Linda was true, and their marriage would be real. If only...

A useless dream.

New York. The house Blake had inherited was not far from her family home. A matter of a few blocks only. The roiling in her stomach increased. She hadn't considered that. What should she do? She could not face seeing them together. And she knew Linda would be calling on her, showing off her luxuries and bragging about her life with Blake. Her stomach knotted at the thought. She would sell the house and—

The passenger car jolted. Her neck jerked. Pain shot through her head, stabbed deep behind her eyes. She winced, turned the handkerchief over to the cooler side and leaned her head against the padded seat back again. If only morning would come and end this torturous night.

A baby's wail rent the silence.

"Shh, little one, shh..."

She opened her eyes, glanced across the aisle. A woman shared a seat with two small children—a toddler curled up asleep on her one side, a small girl sitting at her other side. She rocked the crying infant in her arms.

"I'm tired, Mama." The little girl rubbed at her eyes.

"I know, dear, I know. Our journey will be over tomorrow, but I need you to be a good girl tonight." The woman jiggled the crying baby. "Shh, little one, shh..."

"I wanna lay down."

The little girl was close to crying.

"Shh, Carolyn, don't disturb your brother. He needs to sleep, and I need to feed the baby. You lean against me."

"But I wanna lay down!"

The plea ended in a sob. The woman needed help. Audrey laid her handkerchief on her valise, set it on the floor and slipped across the aisle. "Excuse me. I couldn't help but overhear..." She smiled at the exhausted-looking woman. "And, if it's acceptable to you, my seat is there, across the aisle, and I would be happy to share it with your little girl. She could lie down and be comfortable."

"That is so very kind of you!" The woman tucked a blanket more securely around the infant in her arms. "But I noticed you haven't been feeling well. I don't want to trouble you."

"Please, it's no trouble at all."

"Well, if you're sure." The woman looked down at her daughter. "Carolyn, this nice lady has offered to let you sleep on her seat. You go with her. Mama will be right here."

The little girl's lower lip quivered; she wiped at her teary eyes with her small, fisted hand. "Can you tell me a story?"

"I think I can manage that." She smiled and held out her hand. The little girl scooched off the seat and took hold of it.

"Be a good girl for the kind lady, Carolyn." The mother gave her a grateful smile. "Thank you, miss."

"My pleasure." She lifted the little girl to her seat, slid in beside her.

"Can I lay down?"

"You certainly may. Would you like to rest your head on my lap?"

The child yawned, nodded and lay down, blinked and looked up at her.

Her fingers twitched to smooth back a tress of hair

that was clinging to the little girl's chubby cheek. "Would you like to hear a poem about a kitty?"

"I like...kitties..." Carolyn's round brown eyes closed.

"All right." She smiled, shrugged out of her jacket and spread it over the small body.

"'Pussey-Cat lives in the servants' hall,

She can set up her back, and purr;

The little Mice live in a crack in the wall,

But they hardly dare venture to stir;'"

"'Cause they're...scareded...'"

"Yes." She smiled at the child's word, took a breath and continued.

"'For whenever they think of taking the air,

Or filling their little maws,

The Pussey-Cat says, "Come out, if you dare;

I will catch you all with my claws."'"

She smoothed back the silky hair. Carolyn didn't open her eyes. She softened her voice to a whisper.

"'Scrabble, scrabble, scrabble, went all the little Mice,

For they smelt the Cheshire cheese;

The Pussey-Cat said, "It smells very nice,

Now do come out, if you please."'"

Her whisper faded into silence. She glanced across the aisle. The mother was fast asleep, the baby nursing in her arms. She looked down at Carolyn, at her small little nose, chubby cheeks, soft pink mouth and hair the same brown color as Blake's. The pang in her heart stole her breath. She leaned back and closed her eyes, but there was no way to close out the hurt.

* * *

"This is your room."

Blake balanced Linda's trunk on his shoulder, opened the door and stepped back.

Linda glided into the room, stopped, turned and looked at him. "Blake darling, surely you do not expect me to sleep here? On *that*?" She waved her hand toward the cot. "I thought you said this was a hotel."

"A hotel under construction." Blake set the trunk down between the wardrobe and the dressing table. "This is the only habitable room. I'm sorry about the cot, but—" He stopped, looked down at her hand resting on his shirtfront.

"Don't be sorry, darling. I understand." She looked up at him, smiled then pouted out her lips. "I know you don't want me to be uncomfortable, so..." Her fingers walked up the row of buttons on his shirt, stopped and played with his tie. "...why don't you take my things back to our home and you can sleep here. Hmm..." She tilted her head back.

The invitation was there. But memories of Audrey cooking and baking and cleaning the kitchen, smiling up at him as she poured his coffee every morning, made Linda's presumption in calling the living quarters over the store *our home* irksome. He smoothed down his tie and moved away. "I can't do that, Linda. I have to be there to take care of the store and tend to customers."

"But surely you want—"

He looked at her, and whatever she had been about to say died. She smiled and removed her wrap, dropped it on the dressing table bench. The light from the oil lamp glowed on her throat and bare shoulders. His pulse quickened.

"You're right, of course, Blake dearest. The store must come first." She looked at him through her lashes, glided toward him, the silk of her ruffled gown rustling softly. "After this..."

Her hands cupped his face, gave a gentle tug. He slipped his arms around her, met the invitation. Her lips were soft, warm and *wrong*. He released his hold on her, lifted his head. "It's time for me to go. I have work to catch up on at the store after being gone."

"Of course, darling. I understand." Linda gave him a coquettish look, took hold of his arm and walked beside him to the door. "I'll dream about that kiss all night." Her voice was soft, husky, enticing, but not entirely convincing.

He lifted her hand to his mouth, pressed his lips to the backs of her fingers and walked off down the hall.

The floor was swept clean. The shelves and tables neat and orderly with not a speck of dust on them. Blake stepped behind the counter, his footsteps loud in the silence of the empty store. He pulled the oil lamp down to brighten the circle of light on the counter. The looped chains clinked softly against one another. He scowled, scanned the counter. Every item was in its proper place. The ends of the paper rolls were aligned with the cutter bars. The cone of string was wound, the end tucked into the hole at the top, the scissors on the counter at its base. The flowers in the pitcher were arranged in a pleasing mixture of colors.

He frowned, grabbed the ledgers, tossed them onto

the counter and flipped the top one open. The last three pages were filled with the brief notations of items sold while he was gone. He opened the ledger that listed the supplies he had on order. The items that had come in while he was gone were checked off. He compared the two lists, made note of the items that would need to be included in his next order and closed the books.

The till was close to overflowing. He left enough money in it for operating costs, stuffed the rest in a cloth bag and carried it upstairs to his office. The door to his bedroom gaped open, a reminder of the upheaval in his life. He started toward his dresser, the only piece of furniture left in the room. A vision of Audrey looking up at him, her neat hairdo and clothing all askew, her cheeks pink with embarrassment from having rammed him in the stomach with his dresser drawer, filled his head. It was the only time he'd ever seen her... undone. And the day he'd learned she was not as timid and compliant as she'd always been around Linda. The woman could outstubborn a rock!

He clenched his hands and walked to the kitchen to stoke the hot water heater, then jolted to a halt and swept a disbelieving gaze over the room. The supper dishes were still on the table, uneaten food dried on them. The stew pot sat on the stove, the lid and ladle beside it. Spilled food had dried on the stove's cast-iron surface. The remainder of a loaf of bread sat uncovered among crumbs scattered all over the worktable. What had Linda been doing while he was carrying the furniture and her things to the hotel?

He stacked the dishes, carried them to the worktable and scraped what hardened-on food he could remove into the waste bucket. The hot water was almost cold. He scooped up a shovel full of coal and opened the firebox door on the water heater. A pile of gray ashes mixed with a few black clinkers rested on the grate. He stared at the cold cinders, reached over and turned off the water. He'd have to wait for it to heat once he got the fire going again.

A few live coals flickered among a pile of ashes on the grate in the stove firebox. He coaxed them back to life, added a scoop of coal and slid the scraped dishes into the dishpan of cool water to soak while he waited for the coal to start burning. He took care of the leftover soup, filled the stew pot with water, then wet a cloth and scrubbed at the spilled food on the stove surface before it got too hot.

How did Audrey keep it so clean and shiny? She'd loved the stove since that first day—the morning after they married. He paused, remembering the way she looked as she brushed her hand across the gleaming cast-iron cooking surface, then raised it to touch the blue porcelain doors on the warming ovens. Her hazel eyes were shining—

He pulled in a breath, shoveled a few of the hot coals from the stove to the water heater, added chunks of coal to both fires, closed the doors and adjusted the drafts. Anger simmered in the depths of his gut. How could she just leave him like that? How could she walk away from the home they— No. That wasn't fair. Audrey had left because she thought he still loved Linda.

He turned his back on the work, walked to the window by the dish dresser and looked out. It was too dark to see the train station. He shoved his hands into his pockets, hunched his shoulders and stared at the stars. His betrothed had come back to him. Where was his elation? Why did his gut knot at the thought of Audrey's desertion? He had what he'd wanted. So why was the joy and anticipation of his homecoming gone?

Chapter Eighteen

The horse's hoofs clopped against the cobblestones, the sound blending with the rumble of the carriage wheels. The cab slowed. Audrey looked out at the hustle and bustle of trolley cars and carriages, pedestrians walking by on the sidewalk and crossing the street. She'd forgotten there was so much activity in the city. The carriage moved close to the curb, stopped.

"We're here, miss."

"Yes. Thank you." She lifted her valise from the seat and stepped down from the carriage, handed the driver her fare and turned to face the row of houses. The red brick exteriors looked harsh after the wood buildings of Whisper Creek. She frowned and closed her mind to the memory. That part of her life was over. She needed to concentrate on the future—on selling the house and moving somewhere out West. She had decided that much while watching the scenery pass by on the journey home. She had discovered an affinity for the raw, rugged land. And, though their house was smaller, both narrower and shorter than its attached neighbors, it still should bring a price large enough to enable her to make a new start out there…perhaps open a boardinghouse. There was no reason not to sell the house. Linda would never have need of it—she had Blake to provide a home for her.

She crossed the sidewalk, gripped the cold iron railing and climbed to the front door, every step increasing the horrible hollowness within her. An emptiness nothing in New York could fill.

She set her valise on the stoop, searched through her purse for the key and unlocked the door. The musty smell of a closed, unoccupied house greeted her. She stepped into the small entrance hall, swept her gaze over the table that held an oil lamp and two chalk flowers. Her stomach knotted at the sight of the silver tray beside them. There would be no letters from Whisper Creek resting there waiting to be opened now. She took a breath and closed her eyes. *Please, Lord, let the house sell quickly, before Linda and Blake return to New York.*

The silence taunted her. The rustle of her long skirt and the click of her boot heels against the polished wood floor punctuated her movements. She carried her valise up the stairs to her bedroom and unpacked, choking back the tears stinging her eyes.

The kitchen was as she had left it, her rinsed teacup sitting on the wood drain board awaiting washing. The stove was black and cold and uninviting. Thoughts pounced, painful and unwelcome. Had Blake taught Linda how to use the stove? Was he cooking their meals? He must have learned by now that Linda was helpless in the kitchen. Not that he would care.

She clenched her hands, turned and hurried from the

room, but it was too late. The memories swarmed. The truth ripped at her heart. She wanted to make Blake his morning coffee, to see the smile in his eyes when he took his first swallow. She wanted to cook his meals and sit across the table from him while they ate them. She wanted to help him in the store. And she wanted to share that bedroom with him, and to fill the other bedroom with brown-haired, brown-eyed babies. She wanted to be his *wife*. To truly be his wife!

Tears gushed from her eyes. Sobs burst from her throat, raw and unstoppable. She ran up the stairs, threw herself onto her bed and buried her face in a pillow.

The train whistle blew twice, the shrill notes of the "all aboard" warning muted by the heavy fall of rain on the porch roof. The bell on the door jangled as the last of the soldiers, who had feared running out of chewing tobacco more than getting a wetting from the storm, left the store. Blake recorded the last purchases, placed his ledger and the till on the shelf out of sight and walked upstairs to the sitting room. He'd learned not to look for Linda in the kitchen. "That's the last of the customers, until the next train comes in. I doubt anyone else will brave this storm. Unless Mitch runs out of something he needs for one of his jobs."

"Well, I hope he doesn't." Linda rose from the settee, shook out her ruffled skirt and glided toward him. "You work too hard, darling." She glanced at him through her long lashes, put on a pretty pout. "I've hardly seen you today."

He accepted the wordless invitation and kissed her.

"I'm a storekeeper, Linda. My time belongs to my customers during store hours."

"But there's nothing for me to do."

You could help me. Audrey did.

"You needn't scowl, Blake."

"Was I? I didn't realize it." He smiled, lifted her hand from where she'd rested it on the front of his shirt and kissed her fingers. "I was wondering if there is any coffee?"

"You were thinking about *coffee*. And after I put on my prettiest new dress for you."

The pout increased. She moved a step away, wrapped a blond curl dangling at her temple about her finger and gave him a sidelong look that once would have had him groveling for forgiveness. The emotion that rose in him was irritation. What was wrong with him? He stepped forward, rested his hands on her bare shoulders and placed his mouth close to her ear. "Forgive me, Linda. I should have told you how beautiful you are."

She turned, smiled and slid her arms around his neck. "I forgive you, darling. How can I not, when I love you so much?"

She touched her lips to his in a teasing kiss that should have made his blood boil and his arms pull her close for a real kiss. But an image of Audrey, neat and resolute, blushing as she announced she'd come to Whisper Creek to marry him, destroyed any possible response but the right one. He cleared his throat, set Linda back away from him. "We're forgetting that I'm a married man, Linda."

"Not truly married, Blake. Your union is—"

"Legal and binding."

Her blue eyes flashed. "Then perhaps—"

"Yes?"

"Nothing, dearest. You're right." She touched his arm, sighed and gave him a smoldering look. "It's only that I so long to be your wife, I forget about…propriety." She stepped close, played with a wrinkle in his sleeve. "I thought that was what you wanted, too…for us to marry and share a life together."

Did he? Was this apathy he felt toward her because of his anger at her betrayal? Could he get beyond it to feel for her as he once did? "Yes, of course. But I have saving this store to think about. I have to do this the right way."

"I understand. But surely this store isn't—"

"Isn't what?"

"Isn't as important as me."

That wasn't what she'd been about to say before she stopped herself. He stared at her. She smiled, but there was a gleam in her eyes he'd never seen before. Selfishness?

She laid her head on his shoulder, her soft lips brushing against the skin on his neck. "But please hurry and annul this pretense of a marriage you have with Audrey, so we can have a real marriage together."

Pretense of a marriage? It didn't feel that way. "I'll do my best—for all of us."

Linda lifted her head, gave him a quizzical look, then smiled and strolled to the window. "You poor darling, suffering through all of this, just so we can have a comfortable life together."

"Suffering through what?"

She gave a delicate wave. "Everything. Staying here

under brutal conditions while building the store and these living quarters. Being lonely for your friends. Having nothing fun or exciting to do. Missing me…"

He thought back, remembered. "I was lonely for you. But your letters kept me going forward." He moved close to her, took her in his arms. "I thought I loved you when I asked for your hand in New York before I signed that contract and came to Whisper Creek to build a life for us. But the truth is, I really fell in love with you through your letters. You were different. So…" *Interested in me and my life. So caring.* He pushed the thought away, determined to rekindle the love between them. "I can't describe it. I only know your letters captured my heart."

"And yours, mine, Blake darling. I lived to read them."

He gave her a gentle kiss and stepped back. "I have to eat before the next train comes."

She sighed, pushed her blond curls back over her shoulder. "Surely, the store makes enough profit you can hire a cook and servant for us until—"

He stopped at the door, turned. He was getting tired of her unfinished sentences. Linda was hiding something. "Until what?" His tone demanded the truth.

She widened her eyes and pressed a hand against the creamy skin above her low, square-cut neckline. "Why, until we can return to the exciting life we will have in New York."

"In New York!"

She laughed, rushed into his arms. "You stop teasing me, Blake Latherop!" She gave him another of those coquettish looks through her long lashes.

He clenched his jaw to keep from telling her to stop it. Audrey never resorted to such behavior. She just lifted that little chin of hers and gave as good as she got. Audrey. Just the thought of her took his breath. "I'm not teasing."

She laughed, gave him a playful pat on the arm. "Of course you are! I know you want to go back to New York now that you have that beautiful big house and the means—"

"Meester Blake. Where is laundry?"

Blake scowled, pivoted toward the stairs and stepped to the railing. "I forgot. I'll bring it right down, Ah Cheng." He strode to his empty bedroom, opened the wardrobe and yanked out the bag of dirty clothes. There was a folded letter on his dresser. He pushed it into his suit coat pocket and hurried downstairs. "Here you are, Ah Cheng."

"Bring back two days, Meester Blake."

He nodded, following Ah Cheng to the loading dock. His wife stood holding an umbrella. He watched the two of them walk away, the heavy laundry bag now carried by Ah Cheng's wife while Ah Cheng held the umbrella.

He shook his head, wondered how long Ah Cheng's superior behavior would continue now that the Chinese were in American territory. From what he could tell, Yan Cheng was an intelligent, observant woman. And soon, she would have many American women customers aghast at the way Ah Cheng treated her, and not at all reluctant to say so. But that was neither his problem nor his business.

He turned back to the storage room, shoved his hand into his pocket and pulled out the letter. He unfolded it and looked down at the signature. *Audrey.* His heart lurched. He jerked his gaze to the beginning, hungry to read what she had written.

Dear Blake,

By now, you know I am gone from Whisper Creek, and from your life.

How happy you must be to have Linda for your own once again. I am glad for you both, and wish you every happiness.

I am uncertain as to what must happen now as far as the store is concerned.

Please know that I wish you every good fortune in that endeavor. I enjoyed working in the store. And our time together as "pretend man and wife" was pleasant.

And now to the purpose of this letter. I am writing to tell you that I will not, in any way, oppose an annulment of our in-name-only marriage. You may take whatever action you deem necessary to dissolve those matrimonial bonds.

Goodbye, Blake. I wish you and Linda a long and happy life together.

With affection,

Audrey

His stomach knotted. His jaw clenched. He crushed the letter in his hand, then thought better of it and smoothed it out and folded it. He would need it.

He scanned it once more, shoved it back in his pocket and scrubbed his hands over the back of his neck. She just gave up! The feisty Audrey he had come to know just gave up! Obviously, she didn't think their marriage worth fighting for!

Shock jolted his thoughts to a halt. Did he? The truth slammed into him, sent his heart racing. That was what was wrong. He loved her. He loved his wife!

He yanked the letter out and opened it, read it carefully seeking any slight indication that Audrey might feel the same toward him. He could find nothing, but something about the letter nagged at him. He read it again.

"Blake darling, are you coming?"

Linda. He whipped around toward the stairs, plowed his fingers through his hair. What was he to do about Linda? How could he tell her that he didn't love her and would not marry her when she'd annulled her marriage in order to marry him? When she had lived for his letters? He owed her his fidelity, if not his love.

"I'm coming." He climbed the stairs, faced a pouting Linda.

"I'm hungry and there's nothing to eat."

He looked at her standing there waiting for him to serve her. Fidelity was one thing. He would not be her servant. "There's ham and beets and pickles in the refrigerator."

She gasped, gazed at him, put her hand on his arm. "What's happened, Blake darling?"

If this relationship would work, it had to start with honesty. He took a breath, controlled the tone of his voice. "I found a letter from Audrey."

"Oh. The one where she told you she would not oppose an annulment of your pretend marriage."

"It's not *pretend*."

"Whatever it was, it will soon be over." She smiled, slipped her hand into his. "I'm sure you're relieved to have the letter so you can go forward with—"

"The *letter*!"

"What about it?" Linda's eyes flashed. "What is *wrong* with you, Blake?"

"It's not what she wrote. It's the writing!" Anger churned in his gut. He yanked his hand from hers, clenched it to keep from shaking the truth from her. "You didn't write those letters to me. Audrey did."

"Blake darling, how can you say—"

"The truth, Linda!" Her face blanched. Her lips compressed.

"Very well. I *didn't* write you those letters. I asked Audrey to answer them in my name. But only because Audrey is better at that sort of mundane thing than I, and I didn't want you to be disappointed in me." She stepped into his arms, slid her hands to the back of his neck and tilted her head in invitation.

Her charms left him cold. He grabbed her wrists, pulled her hands away from his hair and moved her back away from him. "Why did you come here, Linda? And I want the truth. I've had enough of your games. Where is your husband?"

"Very well! If you want the truth, you shall have it!" She whirled away from him, her long ruffled skirts flaring out around her. "I don't know where Nigel is. He gambled away all of my inheritance and then left me with a note that said our marriage was bogus, that his friend had performed the ceremony." She pulled a long blond curl forward to dangle against her bare shoulder. "Everyone says that with my beauty I should be on the stage! I came here because I was penniless. And I was sure you would give me enough money to get to San Francisco."

"Because of my love for you." He knew it for a fact before she nodded her head.

"That's right."

"And then you discovered that Audrey was here. And that we were married." He read the answer in her eyes. "She's your *sister*! Why did you change your—" *I know you want to go back to New York now that you have that beautiful big house and the means*— "My inheritance! *That's* the reason you decided to stay and marry me. Audrey told you I was in New York because my father had died and you—"

He couldn't look at her. How had he ever found her beautiful? He walked to the window beside the dish dresser in the kitchen, looked at the coursing runnels of rain on the small panes of glass. Her hand touched his back. He tensed.

"Audrey still has her inheritance, Blake. Mine was gambled away by Nigel. I need—"

"Stop! Don't say another word, Linda." He pulled in air, clenched his hands to control the burn in his gut. "You came to me for money to go to San Francisco and become an actress. Very well. I will purchase your train ticket to California, and give you expense money enough for the journey and one year in a hotel."

"Blake darling! I knew—"

"Halt right there, Linda!" He turned and looked at her, allowed his disgust to chill his voice. "I'll not have you misunderstanding the reason for my assistance. I'm doing so because you are Audrey's sister, and I don't want her worried about you. It has nothing to do with your beauty—that exists only on the outside. I've never known anyone uglier of character. Your sister shines like a jewel in comparison! Now go and pack your things. You'll want to be ready when the next train headed for San Francisco arrives. I will come to the hotel and take you and your trunks to the depot."

"Your shipment of supplies is being stacked in the shed out back, Blake." Asa squinted up at him, spit tobacco juice from the side of his mouth.

"Garret will pick up the supplies tomorrow when the road dries out." He reached in his pocket, pulled out some bills.

"What do you need this time?"

"A ticket for one to San Francisco."

"Pullman passenger car?"

"Yes. There are two trunks here on the platform to be loaded."

"Gimme a minute." The stationmaster slid off his stool, opened the back door, gave a shrill whistle, pointed toward the platform, then returned. He slid onto his stool and picked up one of the bills, passed the ticket and change back to him.

"And a ticket for one to New York City."

Asa peered out at him, then shrugged, took another bill and slid the ticket and change back to him.

He pocketed the New York ticket and change, walked to where Linda stood at the side of the platform and handed her the ticket for San Francisco, a packet of money and a note on a San Francisco bank he did business with for the store. "You'd best get aboard while the rain has slacked off a bit. The train will leave in a few minutes."

"We've only been waiting for you to bring me my ticket." She smiled at a portly gentleman standing beside her. "This kind gentleman is riding the same train and has offered me the shelter of his umbrella as well as his personal protection on my journey. I told him of my destination, and he has assured me that with my beauty I will be a star of the stage in no time. He has friends with the theater, and is eager to help me achieve my dream." Linda glanced at the banknote, smiled and tucked it into her purse with the other items. "Goodbye, Blake. Tell Audrey I will send her tickets for my first show when I become a famous actress." She took hold of the man's proffered arm, lifted her hems and walked away.

He took a long deep breath, trotted down the platform steps and ran for the store to pack.

Chapter Nineteen

Audrey fastened the ties on the bodice of her pale green silk dressing gown and slipped her feet into her cream-colored silk slippers. She stared at her reflection in her dressing table mirror and wished, again, that her long curly hair was blond like Linda's instead of red. And that her eyes were blue instead of hazel. And that she was beautiful. And curvaceous. And all of the things that her sister was that she wasn't. But she was improving. She hadn't burst into tears. She'd cried them all away.

She frowned and gathered her still damp hair at the nape of her neck, tied it loosely with a ribbon, fluffed it across her back so it would dry and left her bedroom. The wayward curls falling on her forehead and dangling at her temples no longer mattered with Blake not around to see them.

The smells of linseed oil and lemon juice hovered in the hallway. A faint trace of the ammonia she'd used to scrub the hall runner teased her nose. She gripped the polished banister and descended the stairs, the hint of various scents bearing witness to the days she'd spent scrubbing, cleaning, polishing and washing.

She cast a satisfied look about the small entrance hall, then turned and made her way down the short hallway to the kitchen. The smell of the vinegar she'd used to wash the windows and make them shine was fading. It would be gone by morning. And there would be no more. She was finished. The house was clean and polished from the top to the bottom. Or almost. She couldn't make herself go down into the cellar.

She pumped water into the teapot and filled the reservoir on the side of the stove, replacing the water she'd used for her bath, added wood to the fire and adjusted the dampers for a slow burn. Tomorrow she would go to see Mr. Ferguson. Her father's old friend would tell her how to proceed with the sale of the house. And then what? She held her thoughts to that question, refused to think of Blake and Linda, and the emptiness of her life.

She walked into the sitting room and went to the window that looked out on the street. Where would she go? She needed to have a destination in mind. And a plan of what she would do when she got there. Wherever *there* was. She turned from the window and glanced at the globe sitting beside her father's favorite chair, but she didn't want to travel. She wanted a home. She wrapped her arms about herself and searched her memory, thought of the towns where the train had stopped. They were all growing quickly and had a different "feel" to them than Whisper Creek. Was it possible to find another place like Whisper Creek? Dare she go even farther west?

Tears stung her eyes. She was only lying to herself. What she was contemplating was an effort in futility. There was no place that would become a home for her. A home was a place that is shared with someone you love.

The knock at the door was so unexpected, so loud in the silence that she jumped. She whirled about, blinked her vision clear and hurried for the front door. It was probably Lily Chaseon, sent by her mother to borrow enough sugar for her tea in the morning. She did that with— She opened the door, stared. Her billowing dressing gown fluttered into folds around her.

"Blake!" She gasped his name, pressed her hand to her chest to stop the wild beating of her heart. "What are you doing here?" She caught her breath, leaned forward to look out on the stoop. "Where is Linda?"

"May I come in?"

A chill slithered down her spine. She grabbed the doorknob, leaned on it for support. "Has something happened? Is Linda ill? Or…"

"Linda is fine. May I come in? Or do you wish to conduct this conversation on your stoop where your neighbors can hear?"

His voice. His eyes… "Yes, of course…come in." She backed up, pulled the door wide. *Don't cry! Don't you dare cry!* "May I take your coat and hat?" She held out her hand, saw it trembling and lowered it to her side again.

"I'll just put them here."

He shrugged out of his coat, folded it over a chair and put his hat on top of it. There was a valise at his feet. Her heart started its wild beating again. She lost her breath.

"It's been a long journey. Have you any coffee?"

"None made, but—yes, of course, I have coffee." She took a breath, tried to order her thoughts and make sense of his sudden appearance. "I'll make some right away." She gestured to her right. "The sitting room is there. But, of course, you know that."

She bit down on her lower lip to stop the inane words and hurried from the entrance to the kitchen. He followed. She did her best to look nonchalant and glanced over her shoulder at him. "Was there something you wanted?"

"The coffee. I figure it's all right for a man to be in the kitchen while his wife makes him coffee."

The coffeepot fell from her fumbling fingers, clanged against the stove. She grabbed for it, but he was faster. Their hands collided. She jerked hers back.

He picked up the coffeepot and turned to the sink cupboard, pumped in water. "Here you are." He handed it to her, then leaned back against the worktable in the center of the room.

She added ground coffee, her hand shaking so hard she spilled it on the table. But she couldn't stop her trembling. Nor could she hide it. The metal post and basket rattled against the metal pot when she fitted them together, clanked when she set it on the stove. *Please give me strength, Lord.* She opened the draft for a hot burn, turned back and brushed the spilled coffee into her cupped hand and threw it in the scrap bucket. "I take it from what you said you have not had our... marriage annulled yet. Is there a problem?"

"You might say that." His eyes fastened on hers. She

lost track of her thoughts. "We need to discuss a few things before we can go forward."

She looked down to smooth her palms against her skirt and froze. She was in her dressing gown! Her hair! Heat burned across her cheeks. She closed her eyes, tried to take a breath. "Then, if you'll excuse me, I'll go upstairs and put on some proper attire. I'll be right—"

"What you have on is fine, Audrey. A dressing gown is proper attire for a wife with her husband."

That was the second time he'd referred to her as his wife. She gathered what inner strength she could muster and looked up at him. He wasn't teasing. His eyes were dark, smoldering. It was a look she'd never seen before. She lifted her chin. "The letter I left you was not sufficient?"

"That's right, it wasn't."

She swallowed hard, forced herself to concentrate. "I'm sorry. I didn't know what to include."

"Not surprising." His gaze burned down into hers. "Forget the coffee. Let's go into the sitting room and we'll talk about it."

Her heart almost stopped when he reached beyond her and closed down the drafts. "Very well." She whirled about and moved into the hall, holding a decorous pace, though she wished she could run upstairs and get dressed and do her hair. Whatever that was in Blake's eyes was making her nervous. She felt...vulnerable. And the sitting room suddenly felt very small.

She moved to stand behind her father's chair beside the fireplace, as if the memory of him could somehow protect her. She drew a breath, pressed her hand against her quivering stomach. What foolishness! This was Blake. Her…her husband. No. Her *pretend* husband. *Blessed Lord, please help me to*— Paper crackled. She turned, looked at Blake.

He pulled a letter from his pocket, ran his fingers along the fold and looked her way. "You started by writing, 'Dear Blake. By now, you know I am gone from Whisper Creek, and from your life.'"

Tears stung the backs of her eyes. Writing those words had cost her a piece of her heart. She breathed hard, blinked.

"You were going to simply walk away." He tapped the letter against his other palm, held it up and gave it a little shake in her direction. "*This* was to have been your goodbye to me. You walked out of the house with your valise and didn't expect to see me again— wouldn't have if I hadn't followed you into the woods."

His voice was soft, conversational. It was his words that ripped her heart apart. "I explained…"

"That's right, you did. How did you phrase it…" He unfolded the letter, looked down and read, "'How happy you must be to have Linda for your own once again. I am glad for you both, and wish you every happiness.'" His head raised, his gaze locked on hers. "What were you doing, Audrey? Protecting your sister and me again?"

"No! I just—I…care about you…both, and I want—" she clenched her hands, dug her fingernails into her palms to control the tears blurring her vision "—I want you to be happy. And—and I was being polite."

"Truly? I would think good manners would dictate

that you allow a person to choose for his or her self what will make them happy."

"That's not fair!" She raised her chin. "Writing those words cost me—" She sucked in a breath, pressed her lips together and crossed her arms, holding in the pain slashing through her.

"Cost you what, Audrey?"

Lord, please! Please help me. Make him stop! She lifted her chin another notch. "A lot of thought! I wanted to say the right thing. Obviously, I was mistaken in my choice of words." She glanced toward the darkness outside, wished she dared go to the lamp stand beside him and turn up the wick in the oil lamp to give more light, instead of this soft glow. "It's getting late, Blake. What is the purpose of this visit?"

"My purpose?" His gaze captured hers again. "I told you my purpose—to discuss your letter and talk about what was not sufficient."

She couldn't take any more. She had to get him to leave before she broke down. "That's not necessary. If you need me to sign—"

"Take this part…" Her letter crackled in his hand. His deep voice read her words, setting her awash in hurtful memories. "'I am uncertain as to what must happen now as far as the store is concerned. Please know that I wish you every good fortune in that endeavor. I enjoyed working in the store. And our time together as "pretend man and wife" was pleasant.' *Pretend* man and wife?" He lifted his head and looked at her. "Our marriage was real, Audrey."

If only! She gripped the back of her father's chair, choked out words. "You know what I meant."

"Yes, this last part makes it very clear." He looked away, and she was able to breathe again. "'And now to the purpose of this letter. I am writing to tell you that I will not, in any way, oppose an annulment of our in-name-only marriage. You may take whatever action you deem necessary to dissolve those matrimonial bonds. Goodbye, Blake. I wish you and Linda a long and happy life together.'" He lowered the letter and gazed at her, his eyes dark, inscrutable in the low light. "What did you think you were doing, Audrey?"

Tears gushed. She blinked and wiped them away. "You know as well as I do what I was doing. I was setting you free to marry Linda."

"Don't you think that should be my choice?" He stepped close, his gaze burning down into hers. "Don't you think it should have been my choice all along? That I should have been told the truth?" That little muscle along his jawbone twitched; flames flickered in the depths of his eyes.

She backed up, trembling, her heart pounding.

"I know you wrote those letters for Linda, Audrey. I knew as soon as I read this letter. I recognized the handwriting." He closed the distance between them. "I am not some toy ball you and your sister can toss back and forth between you as suits your fancy. I am a man with a mind, a will and emotions, and *I* will choose who I will marry. Is that understood?"

Was he saying— Her knees gave way. She caught hold of the front of his shirt, nodded.

"Good. Because I've waited as long as I'm going to, to do this…"

His arms slid around her and pulled her against

him. His heart thudded beneath her hand. He lowered his head and she went on tiptoes, closed her eyes and wrapped her arms around his neck. His lips covered hers, and time stopped; the world fell away. There was only Blake.

He lifted his head, cleared his throat. "I love you, Mrs. Latherop. Will you come home and be my wife in truth, and in love, forever?"

His wife. Mrs. Blake Latherop, in truth. She gazed up at him, let the love she'd kept hidden shine out of her eyes and nodded. "Forever."

"Then we'll need this." He grasped her hand, slipped his other hand into his suit pocket and pulled out an emerald-studded gold band he slipped on her finger.

"And we'll not need this!" He ripped her letter in half and threw it to the floor, bent and lifted her into his arms. She slipped her arms around his neck, touched the crisp hair at his nape with her fingertips, shy in the newness of their expressions of love. "I love you, Blake."

He caught his breath, claimed her lips and seared them in a kiss of love and promise. She trembled, sighed and rested her face against the soft skin of his neck as he carried her to the stairs.

Epilogue

The train swayed around the mountain wall, blasted its whistle, then chugged through the growth of tall pines and entered the long, broad valley, dark and shadowed under a moonlit sky.

"We're almost there." Audrey leaned back against Blake, reveling in the strength of his arms around her. He bent down, kissed the soft skin in front of her ear.

"Almost *home*."

She tilted her head back and smiled up at him. "That sounds wonderful."

"That *is* wonderful. And so are you." He pulled her tight with one arm and grabbed the roof post with his other hand as the train jolted over a rough spot on the rails. "I've been thinking about how blessed I am to have you...to have your love."

"And I, yours."

He kissed the top of her head, then rested his chin against her hair. "And I think Mrs. Ferndale's grandfather was right—God *does* work in mysterious ways. If you hadn't agreed to write those letters for Linda..." He turned her around in his arms, crushed her against him.

She lifted her face, slid her arms up around his neck and met the hunger of his kiss with her own. The world swayed. She didn't know if it was his kiss or the train; she just held on.

The whistle blew twice. The train slowed. Her stomach tensed, fluttered at the sight of the Union Pacific station and the shadowed buildings at the end of the station road. The windows of the parsonage spilled golden light into the night. The store was dark, of course, but a thrill ran through her at the thought that soon the windows would be aglow with lamplight announcing to all that they were home. *Home.*

"Time to get our valises."

She started to precede Blake into the passenger car, then turned back, stared. There were lights shining from the buildings on both sides of the store. "Blake, look at the lights. The apothecary must have come to town while we were in New York."

"It appears that way. We'll find out tomorrow."

The train rolled to a stop. She watched Blake pick up the small valises they carried with them, shove the handles of both into his one hand and offer her his other to help her down the steps. She slipped her hand into his, lifted her hems and stepped down.

The silence of the night settled around them as they walked down the road to the store. The murmur of the waterfall whispered through the stillness. She looked at Blake...remembered and smiled.

"Ah, it came." His hand squeezed hers. "Look up, Audrey."

She gave him a puzzled glance and tipped her head

back, stared at the sign that proclaimed Latherop's General Store. "Oh, Blake, it's beautiful!" Tears welled.

"It does look good up there." His arm slipped around her. "We'll have to come down together in the morning and see how it looks in the light." He dropped a kiss on her temple and escorted her up the steps.

The store was dark, redolent with the scents of various soaps and spices and with a hint of dust. She would clean it tomorrow, before the first train came. She watched Blake light the oil lamp that hung by the steps in the storage room and thought of that first night... their wedding night. It was different now. It was real. Her stomach fluttered.

Blake stepped back, and she started up the stairs, paused and stared. The oil lamp sconce glowed with a soft golden light. She climbed the stairs, glanced toward the sitting room and stopped. The light from the hall fell on the arm of the settee just inside the door. A dark pine-green settee. She spun about. "Blake, something is wrong."

He smiled and shook his head. "I ordered the new furniture the day after you said yes to my proposal. And I delayed our homecoming until it had time to arrive. Garret and Mitch and Pastor and Mrs. Karl took care of the rest."

"But—" She swept her gaze over the pine-green- and rust-red-striped chairs. Tears stung her eyes. "Blake, it's beautiful!"

He grinned, dropped the valise, took hold of her hand and led her to the kitchen. The lamplight fell on the dish dresser, glistened on a new set of white china with a green leaf border. She blinked her vision clear, turned and gasped. A new stove with shining white doors on the warming ovens held place on the end wall. The truth struck—*no blue*. He had done this just for her! A sob burst from her throat. She spun and threw herself into his arms, buried her face against his shirtfront.

"And now, Mrs. Latherop..." He bent and lifted her into his arms, carried her down the short hall and over the threshold into their bedroom. She caught a glimpse of a new dressing table and a coverlet of pale green before he lowered his head and claimed her lips in a kiss that united their hearts forever.

* * * * *

Don't miss these other historical romances
by Dorothy Clark:

HIS PRECIOUS INHERITANCE
AN UNLIKELY LOVE
A SEASON OF THE HEART
FALLING FOR THE TEACHER
COURTING MISS CALLIE
WOOING THE SCHOOLMARM

Available now from Love Inspired!

Find more great reads at www.LoveInspired.com

Dear Reader,

When, in answer to prayer, the Lord gave me the idea for this new series, I was very excited. The unique twists to the familiar mail-order-bride story that came to me intrigued and motivated me. And the comforting truth behind the premises for the stories inspired me.

I *love* the idea that God quietly and lovingly guides His children, even when we think *we* are the ones making all of the decisions. As William Cowper wrote: "God moves in a mysterious way His wonders to perform." How calming and reassuring to know that we truly can rest in Him.

And there was another reason the idea for this series excited me—the research. I've always wanted to ride one of the old trains and experience the sway of the car, the clickety-clack of the wheels against the track and the faint smell of smoke as the steam engine chugs on its way West. I'm doing that now (in my imagination) as I write.

How about you, dear reader? Would you like to come along on my next journey to Whisper Creek? I understand there is a new resident. That the apothecary will soon be open for business. And there is that reversion clause in the contract...

Thank you, dear reader, for choosing to read *His Substitute Wife*. I hope you enjoyed Audrey and Blake's story. I truly appreciate hearing from my readers. If you care to share your thoughts about this story, I may be reached at dorothyjclark@hotmail.com or www.dorothyclarkbooks.com.

Until the next "All aboard" call sounds,

Dorothy Clark

WED BY NECESSITY

Smoky Mountain Matches • by Karen Kirst

Caught in a storm overnight with her father's new employee, Caroline Turner finds her reputation damaged. And the only way to repair It is to marry Duncan McKenna. But can a sophisticated socialite and a down-to-earth stable manager put their differences aside and find love?

THE OUTLAW'S SECRET

by Stacy Henrie

When Essie Vanderfair's train is held up by outlaws, the dime-store novelist connives to be taken hostage by them, seeking material for her next book. But she doesn't anticipate falling for one of the outlaws...or that he's secretly an undercover detective.

THE BOUNTY HUNTER'S BABY

by Erica Vetsch

Bounty hunter Thomas Beaufort has no problem handling outlaws, but when he's left with a criminal's baby to care for, he's in over his head. And the only person he can turn to for help is Esther Jensen, the woman whose heart he broke when he left town.

THE RELUCTANT GUARDIAN

by Susanne Dietze

On the verge of her first London season, Gemma Lyfeld accidently stumbles on a group of smugglers, catching them in the act...and they think she's a spy. Now she must depend on covert government agent Tavin Knox for protection. But how will she protect her heart from him?

———————

REQUEST YOUR FREE BOOKS!

2 FREE INSPIRATIONAL NOVELS
PLUS 2 *FREE* MYSTERY GIFTS

Love Inspired® HISTORICAL

YES! Please send me 2 FREE Love Inspired® Historical novels and my 2 FREE mystery gifts (gifts are worth about $10). After receiving them, if I don't wish to receive any more books, I can return the shipping statement marked "cancel." If I don't cancel, I will receive 4 brand-new novels every month and be billed just $4.99 per book in the U.S. or $5.49 per book in Canada. That's a saving of at least 17% off the cover price. It's quite a bargain! Shipping and handling is just 50¢ per book in the U.S. and 75¢ per book in Canada.* I understand that accepting the 2 free books and gifts places me under no obligation to buy anything. I can always return a shipment and cancel at any time. Even if I never buy another book, the two free books and gifts are mine to keep forever.

102/302 IDN GH6Z

Name	(PLEASE PRINT)	
Address		Apt. #
City	State/Prov.	Zip/Postal Code

Signature (if under 18, a parent or guardian must sign)

Mail to the **Reader Service:**
IN U.S.A.: P.O. Box 1867, Buffalo, NY 14240-1867
IN CANADA: P.O. Box 609, Fort Erie, Ontario L2A 5X3

Want to try two free books from another series?
Call 1-800-873-8635 or visit www.ReaderService.com.

* Terms and prices subject to change without notice. Prices do not include applicable taxes. Sales tax applicable in N.Y. Canadian residents will be charged applicable taxes. Offer not valid in Quebec. This offer is limited to one order per household. Not valid for current subscribers to Love Inspired Historical books. All orders subject to credit approval. Credit or debit balances in a customer's account(s) may be offset by any other outstanding balance owed by or to the customer. Please allow 4 to 6 weeks for delivery. Offer available while quantities last.

Your Privacy—The Reader Service is committed to protecting your privacy. Our Privacy Policy is available online at www.ReaderService.com or upon request from the Reader Service.

We make a portion of our mailing list available to reputable third parties that offer products we believe may interest you. If you prefer that we not exchange your name with third parties, or if you wish to clarify or modify your communication preferences, please visit us at www.ReaderService.com/consumerschoice or write to us at Reader Service Preference Service, P.O. Box 9062, Buffalo, NY 14240-9062. Include your complete name and address.

LIH15

Gatlinburg, Tennessee
July 1887

As a holiday, Independence Day left a lot to be desired. Independence was a dream Caroline Turner wasn't likely to ever attain.

The fireworks' blue-green light flickered over the sea of faces, followed by red, white and gold. She schooled her features and made her way along the edge of the field to where the musicians were playing patriotic tunes.

"Caroline, we're running low on lemonade."

"Then make more," she snapped at eighteen-year-old Wanda Smith.

"We've misplaced the lemon crates."

At the distress in the younger girl's countenance, Caroline relented. "Fine. I'll look for them. You may return to your station."

It took her a quarter of an hour to locate the missing lemons. By then, the last of the fireworks had been shot off and attendees were ready for more food and drink.

The celebration was far from over, yet she wished she could return home to her bedroom and solitude.

A trio of young women approached and engaged her in conversation. As usual, they wanted to know about her outfit, whether she'd had it made by a local seamstress or her mother had had it shipped from New York. Before they'd exhausted their talk of fashion, a stranger inserted himself into their group.

"Excuse me."

Caroline didn't recognize the hulking figure. Well over six feet tall, he was as broad and solid as an oak tree and looked as if he hadn't seen civilization in months. He was dressed in common clothing, and his shirt and pants were clean but wrinkled. Dirt caked the heels of his sturdy brown boots. His thick reddish-brown hair was tied back with a strip of leather. While he appeared to have a strong facial structure, his mustache and beard obscured the lower half of his face. His mouth was wide and generous. Sparkling blue eyes assessed her.

"Would you care to dance?" He spoke in a rolling brogue that identified him as a foreigner.

Don't miss
WED BY NECESSITY by Karen Kirst,
available wherever Love Inspired® Historical books
and ebooks are sold.

SPECIAL EXCERPT FROM

Discovering he has a two-year-old son is a huge
surprise for veterinarian Wyatt Harrow. But so are his
lingering feelings for the boy's pretty mom...

Read on for a sneak preview
of the fifth book in the
LONE STAR COWBOY LEAGUE: BOYS RANCH
miniseries, **THE DOCTOR'S TEXAS BABY**
by **Deb Kastner**.

Wyatt glanced at Carolina, but she wouldn't meet his eyes.

Was she feeling guilty over all Matty's firsts that she'd denied Wyatt? First breath, first word, the first step Matty took?

He couldn't say he felt sorry for her. She should be feeling guilty. She'd made the decision to walk away. She'd created these consequences for herself, and for Wyatt, and most of all, for Matty.

But today wasn't a day for anger. Today was about spending time with his son.

"What do you say, little man?" he asked, scooping Matty into his arms and leading Carolina to his truck. "Do you want to play ball?"

Not knowing what Matty would like, he'd pretty much loaded up every kind of sports ball imaginable—a football, a baseball, a soccer ball and a basketball.

Carolina flashed him half a smile and shrugged apologetically. "I'm afraid I don't know much about these games beyond being able to identify which ball goes with which sport."

"That's what Matty's got a dad for."

He didn't really think about what he was saying until the words had already left his lips.

Their gazes met and locked. She was silently challenging him, but he didn't know about what. Still, he kept his gaze firmly on hers. His words might not have been premeditated, but that didn't make them any less true. He was sorry if he'd hurt her feelings, though. He wanted to keep things friendly between them.

"There's plenty of room on the green for three. What do you say? Do you want to play soccer with us?"

Shock registered in her face, but it was no more than what he was feeling. This was all so new. Untested waters.

Somehow, they had to work things out, but kicking a ball around together at the park?

Why, that almost felt as if they were a family.

And although in a sense that was technically true, Wyatt didn't even want to go down that road.

He had every intention of being the best father he could to Matty. And in so doing, he would establish some sort of a working relationship with Carolina, some way they could both be comfortable without it getting awkward. He just couldn't bring himself to think about that right now.

Or maybe he just didn't want to.

Don't miss
THE DOCTOR'S TEXAS BABY
by Deb Kastner, available February 2017
wherever Love Inspired® books and ebooks are sold.

www.LoveInspired.com

Love Inspired

Love the Love Inspired book you just read?

Your opinion matters.

Review this book on your favorite book site, review site, blog or your own social media properties and share your opinion with other readers!